My Missing Boy

ALSO BY D.L. FISHER

The Perfect Nanny
My Missing Boy

MY MISSING BOY

D. L. FISHER

JOFFE BOOKS

Revised edition 2025
Joffe Books, London
www.joffebooks.com

First published in the USA in 2023 as *Win, Lose or Die*

This paperback edition was first published
in Great Britain in 2025

Cover art by Dee Dee Books Covers

ISBN: 978-1-80573-098-9

To my children (all five of you),
Thank you for being such amazing human beings,
and for inspiring this book with your endless extracurriculars
and tournaments. I may be guilty of sneaking in a few
chapters here and there, but I'm always rooting for you.

CHAPTER 1

GABBY RIZZO

I couldn't tell you what stopped me in my tracks as I dragged myself through our house, barely awake. Maybe it was my husband or son banging around upstairs in a frantic last-minute panic. Perhaps it was just a feeling in the pit of my gut that something was awry.

Whatever it was, I dropped my tumbler of iced coffee, and it exploded everywhere, spraying coffee and cream all over our marble tiles.

What a freaking mess.

It's a little early for the day to go sideways.

"*Gabby*? What are you doing?"

"Christ, Greg." I jump at the sound of my husband's voice, completely caught off guard. "Where did you come from? You scared the living daylights out of me!" I move a hand to my hip, annoyed. Flustered.

"Last time I checked, I do live here. Were you expecting someone else?" Greg arches an eyebrow.

"Yeah, totally," I say, relaxing ever so slightly. No, I wasn't expecting someone else. But I also wasn't expecting him. Not really, anyhow.

My six-foot-three, two-hundred-twenty-pound hunk of a husband has a nasty habit of sidling up when you *least* expect him. It's almost as if he were standing there all along. I keep buying Greg Tic Tacs, hoping he will slip a pack into his pocket so I can hear him coming. I wonder if he's worried he has terrible breath.

"I wasn't trying to send you into cardiac arrest, Gabby. I just wanted to see where you were at with the packing. I've been wrangling together some of Cam's things upstairs and getting my stuff laid out. I can't find his Futures sweatshirt. Is it in the wash?"

He has to be kidding. Sometimes, I think my husband and son look for things with their eyes closed. "The team-issued one? It's folded on his bed, Greg."

"Oh." He juts out his lower lip. "I guess I'll leave you to it, then."

I lower my gaze, then look up to apologize for overreacting. It's too late, though. Greg's no longer standing there, thanks to his Houdini-like knack for appearing and disappearing without ever making a sound.

And *no*, he didn't offer to help clean up the mess. Nor did he even acknowledge it.

I pull my sweatshirt over my head, using it as a makeshift towel to blot the tiles, but it's no use. It appears the tiles are damaged beyond repair.

Much like our marriage, I'm afraid.

I catch my son Cameron from the corner of my eye, watching me as I unravel.

"Hey bud, just about ready." I reach into my pocket and pull out our packing list. I finger it, the razor-sharp edge slicing the skin of my pointer finger with a quick pinch of pain that brings me back. It's as if someone has cracked a vial of smelling salts under my nose.

"Chest protector, cleats, groin guard . . ."

I rattle off the essentials as Cameron looks on with his quintessential teen mixture of amusement and irritation.

"Mooooommmm . . ." — the "oooooooo" — stretches tight like a rubber band until it snaps, his voice cracking from puberty. "God, you've already asked me like a hundred times."

Have I?

He rolls his eyes and throws his hooded Futures sweatshirt on top of an overflowing baseball bag.

"First, we don't take the Lord's name in vain. Clear?"

"Yes, ma'am."

"Second, it's all *in* the bag, right? Not like, you left it out on the bed for *me* to pack?"

Cam throws his hands up in exasperation, then stomps off to his bedroom. There are a few moments of silence, followed by a floor-shaking slam. My stomach clenches, an intense cramp that makes me momentarily grasp my side.

Teenagers.

Cam's just nervous, I tell myself. In no time (hopefully), we will hit the road for his baseball tournament at the Startown fields in Georgia. Only the elite receive bids to Startown — the best thirteen-year-old baseball players in the country. And my boy Cameron is one of them. Not just one of them — he's *the* one to watch.

Cam is ranked first in the nation at shortstop and hitting and number two in pitching for his age bracket. I strongly suspect the boy ranked above him began taking steroids at the age of eight. On the rare weekend that the Futures are off, our phones are constantly ringing with every other baseball organization in the state looking for Cam to fill in. It's all baseball all the time.

My phone vibrates in my pocket, pulling me from my frenzied thoughts. I retrieve it and swipe my thumb on the screen. It's the Futures' parent group chat. I scan the messages — *what time are y'all leaving; ugh, did you see our draw; who's ready to kick some 13U ass?* — I roll my eyes and shove it deep into my pants.

There's too much to think about without giving myself a splintering headache. I already feel the fingers of a migraine teasing my temples.

Last night, I had to evoke game theory to counter every possible scenario we might encounter on the road. Will Cam favor a Drop-5 or Drop-3 this weekend? What if his DeMarini Voodoo cracks when he smashes his first home run of the day out of the park? Which bat then — Meta BBCOR, Cat 9, Nexus, Mashup, Green Zen? The kid collects four-hundred-dollar bats like they're tubes of ChapStick.

I tap my thumb against my chin, thinking. There's more. He needs his infield glove, pitcher's glove, and catcher's mitt. Elbow guard, armband, sliding mitt, bat weight. Cooling towels and Gatorade pods, and headache patches. Turf shoes, just in case.

The list goes on and on and on.

So it's settled — we will have to drag along every goddamn baseball bat and piece of equipment this kid owns. If I'm lucky, there should be just enough space in the truck for my tiny suitcase.

My stomach rumbles, and I lick a bead of sweat from my upper lip. I have yet to have enough coffee for this, and the quarter cup I chugged down before spilling it is sitting like a brick in my gut. I head to the kitchen for a snack. I grab a cookie off the crystal bowl on our waterfall island. But just as my teeth sink into a gooey dark chocolate chip, there's a loud bang, followed by a string of expletives. I startle as if caught in the act.

"Gabby!!!"

I race back into our foyer, where Greg is clutching his foot, a pained expression on his handsome face.

"Think you could maybe *not* throw everything in the middle of the room next time. Is it *that* difficult to keep things organized? I just tripped over Cameron's baseball bag. I think I may have broken a toe."

"Seriously? Let me look. I'm so sorry," I say, meaning it.

"No, no." He waves me off. "I have to run to the office to grab some papers I left behind. Get the rest of our stuff together, and I'll pick you up in thirty minutes."

"You're leaving? But, but . . ."

"But someone has to pay the bills, Gabby. Remember?" He lowers his eyes to the stained floor as he says this. So he has noticed.

Greg starts walking to the door but then abruptly turns to face me. He closes the space between us and brings a hand to my face as if he might lean in for a kiss the way he used to. My skin prickles. He stares deeply into my eyes as he slowly moves his thumb across my cheek, *wiping*.

"Really, Gabby? Cookies for breakfast?"

What can I say? My cheeks flame red as my husband callously pulls away and leaves me standing with my jaw hanging. I chew on my lip, biting back tears.

Greg's office is five minutes away, but an hour passes without a word from him. I check my phone for a message or a missed call. There's one text from a dad on the team — *getting excited,* followed by an emoji wink — but radio silence from my husband.

I need to make myself useful — start bringing our luggage outside to save time when Greg returns. I reach down and slip my arm into the strap of Cameron's baseball bag, which costs twice as much as my sneakers and weighs ten times as much as our dog. I hoist it up, grunting from the effort.

I flip around, and Greg's standing there. *Again.* My heart beats like a bass drum, my pulse throbbing at my fingertips. The bag slips, hitting the ground with a metallic thud that echoes off our walls and eighteen-foot ceiling. I bend down to pick it back up — anything so I don't have to look at my husband.

It takes a few deep, albeit frazzled, breaths to slow my breathing down enough to speak to him.

"Seriously, Greg, stop sneaking up on me like that," I scold him, shaking my head with obvious displeasure. "You're literally going to scare me to death one day!" I clutch Cam's baseball bag close to my chest as if I might hide behind it.

Greg's lips turn up, and his greenish-gray eyes crinkle at the corners. "Here, I'll take that," he says, softening as he eyes me with concern. I swear, any chance my husband gets to be the hero, the guy runs with it.

Still, I smile appreciatively. "Always the gentleman," I say. Though, I suspect we both know this isn't the case.

Greg throws Cam's eighty-pound bag over his shoulder. The veins on his bronzed forearm bulge, and a wave of heat washes over me. I instinctively scratch the peeling pink patch of burnt, freckled skin on my shoulder.

"Cam, honey, we need to go!" My voice rises to the octave of a dog whistle.

Teddy, our twelve-year-old chihuahua, jerks his head and shoots me a stern look for interrupting his early morning nap before settling back into his Burberry-print dog bed. I debated bringing him to the tournament, but our set-in-his-ways pup would just be another thing to worry about. I'm throwing our neighbor ten bucks a day to change his wee-wee-pads and let him out in the backyard in the morning and afternoon.

"You don't look so great, Gabby. Are you sure you're okay?" Greg's eyes crinkle at the corners as he examines me.

Did I say I wasn't okay?

"I'm fine," I lie, straight-faced. "I'll feel better when we hit the road."

"Why don't you sit in the car, and I'll get us all packed up and out the door? Okay?"

"Okay," I agree because I don't have a choice. Not really, anyhow. I'm not sure I can physically stand here much longer without collapsing into a messy puddle on the floor. I've already done enough damage for the day.

Cameron materializes as if on cue, his body filling up more space in the door frame than ever. Overnight, Cam has morphed from a scrappy child into a carbon copy of his father. Same wavy blonde to light brown hair. Same eyes that can be cool or warm, depending upon the color of his shirt. Today he's wearing his navy practice jersey and could freeze me with his glare. Or maybe it's the expression he's wearing — annoyance laced with . . . is that *pity*? Whatever the case, before long, Cameron will no longer look up at me but down. In the figurative sense, I suppose that's already started to happen.

"Ready?" he asks, looking me over with morbid curiosity as if I'm a stranger instead of his loving mother. The look cuts like a knife.

"Help your mom to the car, Cam. I'll grab all the bags."

"Whatever." He shrugs, his sandy hair falling over his hazel eyes. I resist the urge to push it from his face.

My lids feel like weighted blankets, and nothing sounds better than collapsing into the front seat of our Escalade. I follow Cam to the car, keenly aware of my body swaying on the path. He's already stuck in his AirPods, tuning me out. Aside from looking back over his shoulder once to ensure I haven't toppled over on our walkway, I might as well be invisible.

Cam opens the back door and slides into his seat, stretching his long legs wide. I fiddle with my door handle, finding it difficult to pull the latch. Finally, after a few clumsy attempts, it clicks; I throw the door open and sink into the supple black leather of the passenger seat. Greg insisted on black leather because it's top-of-the-line. Unfortunately, it's also obscenely hot.

Still, I sink into the seat like it's a Tempur-Pedic mattress. I'm even more exhausted than I realized. A great deal of time and energy went into planning this trip. I'm grateful Greg volunteered to man the nine-hour drive.

Despite all the stress and fatigue, I'm looking forward to this time away. I promised myself I'd make an effort this weekend, allow myself to let loose, and have a little fun. Just a little. There's a doubleheader tomorrow, dinner, and an after-hours cocktail party for the adults. The boys are bunking up in double rooms with a chaperone in an adjoining suite. Which, thankfully, Greg and I are not.

As I think about the figure-hugging black dress draped on a hanger in my luggage, my lips curl into a smile. The red lace thong. The Brazilian bikini wax.

What could go wrong?

I take a final slow, deep breath and surrender myself to sleep.

Death is the last thing on my mind as my eyes zip shut.

CHAPTER 2

GREG RIZZO

They say you shouldn't live vicariously through your children. I say they don't have a son like Cameron. At two, he was hitting dingers off a tee, and fifty-yard line drives that would leave fiery indentations in the white, picket fence gating in our expansive yard. By four, he could throw a curveball, changeup, and slider. By six, he understood every delicate nuance of the game, calling balks before the umps and pulling observations that I didn't even pick up on.

And now, at thirteen, he's got the opportunity of a lifetime.

I'm not about to let my wife ruin it for him.

Best-case scenario, Gabby will sleep through the nine-hour car ride to Georgia. Then, I won't have to listen to her fret about this and that and pass her nervous energy onto our son. Considering how tired she's been lately, I'd hardly qualify that scenario as a long shot.

Especially after last night.

The way she woke me from a deep sleep, I was certain someone had broken into the house or died.

"Greg, wake up now," she begged, her voice laced with panic.

I opened one eye, only half conscious. I reached for my phone on the nightstand, registering that it was two thirty in the morning.

Two thirty in the freaking morning!

"What is it, Gabby? What's wrong?"

Something had to be terribly wrong for her to wake me in the middle of the night.

"I don't think we should go tomorrow, Greg."

"Go where? To the tournament?"

"Yes, to the tournament."

That woke me up. The mood in the room instantly shifted, and I couldn't disguise the annoyance in my voice.

"You woke me up to tell me we shouldn't go to the tournament we've been counting down the days for since Cam turned twelve?"

"Please, listen to me, Greg. It's just . . . it's too much pressure. I have a really bad feeling about this. I need you to trust me. I can't explain it."

"There's nothing to explain, Gabby. You're being ridiculous. We're going." I rolled over, so my back was facing her. *Not go? Too much pressure?* She was out of her mind. The conversation was over.

Like hell, we aren't going.

Cameron was built for this. He knows what this tournament means; he gets what's at stake. I would move heaven and earth to ensure his success. I would do anything for my son.

Even if that means disregarding Gabby's unexplainable feelings.

Don't get me wrong, I still love my wife, but things between us are different now. The days when one look gave me butterflies, and I would jump through hoops to make her smile are long gone. Those days and the Gabby I fell in love with are distant memories from someone else's life, it seems.

I guess that happens in every marriage — passion gives way to comfort. And trust. Until that's eroded as well.

I would never say as much out loud, but Cameron was both the best and worst thing to happen to our family. When your child is a prodigy like ours, you pour all your time and energy into them, leaving little room for all the other big and little things in life that used to matter.

Like each other.

We can't seem to agree on anything these days where Cam is concerned. Not even a baseball tournament.

I strongly suspect Cameron is the glue holding us together; without him, we will become completely undone. And lately, it seems not a question of if but when.

I glance over at my wife, dressed in her uniform of joggers and a tee, trainers, and her half-blond, half-brown hair haphazardly tossed up in a messy bun. Granted, we'll be in the car for the better half of the day. But still, she puts about as much effort into putting herself together as she does into our marriage.

Sometimes I think about what I've done to my wife and wonder if I'm responsible for crushing her spirit.

Then I think about what she's done to me.

It's strange, knowing someone you love is lying to you without them knowing you know. It's a delicate balance to walk in a house full of eggshells. I'll call her out one day on her deceptions, but not today.

Today, we will show up in Startown as a united front to support our Cameron.

Cameron's coach says he's got more raw talent for a boy his age than he's seen in his entire career.

Entire. Career.

My boy's got a seventy-five-mile-per-hour fastball, a .350 batting average with seven home runs this season, two of which were grand slams, and he has yet to meet a slump he can't swing his way out of. It would be a sin not to capitalize on his God-given talent.

When it became clear that Cam was extraordinary, Gabby sat me down for a heart-to-heart, one of many revolving around our prodigal son.

"Greg, I know he's good," she said.

"He's not just good," I interjected. "He's professional-good, and he's only eight, Gabby. Can you imagine what he'll accomplish if we nurture this gift?"

"But it's *me* who has to nurture this gift, Greg. I have to take him to all these lessons and practices and then practice around the clock with him at home. You're off *working* most of the time." She nearly choked on the word working as if she suspected I was busying myself in other ways.

"We both have our jobs, Gabby."

Her face crumbled. That one hit harder than I intended.

"Look," she said, after recovering from my blow, "I just want Cameron to have as normal a childhood as possible — math tutors, playdates, and birthday parties. I don't want him to feel like he missed out on being a kid."

"Really, Gabby? What's more normal than a love of all things baseball? It's as All-American as grandma and apple pie. Cameron wants this just as much, if not more, than we want it for him. You don't understand."

Therein lies the problem — she'll never understand.

I throw the rest of the bags over my shoulder and head outside. The sun is already blaring, an angry swirl of reds, oranges, and yellows, and it's only 72 degrees. The forecast calls for cloudless skies and a high of 97, not factoring in humidity, making it feel more like 105. I walk back into the house to grab an extra sleeve of Gatorade for Cameron.

Cam should have been pre-emptively hydrating for the past two days, but I can't take Gabby at her word that he has. She seems to get lost a lot in that head of hers, especially lately, and our needs sometimes fall by the wayside.

I swear I heard her talking to herself the other day. And on more than one occasion, I've noticed that her joggers are inside out, or she's got snail trails of mascara running down her face when she and Cameron roll in the door from practice.

Seriously, how do you go out in public like that?

I'm not sure where all the money I'm shelling out for therapy is going. If anything, Gabby is getting worse. But I have to assume Dr. Green knows what he's doing. He came highly recommended, even if his methods are somewhat controversial.

Before heading out of the kitchen, I open our miscellaneous drawer, home to all the random things in our lives lacking a proper place. I never open this drawer unless it's vital, let alone rummage through it. The random mess gives me a full-blown adult case of the heebie-jeebies, as though something living in there is going to jump out and bite my fingers. It's the same feeling I get when I stick my hand in Gabby's purse. That's my wife in a nutshell; she likes to hide things where she doesn't have to look or think of them, where she thinks no one will find them.

I grab a container of Tic Tacs to occupy my mouth on the ride. Gabby will be snoring the whole way, and I'm sure I'll only hear from Cam if he's hungry or has to use the restroom.

There must be twenty boxes in here. My wife has an abnormal obsession with Tic Tacs. Is it a weight loss thing? I know Gabby is self-conscious about her figure. She seems to have blossomed more over the past month than our azalea and rose garden.

Something catches my eye, and I reluctantly push my hand farther into the bowels of the drawer. I give a gentle tug and pull out a plastic wand. I turn it over in my hands, examining it.

A pregnancy test.

Not just a pregnancy test, but a positive pregnancy test.

I scratch my head, confused, in a bit of shock, and slip the test into the pocket of my khaki shorts. I've known Gabby has been hiding something for a while. But this? It's not possible.

Not. Possible.

Cameron is a teenager. How could we start over again? Especially since we've barely made it this far on our first go around. But the test is in my pocket, already burning a hole, singeing the hairs on my thigh. I can't believe Gabby is pregnant.

And I can't even ask her about it. Surely, she's already passed out in the car. Besides, it's not as if we can talk about something of this magnitude in front of Cameron. He may pretend we don't exist, but he's always listening — one of the downsides to having an only child, I suppose.

A wave of nausea washes over me as I wonder if having an only child will become past tense. As in, *remember when Cam was an only child?*

Again, not possible.

I mentally file the test away with the other swirling thoughts and questions running amok. I let myself out of the house, locking the muted, mint-green door behind me. I wanted something bolder — cobalt or burgundy — but Gabby didn't want our home to stick out. She absolutely hates drawing attention to herself. She won't so much as let me post a family picture online. Somehow, my wife missed the memo — it's the twenty-first century. 2022, to be exact. What thirty-two-year-old doesn't at least have a Facebook page? It's bizarre. Even my eighty-six-year-old grandfather has a Facebook page. But that's my wife — the only thing she's okay with shining is our son.

And, once upon a lifetime ago, me.

"Hey, Greg." A voice jolts me back to the present, and I glance up to see my next-door neighbor Matt Baker loading up his car. Matt and his wife Susie are our best couple friends, though there's a heavy undercurrent of competition between our boys. If it weren't for the fact that Cam is a righty and Jake a lefty, thereby mostly relegating them to different positions on the field, the relationship would be untenable. Because, like most kids, Jake is nowhere near as talented as our son. Still, despite their competitive natures — and ours — Cam and Jake are as close as brothers.

"Hey, Matt," I toss back as I heave our bags into the trunk.

Susie pops out from the passenger side of their car, and my stare lingers for a touch too long. She's wearing a too-tight-too-low-cut Futures V-neck, her double-D implants barely held in place by the thin fabric. I can see the outline of her nipples, and I'm reasonably certain she's not wearing a bra.

Susie and my wife are so *different.* Gabby is naturally pretty, not in a head-turning way, but attractive all the same. Susie Baker — now she's the type of woman who elicits stares wherever she goes. She's all fake hair and tits and teeth, and though none of it is real, you still want to touch it. I'd pay to meet a straight man who doesn't.

I imagine she was something to look at before all the work. The longer I've known her, the more she resembles a Barbie doll. Not that I'm complaining about the view.

My shrinking violet and our neighborhood's resident socialite have become the best of friends. Somehow they make it work, even if I have yet to figure out the how or why.

Or a way to put an end to it.

Thou shalt not covet thy neighbor, passes through my head, and I can't help but laugh. Matt and Susie moved in when Jake was a few months old, and Gabby was pregnant with Cam. Gabby sold them the house right next to ours, with a pool, jacuzzi, and built-ins.

Built-in best friends.

The thou shalt not covet ship sailed long, long ago.

"Cam excited?" Matt asks, unfazed by the turn my eyes have taken. It's a road well-traveled, indeed. I struggle to pull my eyes from her, as I often do.

"Sure is," I say, forcing myself to look away. "Jake?"

"I'd say. He's been bouncing off the walls since five a.m." Matt lets out an exaggerated yawn. Since he figured out how to jump out of his crib as a toddler, Jake has taken to jumping into his parents' bed the minute his eyes shoot open.

"How lucky for you and Susie." I wink sympathetically.

That's one thing I do not miss at all, getting up in the wee hours with a young child. Those days were like a bad dream, a Van Gogh blur of warbled days and sleepless nights. Cam was a preemie and didn't sleep through the night until his first birthday. But after that, he caught up to the program, putting on enough weight to leave him satiated until morning. He didn't just catch up; he ripped the damn program apart and wrote a new one.

Jake is older than Cam, but apparently, he hasn't gotten the memo that at thirteen going on fourteen, you do not need to wake up your parents when you can't sleep. *Read a book. Turn on the television. Pour yourself a goddamn bowl of Captain Crunch.* Perhaps Gabby and I are just lucky where Cameron is concerned.

Of course, we're lucky. *There.*

"Well, we'll see you there," I say, letting myself into the car. Matt salutes me as he slips into his Suburban.

I slam the trunk closed and make my way to the driver's side of our car. I slip into my seat, pausing to gather my thoughts. Gabby releases a soft moan, and I push the key start, firing up the ignition. I turn up the air and flick on the radio, hoping to drown out the sleepy noises I once found so endearing. I can't even look at my wife right now, let alone hear her. I wonder what she's dreaming about. Perhaps the knife she stabbed in my back? The child she's failed to mention she's carrying?

Duh, no wonder she's so tired. I shift in my seat, and the pregnancy test jabs into the flesh of my thigh like an exclamation point.

Cameron doesn't flinch when I've finally settled in; my hands clenched too tightly around the leather-wrapped steering wheel. I peek over my shoulder to see what has him so enraptured.

Baseball videos. Cameron's watching baseball highlights from the Little League World Series championship. Because, of course, he is. His dedication to the sport brings tears to my eyes. My lips pull up slightly, though they stop short when I look at my wife.

Matt and Susie wanted to drive down to Georgia together, but with all the luggage and equipment we had to drag along, it would have been a tight squeeze. And now, with this sudden revelation in the kitchen, I'm grateful we opted to take separate cars because there wouldn't have been enough oxygen in the air for the lot of us.

My career in financial management necessitates being "on" all the time, and I'm extremely good at what I do. Most of my clients value their money more than their children. I know how to appease people and tell them what they want to hear. I can smile my way through anything.

But *this*? My wife hiding her pregnancy from me in our junk drawer?

I doubt I could stuff this news down for nine hours while engaging in casual conversation without exploding because that's what happens when you stuff things down. Eventually, you explode.

I take one last look at our beautiful house, with its picturesque white shutters, exposed red brick, and meticulously manicured, sprawling lawn. From the outside, it looks perfect.

Looks can be deceiving.

I fasten my seat belt, a chill snaking up my spine as it clicks into place. Something tells me we're in for a bumpy ride.

THIRTEEN YEARS EARLIER
GABBY'S JOURNAL

I dreamt I was falling last night — a long, deep fall that seemed to last forever. I woke up just before I hit the ground, cloaked in a cold sweat, trembling and screaming. Greg wrapped his protective arms around me and whispered in my ear that he had me, and everything would be okay. That's what he always tells me — everything will be okay.

I want to believe him, but my husband is a terrible liar.

I know it's just a dream, but it feels like it's something more — like a warning. I have this inescapable sense of dread that we are headed toward some earth-shattering catastrophe.

For a few years, that urgent feeling of doom and gloom had all but vanished. The nightmares I'd struggled with since my parents died had mostly waned after I met Greg. For the first time in a long time, I felt safe. But now? Good Lord, it's come back with a vengeance. And the lucid dreams are enough to make me never want to close my eyes again.

The flames are so intense I feel them in sleep. I throw the covers from my body, sweat sticking to me like small fires. Sometimes I'm in the car with my parents. Other times, I'm watching, pinned in place as they burn to death.

And then I wake and realize it's less of a dream than a memory. I'm thinking of my mother and father, though I make it a practice never to think of my mother and father or the fiery car crash that instantly killed them and left me orphaned at the ripe old age of sixteen. After waking from one of these dreams, the thought of my parents' burning flesh sticks with me for days.

As if I've not got enough to worry about, I'm left pondering why life is so unfair.

At least I've got Greg.

We graduated six months ago from college, with big plans for our future. Greg signed a minor league contract with the Richmond Flying Squirrels *(yay!). And I was hired for my first adult job at a prestigious real estate agency (double yay!). I took the real estate course and got my license during our last semester of college. I was all ready to go with my name on a shiny business card by the time I graduated. Gabby Reynolds, Realtor, Houlihan Lawrence. It felt surreal getting dressed every morning in a sharp-looking outfit, coffee tumbler in hand, heading out into the real world.*

I loved everything about it — the action, the houses, the people. I was good at it, too. My boss said he'd never seen a new realtor build her own book of business so quickly. I told myself this was just the beginning of a long, lucrative, gratifying career. I pictured myself buying and selling homes forever, setting my own schedule so I could accompany my husband on the road.

So I could watch him.

But then, surprise! I was a few weeks late, and I don't have to tell you what that meant or how it happened. Suddenly, everything changed. Funny how someone who isn't even here yet has completely altered the direction of our lives.

Before I got pregnant — I was fairly certain I never wanted to have children in the first place. I mean — I loved my husband with all my heart. I knew we would have the most genetically, athletically, and academically blessed kids if we followed the parenthood path. But I was petrified of messing up another human being as my parents did me. They say you eventually turn into your parents. God, I hope they are wrong.

The plan was to float through life with Greg and my career and hopefully make friends and find hobbies to keep me occupied in my idle time. Heck, I might even dabble in volunteer work. I've heard you can hold crack-addicted babies in prison to help them wean off the drugs passed in utero from their incarcerated mothers. So I thought, maybe I'd do something like that. How much damage could I do a few hours a month?

Except, now I'm very pregnant with my own child, who I won't be able to snuggle for a couple of hours and then hand back to the prison nursery. My stomach has grown so large that I'm no longer sure I still have feet and ankles. They must be there, insanely swollen like the rest of my body.

Greg has all too readily taken to leaving me behind while he lives his best life, fulfilling his dreams.

What about my dreams?

I took a spill a few days ago while showing a Cape Cod in Carytown. It was a new listing I'd just secured, and I was the first agent to show the place. So no one should have stepped foot in that house other than me. Yet somehow, there was a slick of water in the foyer, just enough to send my legs flying out from underneath me, throwing me violently onto my back.

It's been a few days, and I still can't shake the feeling someone left that slick there for me to find. Greg says I'm being paranoid. The EMTs didn't report observing any moisture on the ground or anything that looked suspicious where I fell. I explained to Greg that it took twenty minutes for the ambulance to arrive, and I was lying in it, so maybe it absorbed into my cotton maternity dress. He gave me his best patronizing smile. "Don't be silly. The cleaners probably missed a spot. No one is trying to hurt you or our baby."

But what if they are? How can Greg be so sure?

And how can he be so fricking calm when we could have lost our child? Because even if I didn't want this child before, I do now. I love this baby growing inside me more than anything in this world. Maybe even more than my husband. Or perhaps it's just the hormones talking.

After twenty-four hours of observation — of mother and baby — I was released with explicit instructions to stay on bed rest for the remainder of my pregnancy. The doctor also warned Greg to monitor my mental state since, apparently, I'm already exhibiting signs of pregnancy paranoia. There's the potential for postpartum depression or, worse, psychosis.

I googled postpartum psychosis, and holy crap, that's scary. I can't imagine what would lead anyone to believe I might be a risk to myself or my unborn child.

I'll admit, I'm out of sorts. But that doesn't make me paranoid or crazy. Leave it to my husband and a male doctor to make that diagnosis. I'd love to see how they'd react if they were the ones in my maternity jeans. I'm sure they have my best interests at heart, but I also know I didn't imagine it. There was water on that floor. The cleaning crew was there two days prior. I was wearing flats. I may be pregnant, but I'm not a clown. I didn't trip over my own two feet.

Yet, here I am.

It isn't easy lying in bed, swollen like a whale, while your husband is living his best life on the road. We have no family other than each other, with me being an orphan and Greg cutting off his parents when he chose to marry me. I doubt they even know I'm carrying their grandchild.

Thank God for my neighbor and best friend, Susie Baker. Sometimes you meet people in life, and you just know. I knew from the moment I showed her the house next door to ours that we would be forever friends.

She's a fantastic cook and baker (ha-ha) — her chocolate-chip cookies are literally to die for! Okay, maybe not literally, but still, to die for. I bet she could make a small fortune if she sold her secret ingredient.

She's been checking in on me every day, sitting by my feet like a faithful dog and telling stories about our neighbors that have me laughing so hard I've almost peed the bed. What did I do to deserve a best friend like Susie? I couldn't possibly survive the next three months without her.

CHAPTER 3

GREG RIZZO

Only two hours into our nine-hour car ride, Cam is already complaining he's hungry. Unfortunately, I have no idea where Gabby packed the snacks, and I'm preoccupied with maneuvering our Escalade through bumper-to-bumper traffic.

Navigation announces, "Traffic accident two miles ahead" in her distinctive British brogue. I'm not sure why our navigation has a British brogue in the first place. Our car was manufactured in Arlington, Texas, and we live in Richmond, Virginia. I suppose it has become somewhat charming — that is, when there's no accident slowing traffic to a complete standstill and a hungry teen complaining on repeat in the back seat.

"Dad, did you hear me? I'm starving. Like my insides are literally eating themselves. Don't you care?"

"A little dramatic, Cam. And your insides can't eat themselves. Not literally, anyhow."

I watch Cameron roll his eyes in the rearview mirror.

I'm stuck between a rock and a hard place, well, a Fiat and a camper van, but the same thing. I want to let Gabby sleep — I mean, I *really, really* want to let her sleep — but I can't very well let my growing boy go hungry. Cam goes from zero to hangry in seconds. The last thing I need is for my son to be in a foul mood when we finally arrive in Georgia.

We all need to be on our best behavior.

I give Gabby a gentle nudge. She lets out a sleepy sigh, but her eyes remain glued shut. "Gabby," I whisper, prodding her slightly more forcibly this time, but she doesn't budge. She's out cold. If it weren't for the gentle rise and fall of her chest and the occasional animal-like whimper, I might worry she was dead.

Perish the thought.

I tighten my grip on the steering wheel so hard my hands hurt. It takes but a few seconds for my fingers to lose color.

Desperate times call for . . .

I cut off a red BMW, cringing as the driver lays on his horn while sticking his middle finger out the window and hurling an Urban Dictionary-worth of expletives at me. I throw up a hand to apologize, my own middle finger twitching in agony, desperate to respond. I remind myself that Cam is in the car. I'm all about setting a good example for my son where I can.

I'm not perfect. But then, who is? I bet if you asked Gabby, she'd tell you that her best friend, Susie Baker, is perfect. I glare down at the steering wheel, cursing the indentations my nails have left in the expensive leather.

Then I pull off the next exit to a rest stop. Now's as good a time as any to top off the tank, piss, and grab some food. Hopefully, that'll buy me at least a few hours without complaints. Assuming, of course, Gabby doesn't stir. She's been so tired lately; I'd bet the farm she won't.

I'm angling our SUV into a spot when the beeping starts. It's incessant, like a car-horn rendition of Frère Jacques.

Did the red BMW trail us off the exit? The last thing I need right now is to get tangled up in a road rage incident. We still have seven hours left to drive, assuming the traffic clears while we're stopped. I take a deep breath and ready myself to apologize profusely for cutting the asshole off.

I glance into the rearview, my fingers trembling on the door lever, and I see two sets of hands maniacally waving. There's no red BMW, just our neighbors in their white Suburban. I let out a long sigh of relief. I'm not sure how they wound up behind us, considering they left about ten minutes before we did, but here they are. At least I don't have to worry about a fistfight.

"Jake's here," Cam says enthusiastically, pointing behind us, his life-threatening hunger instantly forgotten. He jumps out of the car before I've had the chance to shift it into park.

Matt pulls into the spot next to us, and Susie hops out of the passenger side. She stretches her arms overhead, exposing the tanned skin on her abdomen. I try not to look. I always *try* not to look. But, like most things in life, easier said than done.

Matt emerges from the car, an easy smile on his face.

"Fancy meeting you here, neighbor. I mean, what are the chances?" He winks, and I wonder for a moment, what *are* the chances? It's a silly thought. We *are* going to the same place. It's not like they've randomly followed us to some abandoned diner in the middle of nowhere. This is a popular rest stop off I-95. It's a logical place to stop, especially in light of our current traffic situation.

Sometimes, I think Gabby's incessant paranoia is wearing off on me.

I had hoped not to talk to anyone, though, especially Matt and Susie, not until I'd had a chance to collect my thoughts, to process the pregnancy test properly. But, of course, I can't very well come out and say that to our best friends. Although I wonder, momentarily, if Susie already knows. Did Gabby tell *her* before telling me? I wouldn't be surprised. My wife tells her best friend everything.

"Cam was starving," I offer, shrugging my shoulders. "You know how it is. Couldn't very well let him die of starvation, could I?"

Matt nods knowingly. "Sounds like y'all had the same conversation we did in our car."

I swear, these boys are so alike it's unreal. But then, what thirteen-year-old boy isn't complaining about starving every two hours? A road trip with a teenage boy is worse than traveling with a pregnant woman. I taste the bile rising in my throat. As if on cue, the pregnancy test gives me a sharp jab in the leg.

"What about Gabby?" Susie asks, cupping a hand over her eyes and searching for Gabby through our heavily tinted windows.

"She's asleep in there. You probably can't see her." *Precisely why I upgraded our windows to the darkest tint legal under Virginia Commonwealth law.*

Susie rolls her eyes. "What are you doing to that poor woman, Greg? She's been so tired in the mornings lately." *And afternoons and nights.*

I clench my teeth. I know what Susie is implying. And no, Gabby is not conked out from the mind-blowing sex we didn't have last night. And yes, I've asked myself the same question over and over. Why is she so tired? I even called Dr. Green, and while he won't discuss what my wife has told him because of patient confidentiality, he at least let me voice my concerns. He even suggested a couples' session to work through those concerns together.

Well, at least now I have my answer.

I wonder if *he* knows my wife is pregnant.

Not that I plan on sharing any of this with Susie. She knows far too much about our lives as it is. Susie and my wife are like sixty-year-old yentas the way they gab, gossip, and vent. I've overheard one too many conversations I shouldn't have been privy to — I don't always like what I hear.

Cam has already disappeared into the rest stop with Jake and Matt. I'm debating leaving Gabby passed out in the parking lot with the car running. Or, I could kill the engine and open her window. But the temperature has risen at least fifteen degrees in the past two hours, the humidity hovering around us like an aura. Beads of perspiration line the waistband of my shorts, and I check to ensure I haven't sprouted wet marks in the armpits of my tee. Even with the air conditioner on blast, Gabby's hair is matted to her forehead.

Can I leave her?

All it would take is a split second for someone to jump in the driver's side and take off with my car, my wife, and all of Cameron's baseball equipment. Not that they'd get very far with all the traffic, but still. I could lock the doors with Gabby inside, but what if we can't wake her to let us back in?

Why does my wife have to be so goddamn difficult?

I'm lost in thought, practically sweating to death, as Susie and I stand awkwardly, melting in the parking lot. I debate reaching into my wallet and throwing her a twenty to buy Cam some snacks, but I need to use the restroom while I can. I'd prefer not to stop again. It would be nice if we made it to Georgia at some point today.

"Hey, would you mind waiting here with the car while I run inside?"

Susie tilts her head back and laughs. The sun glistens off her blonde hair, and the angels sing. Well, there's music — I definitely hear music. Is Gabby awake? *Nah,* I think. It can't be Gabby. She's as good as dead to the world in there.

Still, my heart jumps in my chest for a moment until I catch a Mustang zooming by us with its radio on full blast. Then, only somewhat relieved, my eyes flick back to the car nervously as if I've been caught doing something wrong. It's a familiar sensation where Susie is concerned.

Thou shalt not covet thy neighbor's wife.

I try not to stare, not to make it obvious to Gabby how wildly attracted I am to her best friend. But I wonder if it is obvious. I mean, who's not wildly attracted to Susie Baker?

I do not doubt if my wife were a lesbian, she would've left me for her best friend ages ago. Of course, I would never tell Gabby this, but I worry she's borderline obsessed with Susie.

I may not know much about the inner workings of female friendships, but I know a thing or two about my wife.

"Wait, let me get this straight," Susie says with a girlish giggle that sends me back to middle school. "You want me to babysit your wife? What's the hourly rate?"

"When you put it that way . . ." I run a hand through my hair, aware of the color spreading across my cheeks. Susie makes me nervous in a way I struggle to make sense of.

"I'm joking. Go on in. I'll wait with Gabby."

"Are you sure?"

"Yes, Greg, I'm sure. Now go before I change my mind. It's hot as an oven out here."

"Thanks, Susie. You're the best."

I feel her eyes on my back as I walk away. I'm glad Gabby is conked out in the car. Because what would she think watching her best friend devour her husband with her eyes? And if she knew just how much I enjoyed it? And Matt? It can't be easy having a wife who looks like that.

Not your problem, I remind myself.

Clearly, I have my own problems.

CHAPTER 4

GABBY RIZZO

I awake with a start to the low hum of our engine and an ice-pick headache behind my right eye. My face is squished against the seatbelt, drool trickling out the side of my mouth and dribbling down my chin. I don't need a mirror to know how mangled I look. If it's even half as bad as how I feel, I should probably phone it in and lock myself in our hotel room until the end of the tournament.

My eyes take a few minutes to adjust to the bright light of the afternoon. I blink several times to push out the remnants of sleep, and my vision finds Greg standing in a parking lot. I check the time on the dash and realize we must be at the hotel. Holy crap, I must have slept the entire way. And yet, I don't feel any more rested than I did before we left. Greg is talking to Matt and Susie, his posture comfortable and his face relaxed as if he hasn't a care in the world. I swear this man doesn't get nervous at all, like ever. It's not normal that he doesn't sweat. I wipe a hand across my forehead. Even in sleep, I'm anxious. Even in sleep, I sweat.

I guess I just have more to be anxious about than my husband.

I fan out my shirt, attempting to dry the swimming pools that have formed in the underbelly of my breasts. Then, against my better judgment, I pull down the passenger-side mirror to steal a peek at my reflection. Despite what my husband thinks — and I know he thinks this — I actually care about my appearance. I just don't have the time or energy to do anything about it. It seems I'm always running from one place to the next, catering to his and Cam's needs, only occasionally my own. A part of me likes the constant motion, though, because it's in the stillness that the dark thoughts come.

The dark thoughts, replete with flashes of flames. I physically shake off the images. I cannot afford to think about my parents this weekend.

I lick a finger and run it under each eye to catch any remnants of day-old mascara. I should splurge on eyelash extensions like Susie, so I look more human than raccoon in the sweltering summer heat. I give my cheeks a sharp pinch each and throw on a coat of clear lip gloss. For now, that will have to do.

My phone rings in my purse. I slide my hand in and silence the ringer. My eyes momentarily flick down to the screen. The parent group chat is abuzz. There's a text from Colton Miller's dad, Steven — *Carla isn't feeling well. She won't be making it to the tournament.* I register another ten or so other texts I have zero intention of answering. I loosen my grip and let the phone fall to the bottom of my bag, where I don't have to think about it.

I take a deep breath and open the car door. Susie's laser gaze immediately darts in my direction. She always seems to know where I am, as if she's got a radar on me. Gabby radar. *Gabdar.* I chuckle to myself. I should write that one down when we get home. I think longingly of my journal, tucked safely between the mattress and box spring of our bed, the one I haven't had time to write in for the past year.

Because there's never enough time.

Susie sashays to my side, her hips swinging back and forth like a pendulum. I take in all five foot three of her and curse under my breath for not putting forth more effort. Susie is so blond and so tan, and her shorts are so short, and her legs are so long. I've never been the jealous type, but then I've also never been best friends with a woman who has a plastic surgeon on speed dial and drips confidence.

"Daaarliiin," she says, stretching out her vowels and kissing each of my cheeks in a slow, deliberate motion. Apparently, while I was sleeping through the nine-hour drive to Georgia, Susie was busy picking up a Southern drawl. Because, of course, she was. She's Susie.

"We thought you'd neeeveeer wake up."

Oh, and who are we? I chew on my lower lip just long enough to feel a trickle of blood break through the surface. I lick it away, wondering if I was the source of Susie, Matt, and Greg's easygoing conversation. I mean, what's a little laugh among friends at Gabby's expense, right?

A sharp pain shoots across my jaw as I grit my teeth. And then I force a tight smile because although I've woken up, it feels as though I'm still on the tail end of a major bender.

"Yeah," I say. "I guess I was a little tired." *Understatement of the century.* I stretch my arms overhead and half stifle a yawn for good measure.

My limbs are like gelatin, and I literally could not keep my eyes open, I could add, but I don't. Susie doesn't need to know about the waves of bone-crushing fatigue I've been experiencing lately. Not when she's shifting from side to side like the Energizer Bunny with a fresh set of batteries. I wonder if there's something wrong with me and if it's time I pay another visit to my internist. Or will Dr. Green say for the millionth time that it's all in my head?

Plenty of time to worry after the trip.

I add health concerns to my growing list of things to worry about *after* the trip. Then I take another deep breath, trying to shake the exaggerated sense of doom clinging to my body like a pair of Spanx.

I promised Dr. Green I'd utilize his 3-3-3 strategy in situations like these. Name three things I see, three things I hear, and three things I feel. I'm not confident he knows what he's talking about half the time, *but oh, what the heck*, I'll give it a whirl. I see a palm tree, Susie's Tory Burch sandals that have exploded in popularity since she got them, and — my eyes travel up — her unnaturally large breasts. I hear birds chirping, an engine revving, and lastly, I hear my best friend's voice in my ear.

"Come on, Gabby." She grabs my arm, shattering my internal dialogue before I can get to the three things I feel. No need to remind myself that I feel like crap.

Susie pulls me along like I'm her Bichon Frise, and she's got me by the leash. It often feels that way — it's Susie's world, and I'm just living in it, along for whatever ride she chooses to take me on. I don't mind it too much, though, most of the time. It's not like she's going out of her way to make me feel like this. With all my time and energy exhausted on Cam, I've mostly forgotten what it's like to have my own interests. My best friend has plenty of interests that she's more than happy to share with me. Life wouldn't be half as interesting without her in it.

"Earth to Gabby." Susie snaps her recently manicured nails in front of my face, bringing me back to the present. They're a pale pink — *Let's Be Friends*, I think — with a strip of bright red across the top, as if they were dipped in blood. I've never seen a French manicure like this, but I'm sure all the baseball moms will be sporting it by the next tournament. "Gaaaabyyyy, are you listening to me? You have to see this place. It's just absolutely aaaamaaaaziiing."

Of course, it's absolutely aaaamaaaziiing; Susie was the one who picked the place. So our team is staying here while all the other teams competing in the tournament are staying in local inns and motels much closer to the fields. Not that I'm about to complain. The last thing I would ever want to do is hurt Susie's feelings. And besides, this place does have all the bells and whistles the others do not — indoor and outdoor pools, fine dining, and spa services. Plus, Susie secured a ridiculously low rate for the stay. All it takes is one look, and it's impossible to say no to Susie Baker. She can be very persuasive.

I twist my neck around to find Greg, but he's no longer chatting with Matt. Cam is missing too, so I assume they've gone to the reception desk to check us in. Better that way, so I have a chance to get my act together.

I let Susie drag me down a literal red carpet to the entryway until we're standing in front of a sign that reads *Foxcroft* in a looping script.

"Wow," I say because I can't find another word to describe the resort's main building. It's quite stunning, but with a definite side of creepy. I researched this place before the trip — the building is old as sand, constructed centuries ago for a wealthy plantation owner. It's like a giant mausoleum, with its whitewashed stone and triangular entryway. It survived the Civil War and the slavery era, and I can't help but wonder how many bodies were buried here.

I swallow the thought and follow Susie through the archway into the lobby of our home-away-from-home for the next five days. I exhale a sigh of relief when no crypts or tombs present themselves. To my surprise, the inside is modernized, with shiny wood floors emblazoned with the Foxcroft logo in bright red letters and glossy walls decorated with various abstracts, mixed-media paintings, and black-and-white prints.

It's not what I expected for a centuries-old Southern resort. That's part of my problem, or so I've been told — too many expectations. My expectations and reality often collide. Still, it's safe to say Foxcroft needs to update its website.

And don't get me started on the staff. The employees are all dressed in head-to-toe black — down to their nail polish and hair ties. *Very un-Southern*, I think. I can't shake the feeling I've walked in on a funeral.

A sense of apprehension unfolds in my stomach just as a hand digs into my shoulder. I whip around, and my heart does a jig in my chest. My face turns the precise shade of the Foxcroft logo, and I want to cry.

I *really* want to cry.

"Greg, how many times do I have to tell you to stop sneaking up on me?" My voice is shaking almost as much as my hands.

I dig my nails into my palms and take a deep, deliberate breath. *Stop overreacting*, I tell myself. The combination of Greg startling me for the second time today and Susie standing by my side to witness it has me flustered. It's bad enough that there are cracks in our marriage; I don't need other people to see them. Especially my best friend Susie, who would no doubt maintain her composure in a shark tank.

I've often wondered how she does it — confronting life with the steely self-control of a Buckingham Palace guard. Then the nagging thoughts creep in, the ones that always seem to surface when it comes to my best friend. I wonder if I will ever look as good as she looks, cook as well as she cooks, or be as good a mom to Cameron as she is to Jake.

I wonder if my husband will ever look at me the way he looks at her.

It's strange how you can love and hate someone so much simultaneously.

"I'm so sorry, babe. Just wanted to let you know we're all checked in. Is everything okay? You're awfully edgy today." He digs his fingers into my shoulder, and I flinch.

"Gosh, she sure is." Susie plants a hand firmly on her hip and nods her blonde head in wholehearted agreement. She has expertly colored hair made to look like she has natural sun-kissed highlights. I'm suddenly self-conscious of my mousy brown roots dipped in a golden-bordering-orange hue that looks like it's never seen a bottle of toner. I'm tempted to grab a chunk of Susie's hair in my hand. I love my friend, but she is such a pick-me girl sometimes; it feels like I'm back in middle school.

I grit my teeth and smile as widely as my jaw allows. My teeth are clenched so tightly, and my cheeks pulled so taut, I must resemble a ventriloquist's dummy. Totally the look I was going for today.

Totally.

My gaze drifts to the keycard in Greg's hand and then to the body behind him. Cameron's standing there, staring at his shoes, a peculiar expression on his face. I hate that he is watching me melt, sweat dripping down my face like the hot wax of a candle.

I must pull myself together and do damage control for my son.

"Hi honey," I say, my voice so sickly sweet that I make myself nauseous. "Dad just gave me a little scare."

"Whatever," he replies, refusing to meet my gaze. *Whatever.* My sweet baby boy's new favorite word. My heart clenches, remembering when that word was *mama.*

I wish someone had warned me how much my loving child, the little boy who cried every morning for an entire year when I dropped him off at preschool, would want absolutely nothing to do with me a decade later. My heart aches, but I would still do anything for him. *Anything.* I guess that's parenthood in a nutshell.

I try to infuse some light into my voice. "Did you see your room yet, Cam?"

"Nah, not yet."

"Come on," I say, suddenly desperate for a reprieve from Greg's and Susie's assessing stares. I know they're both worried about me, but still. It feels like I've been flattened against a slide and squeezed under a microscope.

"What do you say we go find Jake and get you boys situated?"

Cam nods, his sandy hair once again fanning his forehead. This time, I can't resist. I bring a hand to his face and push the hair away.

"Mooooommmm," he complains. I quickly move my hand away, not wanting to embarrass him, but not before I catch the corners of his lips twitching ever so slightly. I'm learning the teen years are a delicate dance, the choreography complicated and constantly changing. You either move along with it, follow the steps as best as you can, or risk getting booed off the stage. There's no room for complacency in motherhood. Just when you think you know your child and have it all figured out, they flip the script and throw you for a loop.

It's small moments like these, though, that feel like big victories. I am trying to enjoy these moments as they come because there haven't been many lately. Not with Cam. Certainly not with Greg.

I spot Matt and Jake in conversation with Cam's coach on the other side of the lobby.

"Let's go," I say, reaching out a hand but thinking better of it and pulling it back. *Dance, Gabby, dance.* Lately, it feels less like dancing and more like balancing on a paper-thin tightrope.

I feel Greg's and Susie's eyes on my back as we walk away from them. Once again, my cheeks flame red. I'm not sure when my best friend and husband started making me so uncomfortable. I must try not to think about it because I don't have the time or energy to tumble face-first down Alice's rabbit hole.

Not this weekend, anyway.

Cameron grins widely as we make our way across the lobby. It's the first time I've seen him smile all day, which makes me think, at least momentarily, that this trip is all worthwhile, despite how awful I currently feel.

"Hey there, slugger." Coach Bob holds up a hand, and Cam readily slaps it. Bob shakes it off, feigning a look of pain as if Cam just broke every finger with his superhuman strength. There's no denying that Coach Bob has a way with these boys. He taps into something we, as parents, can't touch.

Unless he doesn't like you. Then you don't want to know him. Thankfully, that's not a problem we've ever had to contend with.

"Hey, Coach Bob." Cam's grin stretches from ear to ear, his face shining like the sun.

"How's that arm feeling, ace?"

"Feeling like it's ready to throw another no-hitter."

"Now that's what I like to hear. You know we're all counting on you to bring home the championship rings."

As my boy and his coach talk shop, I feel a swell of happiness and pride. *It's going to be a great weekend,* I think. Until I glance over my shoulder at my husband and best friend. Susie has one manicured hand draped over Greg's shoulder while her ruby-red lips are pressed against his ear.

CHAPTER 5

GREG RIZZO

I don't have to look up to know Gabby is watching me. It's a sixth sense I've developed over our ten-plus years together. I used to relish her stare — as I stepped up to the plate or wound up at the mound — but now, it feels accusatory and intrusive. It feels loaded, like a gun.

I delicately extricate myself from Susie. She's standing too close, whispering in my ear. Usually, I'd marinate in the attention, but not when I know my wife is watching.

"Do you think Gabby is acting strange, Greg? I'm really worried about her. She's been all over the place lately."

Maybe she doesn't know.

I force a small smile. "Gabby is just tired, Susie. It was a long drive down." I leave out the part where she literally slept the entire way. Because it's totally normal for a grown adult to take a nine-hour nap, right? "I'm going to go check on the boys," I offer instead as I walk away from her.

Sometimes I wonder if Susie truly cares about my wife or if it's all a ploy to get her recently filled lips close to my face. Either way, I can't say I mind the attention. I am a hot-blooded man, after all. All I ever wanted was Gabby's attention and affection, but now, that's reserved for Cam.

I jam a hand into my pocket, wrapping my fingers tightly around the positive pregnancy test. I'm positive it isn't possible, but here I am, gripping it so tightly it threatens to snap.

I decide I'll confront Gabby tonight. I need alcohol to loosen my thoughts and words. I wonder if Gabby will have a cocktail. She probably shouldn't, considering, but then I probably shouldn't say anything because I'm not supposed to know.

Because she didn't tell me.

I plaster on the most convincing smile I can muster as I approach the cluster of bodies gathering around Coach Bob as if he's a goddamn celebrity. I'm not surprised to find Matt among the crowd of fans. He'd gladly move into Bob's ass if humanly possible. I guess that happens when you have a mediocre child; you have to suck up to keep them relevant. We don't need to remind anyone how relevant our Cam is; his performance speaks for itself.

Always has.

Always will.

Matt is busy talking strategy with Bob, his hands animated, moving in all directions. I roll my eyes. He should stick with computer programming or whatever it is that he does. I once overheard Susie tell Gabby that her husband is better with computers than people. I'm not sure if that's a fact, but I can say I've never met a man who knows less about the sport of baseball. The gist of the conversation is that Jake should start at pitcher in the first game tomorrow so he can pitch again in the last. But it's an elimination tournament, so that's a risky move. Jake has speed, but he's spotty and wild. It makes more sense to put in a sure thing, like Cam.

As if in my thoughts, Coach Bob agrees. "I hear you, Matt, I do, but I'm gonna save Jake for a little later in the tournament. Cam is starting tomorrow." My insides smile. Coach Bob doesn't say that if they make it that far, it's Cam he wants in the championship game on the mound. Not Jake.

Some things in life are better left unsaid.

Matt's eyebrows turn in, and his mouth pinches into a tight line. "You know best, Coach." There's a razor edge to his voice that I don't like. If he notices, Coach Bob doesn't let on. He's Switzerland when it comes to player politics. He's used to parents telling him how to do his job, especially when it's their kids involved. Because every parent thinks their kid is the best. Special. That's what separates us from them. We don't think; we know.

Since he was seven, every one of Cam's coaches and instructors has told us they haven't seen this level of raw talent and potential in a child since (insert any major-league ballplayer name here). The players may change, but the implication remains the same — our boy, Cameron Rizzo, is destined for major-league stardom.

They once said the same thing about Greg Rizzo, too. It still stings like alcohol poured on an open wound.

Matt's voice snaps me out of my thoughts. "Well, now that we have that sorted out, I guess I should bring the boys to their room." I watch as he slips one protective arm around Jake and the other around Cameron, his displeasure over Cam starting over Jake seemingly forgotten. I'm not surprised that the boys are rooming together. They're so close; it's as if they shared a womb. I suspect that Matt treats Cam as if he's his own, partly because he wishes he were.

Considering this morning's surprising turn of events, I'm grateful it's Matt staying with them, not me. I wouldn't want Cam to see what I'm going to do if . . . I shake my head, trying to loosen the thought. The truth is — I don't know what I will do. For once, I don't have a plan or an end game. *Smooth things over with Gabby? Leave my pregnant wife?*

My gaze finds Gabby smiling and laughing along with the other parents. I wonder how she can act like everything is status quo when hiding something as big as this from her husband. Then I remember that my wife is good at hiding things.

This tournament seems to have brought out the worst in me. And yet, I can't shake the feeling that there's worse to come. It's sticking to me like a cotton tee on a hot summer's day.

I'm being paranoid. It's probably just a case of pre-game jitters. Nothing more.

Well, other than the positive pregnancy test stuffed in the back of our kitchen drawer, obviously.

I turn to Gabby. "I'm going to go with the boys to check out their suite. Why don't you get settled, and I'll meet you in our room, okay?" I reach into my pocket to grab the keycard, my fingers hovering momentarily over the pregnancy test.

"Sounds like a plan," she says, taking the card in her hand.

"Room 2-0-0-2," I tell her as I turn to follow Matt, Jake, and Cam.

"Room 2-0-0-2," she repeats as if trying to grasp the numbers tightly so she doesn't lose them. I wonder if she'll be back at the front desk ten minutes from now, asking for our room number. My wife has been incredibly forgetful lately.

Not my problem.

Cam is my problem.

The pregnancy test is my problem.

Her lies are my problem.

And the thing about problems is that, at some point, they need to be fixed.

TWELVE YEARS EARLIER
GABBY'S JOURNAL

Greg has been acting so strange lately. Distant. I can't help but feel like I've done something wrong. But what could I have possibly done wrong?

I'm probably just being paranoid.

That happens a lot more than I'd care to admit. Certainly, more than I'd ever admit to Greg. Susie says it's the post-pregnancy hormones. She suffered through it as well and nearly left Matt. Eventually, it got better for her. I'm still waiting for it to get better for me.

I know it's been hard for Greg lately.

All he ever wanted was to play ball. I remember how he swelled with pride the first time we watched his Little League tapes together. High school. College. Of course, I was at every college game, but there's nothing quite the same as watching a highlight reel of the best moments starring your gorgeous, talented husband.

But I'm not going to lie; I wanted my husband home with our son and me. I guess I just didn't expect him to be so miserable. It all happened so quickly as if someone hit the fast-forward button on our lives. In one frame, Greg was pitching a no-hitter. In the next, he couldn't lift his arm. Then the surgery. Then the unexpected retirement from baseball. I can't help but feel like he blames me. Perhaps he's just desperate for someone to blame other than himself.

I support him; of course, I do, but he shouldn't have done what he did — end of story.

And now, he's suffering the consequences.

I encouraged Greg to put together a résumé and send it out to some banks and Fortune 500 companies, just in case. What if the surgery wasn't a success? What if he couldn't pitch the way he pitched before? What if the major-league teams decided not to take a chance on a minor league ball player coming off the injured reserve and surgery?

Greg didn't want to consider such a possibility, but he grew tired of my voice in his ear telling him he needed a backup plan. Thankfully he eventually relented. While Greg was working his ass off trying to get back on the diamond, he was also fielding multiple offers from high-profile companies.

Good thing, too, since he never made it back out there.

When he was alive, my father always warned me, "Be careful what you wish for." He was right; I hate that he was right. While I wanted Greg home with us, it's been rough having him here. I expected things to be different — for Greg to be more hands-on, more emotionally invested in our day-to-day life. But, instead, he's completely withdrawn from me.

He's thrown himself head-first into his new career, which I guess is a good thing, but it's not quite what I had expected. What I had prepared myself for.

Susie says men build their identities and self-worth around their careers, whereas women can be fulfilled with just their families. More than a little sexist and completely outdated, but I would never say as much to her. Susie certainly seems to know the opposite sex better than I do. You should see what it's like when we go out in public together — all the stares, whispers, and catcalls. I'd like to think maybe one out of the hundred men that stops us on the street is looking at me. But I realize chances are they're not.

And then I remind myself I have a breathtakingly handsome, successful husband. Greg could have had any woman he wanted. But he chose me. I'm not sure why he chose me, but he did.

Not Susie.

Me.

CHAPTER 6

GABBY RIZZO

The hallways are cloaked in low light, barely illuminated by strategically placed decorative torches affixed to the dark walls. Black, wrought iron — they remind me of medieval times. All that's missing is the knight armor statues. The carpets are a brilliant red, cropped low like a crew cut. I'm not sure what vibe they're going for, but now, I'm overwhelmed by the sensation of stumbling onto a crime scene.

I realize I'm incredibly out of touch with what's "in" and think perhaps goth chic has made a comeback while I've been busy at home raising my son. I picture the shiny magazine cover on Susie's kitchen island that I flipped through while she made us mimosas yesterday — Gigi and Bella Hadid with half-shaved heads and bleached eyebrows.

Yes, that must be it.

It was one of our usual days, filled with new recipes, face masks, Mahjong, nail painting, copious amounts of wine, and all the other things girlfriends do. She was filling me in on the latest gossip in our upscale community.

"Allegedly," she said, draining her wine glass in a large gulp and leaning in close as if our neighbors were listening. "The Edens and the Lees are swingers."

"Stop, no way. You are totally making that up."

"Am I?" She arched an eyebrow and drew a cross across her chest.

"Wow! I had no idea. I would never have called that one. The Edens, maybe. But the Lees? My mind is officially blown. What would I do without your intel, Susie?"

She laughed. "Speaking of swinging, did you pack for the baseball trip?"

"If you could call all of our stuff strewn all over the house 'packed,' then yes, I suppose I did."

"Well, what are you wearing to the banquet?"

"A little black dress. You?"

"I haven't a thing to wear," she said, throwing her head over her shoulder and draping a hand across her forehead.

"Lucky for you, I just so happen to have the new Neiman Marcus collection at my disposal."

Susie clapped her hands and squealed like a little girl.

We walked next door to my house so she could fan through my racks of overpriced dresses, looking for something to wear to the banquet. My closet is filled from top to bottom with designer clothing, high-end shoes, and trendy accessories I'll never wear. Susie is much more interested in those sorts of things, and perhaps if I had the figure of an eighteen-year-old yoga instructor, I would be, too. But, unfortunately, pregnancy hasn't agreed with my body the way it has hers. Everything looks fantastic on her, even if the dresses pull too tightly around her ridiculous breasts. Sometimes I wonder if I should bite the bullet and ask for her plastic surgeon's number.

"You should go with the white one," I suggested. "Maybe pair it with the Stewart Weitzman crystal sandals? It makes you look angelic. Like a virgin." I winked conspiratorially. Susie is a lot of things — virginal not being one of them.

She giggled. "How very Kanye West of you. But I'm gonna go with this one."

She held out a red strapless number that I had only recently acquired. It looks like a stripper dress but retails for over one thousand dollars. I didn't bother telling her she'd be one deep breath away from a major wardrobe malfunction in that dress. We both knew that's why she chose it.

I debated handing over my red tango La Perla thong to go with it. It would look much better on Susie than it would on me. It's satin and lace and just the perfect shade to compliment any skin tone; at least, that's what it said on the website. Susie would surely look like a Victoria's Secret runway model in the thong.

But I need that underwear. I need something to wrangle my husband's attention. We haven't been intimate in ages, so I know he won't be expecting it.

I check the numbers on the doors until I find 2002. Greg over-annunciated them as if I couldn't comprehend what he was telling me. I don't know when he started treating me like a challenged child instead of his spouse. Perhaps it was always like this, and I was too enamored with his attention to notice or care. I used to find it endearing that he was always looking out for me. I find it oppressive now as if his hands are wrapped snugly around my neck.

Feel three things. I swallow to prove I still can, jiggle my pointer finger, and chew on my lower lip until I draw blood. Then I press the gray plastic card against the magnetic chamber. The mechanism beeps, and a light flashes green. I take a deep breath and turn the door handle.

I let myself into the king-sized room, which smells of freshly cut roses. The lighting is ampler here, the purplish-pink swirls of a setting sun streaming in. I don't have to force the smile that spreads across my lips as I look around the room. The tension drains from my body as I take in the lacy white shades, fluffy eyelet duvet, and gold-wrapped chocolates on the pillows atop a family of towels folded like swans.

This is what I had in mind when I booked the trip. It feels like I've stepped into the pages of a romance novel where a lost couple reunites in a Paris hotel room and reignites their once-passionate flame. Okay, so we're not in France, but in a small town in Georgia, and we haven't lost each other in the literal sense, but still. This room feels full of promises of a second chance at love and happiness. It fills me with the hope that I can make my marriage better. That I can save it.

Something out of place on the floor catches my attention. I screw up my eyes, trying to identify what it is. It's smack dab in the middle of the room, a dark stain against the carpet, which is more a dusty rose than scarlet. Maybe housekeeping dropped a cleaning rag, or a stray sock got overlooked. A little careless for a four-star resort, but I suppose these things happen.

Human error.

I move closer, tentatively.

I can't tell what it is I'm looking at. Or maybe, subconsciously, I'm trying not to. My legs won't listen to my brain, screaming, "Stop, Gabby, stop," and they keep propelling me forward until I'm hovering over the object. This is the part where I wish I could rewind ten seconds and go back to not knowing what it is. Maybe a full minute before I walked into this room. How about half a day before we left home for this trip?

I'm staring at a dead rat.

It's about half a foot long, cut straight down the middle as if dissected for a biology class. And it's definitely deceased. Its innards are spread across the floor, blood trickling, seeping into the carpet.

I hold a hand over my mouth and gag.

And then I scream at the top of my lungs like a crazy person. It's a sound I didn't know existed within me — deep and visceral — the sound of someone who has stumbled upon a murdered rodent in a fancy hotel room. Not something you see very often or, if you're lucky, *ever*.

And yes, I said murdered.

What the serious fuck?

I want to run from the room, but my feet feel like they've been dipped in cement. So I stand rooted in place, unable to put distance between myself and the dead rat or to avert my eyes from its corpse. The rat that met a brutal, deliberate death. The rat that, I can only imagine, someone left here for myself or Greg to find.

Greg.

I think about how Greg handed me the keycard in the lobby, insisting I go to our room alone. He needed to get Cam settled into his room, even though Matt could fully escort our boys. Was Greg in this room before me? Did he leave a dead rat here for me to stumble upon? Did he drive the nine-plus hours to Georgia with a dead rat in his luggage tucked away between his expensive boxer shorts and no-wrinkle tees?

I shake my head, berating myself for the ridiculous thoughts. My husband may be inconsiderate at times, and we may live more like Craigslist-matched roommates than lovers as of late. But still, I know Greg would never do something as twisted as this. My husband is not a psychopath.

But someone is.

Some people will do *anything* to win.

Is that what this is about?

I wonder, did one of the other parents break into our room? Did they leave this here to scare us off? Were they hoping we would abandon the tournament with Cameron in tow? Would anyone go this far for their kid to get playing time and, with the spotlight off Cam, possibly scout attention?

This possibility seems almost as improbable as Greg planting a dead rat in our room. Yet, I nonetheless struggle to come up with any other explanation. Because, again, I'm staring at a dead rat in our room.

I keep screaming bloody murder because I don't know what else to do. The door swings open, and a slight woman in a black housekeeping dress pushes into the room, propping the door open with her cleaning cart. She moves cautiously toward me.

Like everyone else in my life, I imagine she's assessing me. Asking herself, *Has this woman gone mad? Does she need to be evaluated by a medical health professional?* Wondering, *Should I call management? 911?*

But when her eyes flick down to the floor, she starts screaming along with me. I'm not crazy. There's a murdered rat sprawled out by our feet.

We stand frozen, two adult strangers hollering in unison, like small children who've spotted a spider on the slide at recess. Eventually, she pulls herself together enough to grab me by the arm and drag me out into the hallway away from the deceased rodent.

Grateful is the understatement of the century.

I try to lean against the hallway for support but wind up sliding down, collapsing in a heap on the floor. I realize I'm hyperventilating, so I hold my breath for ten seconds and then exhale through pursed lips. I do this exercise repeatedly until my breathing slowly returns to normal. Then I bury my head in my hands and rub my eyes, trying to erase the image of the deceased rat, its silver fur matted with patches of dark red.

Fat chance of that. It might as well be tattooed on my inner eyelids.

The housekeeper babbles in Spanish over her walkie-talkie. *Rata muerta, rata muerta, rata muerta,* she says repeatedly.

Within minutes, it seems the whole front desk and hotel staff have funneled into the hallway, taking turns traipsing through my room, verifying the existence of the rata muerta. Now there's a Spanish phrase Lord knows I'll never forget.

That and: *asesinada.*

Murdered.

Apparently, I'm not the only one who thought so.

I watch from my perch on the blood-red carpet as a tall man wearing a severe black suit and an equally severe face walks into the room with a Hefty bag. He emerges moments later with the rat in his possession. He wordlessly drops it into the housekeeping bucket and motions toward the cart for someone to wheel it away.

And just like that, it's gone with a flick of the wrist.

I wonder if something like this has happened here before, and I don't know if I should feel better or worse if that's the case. Perhaps better because that would mean it wasn't left here for me to find. But maybe worse if murder is an acceptable activity here because that would make this a dangerous place.

I want to get in the car, drive home, and pretend this little trip never happened. But, obviously, that's not an option. We are here for Cam. Greg doesn't know this, but we are also here to rekindle the spark that's flickered out in our relationship.

New room, new bed.

Dead rat on the floor.

Asesinada.

I can't believe the turn the day has taken.

"Madame?" The collector of the rat is hovering over me with an arm outstretched. I slip my hand into his and allow him to help me to my feet. His wrist cracks loudly, making me jump, and then I remember where that hand has been, and I fight the urge to barf.

"Are you okay?" he asks, eyes wide and probing, and I nod unconvincingly because clearly, I am not okay. I'm not sure if I'll ever be okay. I'm unsure if I'll ever walk into another room without picturing a rat in rigor mortis with a bloody gash lining its underbelly.

"I am so sorry for any distress this has caused you. Nothing like this has ever happened here before. I can assure you we do not have a rodent problem."

So it was left here for me.

I'm not sure how to respond. *Clearly, you do have a rodent problem? Clearly, I have a rodent problem?* Because clearly, we all have some sort of a rodent problem.

He continues before I have a chance. "I am having your stuff moved to a different room, obviously. Room 2010 — just down the hall. Your room will be comped for the night, and I'd also like to offer you this complimentary pass for free drinks this evening."

He hands me a card, and I respond with a surprisingly natural smile, considering the circumstances. It's as if he's handed over a nugget of solid gold. After what just happened, an alcoholic beverage sounds better than a diamond necklace.

Though I shouldn't be drinking.

"Thank you," I say, taking the free drink voucher. "If my husband comes to the front desk looking for me — his name is Greg Rizzo — could you please let him know he can find me at the bar?"

"Yes, ma'am, of course. Is there anything else I can do for you?"

Where do I even begin? I shake my head and offer up a weak smile.

I can already taste the alcohol swishing in my mouth as I turn from him and speed walk to the elevator. I whip my head around twice to make sure there are no rats following because, really, I need something else to worry about.

I wonder what Dr. Green will have to say about this. Will he tell me I'm overreacting? Making something out of nothing? For a brief moment, I question, *am I?* No, I am decidedly not. There's no overreacting over a murdered rat. There's no misinterpreting the mark of a box-cutter blade.

The doors to the elevator open, and Greg steps out just as I'm about to step on.

His lips turn up when he sees me, but then his eyes travel down the hall to the throng of workers congregated outside our room. A concerned look spreads across his handsome face like a dark cloud covering the sun.

Greg couldn't possibly have done this.

He places a protective hand on my shoulder, and heat rises to my cheeks. Greg rarely touches me anymore. As his fingers begin working their way through the knots in my neck, I realize how much I miss the feel of his hands on my body.

While his eyes search mine for answers, goosebumps spread across my skin.

I draw a deep breath, steadying myself.

"There was a dead rat in our room."

"Wait, what?"

"I know, it's crazy. It was just lying there on the carpet."

Greg's eyebrows bend in toward one another. I can't read the expression on his face. This says a lot about how our relationship has shifted, and a wave of sadness washes over me. We used to know each other's thoughts before we thought them.

"I'm sorry I didn't check the room first, Gabby. I . . . I should have been here with you."

"It's not your fault," I say, meaning it. "You were with Cam."

Alas, the story of our lives.

"Well, I'm here now. Were you coming to look for me?" Greg's hazel eyes are wide and expectant, like a puppy dog's, and there's a warmth in them I haven't felt in a while.

"Actually, if I'm being honest, I just wanted to get as far away from this room as possible. The manager gave me this drink voucher. I thought I'd go sit in the bar."

"May I join you, Mrs. Rizzo?"

"You certainly may, Mr. Rizzo." I find myself batting my eyelashes at my husband. *Flirting.* I'm actually flirting with my husband.

It's been a long while since we've enjoyed such easy, amorous banter. I can almost pretend that we don't have more issues between us than *Sports Illustrated*.

Almost.

Once upon a time, our relationship was perfect, like a page from a romance novel. We met at college orientation and were practically attached at the hip from that day on. Greg was my world. I sacrificed friendships so I could be there to support him at every game, feed him after every practice, and keep him company at the gym during the off-season. I did it because I loved him, but also because I believed in him. I believed in us.

Little did I know at the time that our relationship would come to more closely resemble a thriller.

Because then he cheated on me.

And then I forgave him. Well, I sort of forgave him. But I haven't forgotten.

The elevator door has long since closed, and Greg presses the button on the wall to summon it back. An awkward silence stretches between us, similar to those early days of dating when you can only guess the other person's next move, like a game of chess. When the door opens, we step into the elevator together in sync. Though, I suspect that's more conditioning than anything else.

As the elevator lurches, my stomach drops, not just from the lift dipping to the floor below. I look in Greg's direction and realize I have butterflies swarming in my stomach. It's a sensation I haven't felt with my husband in ages. It's a welcome and wondrous feeling until I picture the dead rat. Then, I wonder if what I'm actually feeling is a warning siren.

TWELVE YEARS EARLIER
GABBY'S JOURNAL

I nearly choked on my coffee when I picked up the Richmond Times *this morning.*

The headline read: Rizzo — What a Dope.

What were the chances they were talking about a different Rizzo? About anyone other than my husband? I quickly read through the article as I listened to the sounds of a waterfall upstairs as Greg showered, oblivious to the bombshell sitting in front of me.

It was bad. Really, really bad.

> Minor League player and Major League prospect Greg Rizzo is the latest in a string of athletes to fail a drug test. Rizzo has been on the injured reserve list for the past three months and was slated to return to the diamond after a successful surgery repairing his shoulder. Now, after testing positive for performance-enhancing substances, he is facing the prospect of being permanently banned from professional baseball.

I crumpled the newspaper and buried it in the bottom of the recycling bin, knowing Greg would go absolutely ballistic if he saw it. Maybe this was the only article of its kind. He was a bit of a local celebrity, so it didn't come as a complete surprise that the Richmond Times *would run a story covering him. They did when he got injured in the first place.*

Maybe this was all some horrible mistake.

We'd weathered bad press before — senior year of college when Greg recklessly hit the number one player from Appalachian State, fracturing every bone in his hand and wrist — we could weather it again. Together.

Though I told myself this was the only one, the pit in my stomach was growing by the second. Against my better judgment, I grabbed my iPad and ran a Google search for Greg Rizzo, bracing myself. The screen flooded with headline after headline — Drugs End Rizzo's Run, Failed Drug Tests Fuel Early Retirement, From Perfect Games to Permanent Ban — *I could go on all day.*

The room was spinning, and I grasped the kitchen island for support. My darling husband had promised me this was all some big mistake. And I foolishly believed him. I couldn't help but wonder if he's lied to me about this; what else was Greg lying about? What else was he capable of?

CHAPTER 7

GREG RIZZO

I don't let my face betray my worry. I've gotten good at hiding my emotions. I learned from the best, I suppose.

I can't help but feel responsible for sending Gabby to our room alone. I mean, I was responsible, right? Yes, I wanted to make sure Cam was settled in, but more than that, I've been avoiding my wife as much as possible since we arrived here. Because I know, at some point, I will have to bring up the pregnancy test. I can't imagine any scenario in which I like what she has to say. And therein lies the conundrum I'm facing — when and how to confront my duplicitous spouse.

Part of me wants to tell Gabby she shouldn't be drinking. Another part wants to put off the conversation until after the tournament. I'm not certain which part will win.

"Maybe it's nothing," I say, trying to work it all out in my head. "Sometimes places get a stray mouse or rat. I'm sure even in luxury hotels. Remember how that fancy hotel we stayed at in Paris had an outbreak of bedbugs?"

Gabby shakes her head and scratches her arm at my mention of the bedbug incident we were to never, ever discuss again. Our honeymoon ended with us burning all our luggage and practically bleaching our skin to ensure they were gone. During that trip, we spent quite a lot of time on the king-sized mattress. Us and the bedbugs, apparently.

"I remember," she says, frowning. "This isn't the same thing. The rat was murdered, Greg."

Murdered? Surely she must realize how ridiculous she sounds.

"Is it possible you're being — hear me out — just slightly melodramatic? I mean, really, Gabby, why would someone murder a rat?"

"I don't know, Greg. Why do people do any of the fucked-up things they do?"

I don't have an answer to that. Why do we do any of the fucked-up things we do?

Gabby is looking at me as if I'm the one who's done something fucked-up. We are teetering dangerously close to a blowout altercation. We've reached a tipping point in our relationship, and it feels like I'm frozen on the tracks watching an oncoming train.

"Okay, okay." I put my hands up in surrender. "Tell me everything. What makes you think it was murdered?"

She blinks rapidly as if trying to simultaneously recover and rid herself of the image.

"It was on its back," she says. "Its stomach . . ." She pulls a hand to her mouth.

"What about its stomach?"

Gabby swallows hard, and I can see how difficult this is for her. Could she be right, thinking this was intentional? Why would anyone go to so much trouble to plant a dead — sorry, murdered — rat in our room? The logistics of killing a rat, transporting its carcass, and then breaking into our room to plant it are enough to make my head spin. Or perhaps the murder was committed right here at the hotel in our room? Ridiculous.

I reach out a hand to comfort her, but she blocks it with her own.

"I'm okay," she says. I don't dare tell her she's not. "It was sprawled out on its back. I can't explain the exact position, but it didn't look natural. It had a gash up the middle of its stomach. It was a perfectly straight line, Greg, like someone sliced it open with an X-Acto knife."

Her eyes meet mine, and I feel a familiar twinge of protectiveness shoot through me. No one messes with my family, with my wife.

The elevator dings, the doors open, and we step off before I've had a chance to respond. An older couple takes our place, and I wonder if that'll be us one day or if life will rip us apart long before then.

I have a sudden epiphany.

"CCTV!" I exclaim.

"What?"

"Surveillance footage. You know, Gabby, CCTV footage. They must have cameras in the hallways. They could probably rewind the tapes and see who was in and out of our room aside from you. Right? Then we'll know how it got there."

Hmmm, maybe by burrowing a hole through the wall?

I'm not convinced someone planted a dead rat in our room, though Gabby seems so sure of herself. I can't believe the tapes will show anything different. Anyone else, other than my wife walking into our room.

"Oh my gosh, Greg, I hadn't thought about that," Gabby admits, her eyes flashing with hope. "I bet you're right. Let's stop by the front desk and ask."

I feel a pinch of pride because my wife doesn't defer to me like she used to. She used to confide in me about everything before Susie came along, or at least I thought she did. But now, I ride her chemical ups and downs like a spectator instead of an active participant.

And her lies.

We approach the front desk, and I ask to speak to the manager.

"Just a second, sir," a young woman with dark hair and darker clothing says before disappearing behind a red velvet curtain. She emerges moments later with a tall man, similarly dressed in head-to-toe black. Come to think of it, *everyone* who works here is dressed in head-to-toe black. It's professional, I suppose, but bordering on morose. It makes me uneasy in a way I can't explain. Like perhaps it's an omen. Or maybe it's the fact that my wife thinks a rat was murdered in our hotel room that has me so ill at ease.

I shift in place and feel the sharp jab that seems to present itself at just the right moments. Because let's be honest, that's what's really getting to me. Not the rat that may or may not have been murdered and left for us to find in our room. It's the pregnancy test. It's the fact that my wife has not told me she's pregnant. It's the fact that she's pregnant in the first place.

As the man approaches, a chill descends, and I shiver. I look up and spot a fan spinning wildly above us, though it doesn't feel like that's the source of my disquiet. I watch for a moment as it rotates unreasonably fast, as if it might fly off its hinges at any moment.

The irony is not lost.

Gabby breaks through my thoughts.

"Hello, again," she greets the hotel manager, whose name tag reads Tomas. "I wanted to see if you have more information about—" She leans in closer and mouths, "The incident."

"Thank you for your discretion," he says, his face void of expression. "Obviously, if word of this got out, it could cause quite a commotion here. However, if you're asking if I know how the unfathomable creature found its way into your room, I'm afraid I do not have any additional information. I do hope you can enjoy your drink voucher and put it out of your mind. Was there anything else I could help you with?"

If the rat was murdered and intentionally left for one or both of us to find, I doubt a bottle of Glenlivet would make her forget.

"Do you have any cameras here?" she asks. "Maybe we could look and see who's had access to our room."

Tomas clears his throat again and steeples his fingers under his chin. "Now, that would be helpful, but privacy is highly valued here, so . . ."

"Seriously? So no cameras?" Gabby turns to face me, hope replaced with a look of defeat. Like, where do we go from here?

Where *do* we go from here?

"I'm truly sorry I can't be of more assistance. We've really tried to keep this place as authentic as possible." *Authentic?* That would explain the paper-thin walls and wooden doors they preserved, but everything else? Someone should inform Tomas that he'd benefit greatly from a history lesson.

"Thank you anyway," I interject as I place a hand on my wife's back and navigate her away from the reservation desk. I'm not sure if she's feeling it too, but I can't get away from there quickly enough.

"There's something I don't like about him," she whispers. "Très creepy."

"I agree."

"Should we go check on Cam?" she asks.

It's such a typical, innocent question, yet a familiar one that leaves me with the stubborn sensation of losing my wife to our son. I try to imagine what competing with another child might look like, but I can't. The truth is — our marriage is hanging on by a gossamer thread, and I doubt it would survive the weight of another human being.

"Nah," I say, keeping my voice as even as possible. "Cam's with Matt and Jake. I'm sure they're fine. I'd rather he not know about this before he plays ball this weekend. Don't you agree?"

"I guess you're right. I wouldn't want Cam to worry."

Gabby looks worried, and I can't say I blame her for that. Something about this place has me feeling untethered as well, aside from the dead rat in our room, the pregnancy test in my pocket, and the precarious state of our relationship.

We walk to the hotel bar in silence, and I wonder what thoughts are going through my wife's head. Maybe, if she could loosen up a bit, Gabby might share with me again like she used to. She's put up this fortress around her heart, a sky-high wall between us that feels insurmountable.

When we arrive at the bar, it feels like I've taken a punch to the gut. Susie is perched on a stool, tumbler in hand, laughing at something the twenty-something-year-old bartender just said. Susie Baker is a walking spectacle, and I wonder for the hundredth time how she and my wife became such close friends.

Gabby would like to believe Susie shits butterflies and rainbows, but there's an undercurrent in their friendship, aside from our boys, that I don't like. And fine, I don't like how much Gabby has come to depend on her for *everything*. The more Susie takes from her, the less she has to give me. Instead of making Gabby's life fuller, she's hollowing it out. And it doesn't help that I can't stop thinking about her, *fantasizing*.

Susie abruptly stops laughing and swivels in our direction as if she sensed our presence. She waves us over, and I watch as Gabby plasters on a broad smile, the one reserved for her best friend, and leaves me standing by myself in the open archway to the bar.

Gabby doesn't look back to see if I'm following her. It's like I've already been forgotten. You'd think I'd be used to it by now. But it still stings just as sharply as it always does.

Just as sharply as it did the first time my wife chose Susie Baker over me.

It was the night before we welcomed Cameron home from the hospital after he had spent weeks in the NICU. Gabby and I hadn't been intimate since her C-section. So imagine my surprise when I walked into our bedroom to find her sexed up on the bed in a lacy red negligée with her legs spread-eagle. I'm pretty sure my jaw hit the floor. I froze for a millisecond and then pounced on my wife.

After we made love, I reached over to my nightstand, opened the drawer, and pulled out a small red box. "I love you, Gabby Rizzo," I said, handing over the box as we lay naked, still panting, in bed.

Her fingers shook as she opened it. Gabby doesn't do well with surprises, a fact I learned the hard way early on in our relationship when I popped out from behind a bush to surprise her with roses after a class. It took several days to convince her I wasn't trying to kill her.

But this was a good surprise. I knew Gabby would love it. Sitting inside the box were two blinding four-carat diamond earrings. They were almost as beautiful as my wife, the mother of my child, and Gabby said she would never take them off. "I want to be buried in them one day," were her exact words.

I slipped the sparklers into her earlobes and handed over my phone, so that she could take a look. "Wow, just wow," she said. They cost a small fortune but were worth every penny. They looked stunning on her. I loved lavishing gifts on Gabby, even more so now that she had given me a son.

Gabby said she wanted to show me her gratitude for my thoughtful, generous gift. So I leaned back on our bed, tucking my arms under my head on the pillow. Her hand was sliding down my trunk, wrapping around my — you get the drift — when the doorbell rang.

"Fuck." I jumped out of bed, pulled up my boxer briefs, threw on a pair of shorts, and ran down the stairs. Gabby followed closely behind, wrapping herself in a robe, flushed, her hair wild like Medusa's.

I looked through the peephole of our front door to find Susie Baker staring back at me. Talk about terrible timing. I opened the door a crack — I mean, I was standing there bare-chested, hot and bothered, feeling like we'd just been caught in the act. I noticed a twitch on Susie's face, but she recovered quickly.

"I'm so sorry to interrupt," she said, pink still coloring her remarkably high cheeks. "I didn't think so soon after . . ." Her words trailed off, and it felt like we were in trouble, on the cusp of being grounded by our parents after getting caught making out in the basement on a school night.

Gabby pushed past me, fully opening the door for her friend. Susie handed over a bouquet of vibrant flowers, a small gift box, and a Tupperware full of her famous chocolate-chip cookies that Gabby never stopped talking about. I'd decided Susie either thinks she's Martha Stewart or Gabby's best friend was trying to make her fat.

"Thank you so much, Susie. What's this?" Gabby asked, fingering the box.

"You'll see. Open it," Susie said excitedly.

Gabby gently ripped the gold, lamé wrapping paper and studied the red box, identical to the one that held her diamond studs. *Odd.* There were at least a half-dozen jewelry stores in town. What were the chances she just so happened to pick the same one as me? Had Susie followed me to the jeweler to pick out her gift?

I watched as Gabby opened the box, her fingers trembling with Gabby-like trepidation. She slowly pulled out a shiny, sterling silver locket with Cam's name etched on the back. Susie held out her locket, the same as Gabby's, but with *Jake* scrawled across in script.

"Best friend necklaces for new mom best friends."

"Wow, I just don't know what to say, Susie. It's beautiful. This is too much."

"Nothing is too much for my best friend."

It was as if I weren't even there, and I suddenly felt like I was intruding on a private moment. I quietly backed away toward the stairs.

My wife was oddly silent, off to some place in her head only she knows. She must have been quiet for too long because Susie asked, "You don't like it? Have I upset you?"

"No, no, it's not that," Gabby said. "It's just, it's just the nicest thing anyone has ever done for me."

The nicest thing anyone has ever done for her? Jealousy tore through my bones with its jagged little teeth. Could Susie's pendant cut glass like my diamonds? Did it matter? Gabby's reaction to her best friend's gift cut straight through my heart.

Gabby gave Susie a big squeeze and told her she'd call her just as soon as we got back from the hospital so she could come over to meet Cameron. Of course, she would.

I stood stock still, staring at them from the stairwell. I didn't talk to Gabby for the rest of the night. You'd think she'd have asked what was wrong or pick up where we left off, but no. The only thing she asked me to do was to close the clasp of her chain, which I did begrudgingly. Not that she noticed. She hummed and danced around the room, rubbing her locket between her thumb and pointer finger. One of the backings wasn't fully screwed in on her earrings. Despite its four-karat brilliance, it hung pathetically from her ear.

This is how it is between the three of us — a constant magnetic pull for Gabby's attention that has grown stronger with each passing day, month, and year.

My hands curl into fists at my side, and I start to sweat. I take a deep breath and count to ten. I don't like whatever this is I'm feeling. I stand rooted in place for a while, watching them, before I reluctantly head over to join my wife and her best friend at the bar.

CHAPTER 8

GABBY RIZZO

I'm shaken like a sour apple martini after the dead rat incident. Suddenly, the last thing I feel like having is a serious conversation with Greg. Because that's where this was headed.

I'm relieved when I see Susie at the bar, as now we have a buffer. I'm not ready to lay all my cards on the table. To force Greg's hand.

I'm also not surprised to find her here. There's always alcohol where Susie is involved.

"Daaarliiin'!" Susie waves me over, just as happy to see me now as she always is. I wish I could say the same for my husband and son.

I should feel grateful that I'm on the receiving end of Susie's friendship, but I'm overtaken by something else altogether that I can only package as jealousy.

The Southern drawl remains, but Susie's voice is now infused with vodka, emphasized by an ant line of empty shot glasses on the bar in front of her. If looks are any indication, a tap on the shoulder or a slight breeze will knock her straight off her barstool.

"How early did you start?" I ask, half joking, half serious, half concerned, half jealous. I know that's four halves, but who's counting? Not Susie.

"Oh, Chuckie and I just did a few shots."

"Chip," the bartender says, rolling his eyes, visibly offended. "My name is Chip."

Chip can't be a day older than twenty-one, if that. He's wearing a tight black T-shirt, biceps bulging through the taut fabric. I glance at Susie chewing on her lower lip like a cougar, ready to pounce on him. I shake my head in mock disapproval. Susie does what Susie wants.

"As I said, Chippy and I did a few shots." She winks in his direction, and I watch Chip's demeanor instantly relax. Susie has that effect on people; on men in particular.

It looks like she's had more than a few, but I don't bother correcting her. Because, again, I feel that familiar stab of jealousy. Susie is so carefree while I walk around with the world's weight on my shoulders. I wouldn't mind trading places with her for the night. But then, I'd have to deal with having me as a best friend. Considering how much Susie does for me and how little I offer in return, it certainly feels like she pulled the short end of the stick.

My mouth is suddenly arid like a desert, my tongue dry and wooly, and I take a large gulp of water to quench what feels like an insatiable thirst.

Susie turns to me, her face serious. "Did you hear Levi Hertz is starting in center tomorrow? I mean, *really,* that kid couldn't field a fly ball if it were equipped with a freaking tracker."

I can't help but laugh, and water sprays from my mouth like a fountain. Susie is so unfiltered and fiercely competitive. I don't have the heart to tell her that Levi is, in fact, a much better center fielder than Jake. There's such a thing as being too honest. I tell myself that's why I keep the secrets I keep, because at the end of the day, sometimes the truth hurts worse than any lie you can tell.

"I'm sure Coach Bob has his reasons," I say. "Maybe he wants Jake in left? Or, he has Jake in the bullpen so he can relieve Cam if his arm gets tired?"

My son has been pitching full games since he was eight, so the chance of him needing relief from Jake is slim to none.

"I don't know," Susie says, twirling a piece of white-blond hair around a finger while she licks her lips and winks at the bartender. Crimson crawls up the back of his neck.

She turns back to me, stone-faced. "I honestly wouldn't be surprised if Sandy blew the coach."

I think about Sandy Hertz for a moment, with her smart bob and mom jeans, and her giving Coach Bob a blowjob is as far-fetched as Jake starting at pitcher over Cam. Carla Miller is the only mom I can think of less likely to engage in extramarital activities with the coach. I'm not disappointed that she stayed back from the tournament. Susie, on the other hand, doesn't care at all about the Millers or their son, Colton. Probably because he plays third base and bats last.

I stifle a giggle and shrug my shoulders.

I'm not sure what the big deal is anyway. At least Jake is playing. Greg and I have raised our boy to be a utility player, to treat each and every position as if it's the most important. Because you never know where the ball might drop, every position *is* the most important position. I remember swelling with pride the first time I heard Cam tell a coach, *I'll play wherever you need me, Coach*. But Matt and Susie have raised Jake with a sense of entitlement that is far from deserved.

I doubt Jake would have even made the team if it weren't for our almost incestuous relationship with the Bakers.

Not your problem, Greg would say. But he doesn't understand what it's like to have a best friend like Susie. She's so incredibly extroverted and popular and has a son the same age who does every last thing our son does. Greg is off working and traveling for business, so he's sheltered from the day-to-day. I love her dearly, I do, but sometimes it feels like I can't get away from her even for a minute. She's always there, reminding me with her baked goods and considerate gestures of what a failure I am.

Except for Cam.

Susie orders another round of shots, placing a glass full of glittery liquid in front of me. Goldschlager, if I'm not mistaken, but that's not a liquor you ever forget. My stomach churns just looking at it. I still half-remember a few Goldschlager-laced nights in college when our biggest concern was how big of a hangover we'd have the next day. At least it was until Greg didn't come home that night.

I try not to think about that night, but it often finagles its way into my thoughts. Sometimes I wonder if I hadn't gotten pregnant if I would have forgiven Greg for cheating on me.

If I would have stayed.

"To friendship," Susie says, holding out her glass and interrupting the thought. It's a welcome interruption.

"To friendship."

We clink our shot glasses, and I bring mine to my lips. The liquor is warm and burns as it slides down my throat. Susie doesn't flinch. Holding her liquor — yet another thing she's better at than me. I cough a few times and then quickly chase the shot with one of the glasses of water Chip has so kindly refilled for us. I drain every last drop as if I've stumbled across an oasis in a desert.

Greg is in my head. "Hydrate, Gabby."

As I often do, I swivel around on my barstool and look over my shoulder, sensing someone is there. *Paranoid.* I wonder, is it paranoia if it's real?

Because Greg's not in my head. He's standing behind us, telling me to drink more water. Heat rises to my cheeks — both from the alcohol and the advice. He makes me feel like a child. And just like that, the jovial mood starting to form is killed. It makes me think of the murdered rat in our hotel room.

"Loosen up a little, Greg," Susie says as she orders another round. "YOLO." She pumps her fists in the air as if we're on a dance floor at the Jersey Shore.

"Loose as a goose," Greg replies, though his words are icy and his jaw tense. There's an awkward silence, and I wish the floor would open up and swallow me whole.

I'm not sure what it is, but lately, it feels like the three of us cannot be in a room together without the tension building like a smoldering volcano. My husband and my best friend. My best friend and my husband. They seem to have a love-hate relationship that I don't understand. I can't stand being in the middle of whatever is going on between them.

I suck down another shot, warmth spreading throughout my body like tiny electric shocks.

"Slow down," Greg warns.

I'd like to tell him where he should stick his warning, but I bite my tongue. Not in front of Susie. Not this weekend.

I glance up at the clock on the wall instead, a sleek black circle with its hands illuminated in red lights. 8:03 p.m. I'm not sure where the time has gone. Cam will be going to bed soon to rest his mind and body for the doubleheader tomorrow. I have an indescribable need to hold my baby in my arms, to cling to his neck like a life preserver. I imagine that's not something that time or age can erase.

"I'm going to go say goodnight to Cam," I decide aloud, desperate to see him. Desperate to get away from them.

I'm not sure if it's Greg or Susie I'm talking to, and I'm not confident either one is listening. They are taking a shot without me this time, and I feel their mood loosening.

I should stay.

I should go.

I'm not sure what I should do.

I rise from the barstool, and my knees buckle.

"Christ, Gabby," Greg says, grabbing my arm to stop me from falling. "You're wasted. How much did you drink?"

I open my mouth to tell him I'm not drunk, but then the room spins, and I think maybe he's right. I have had too much to drink. Except, I only had two shots. So why does it feel like I single-handedly drank a bottle of Tito's?

"I don't feel so good," I start to say. Then it all comes out, a waterfall of alcohol and the extra hydration all over Greg's shoes. I immediately regret doing the shots. I regret coming here. I regret a lot of things, if I'm being honest.

"What the fuck, Gabby? Did you forget where you are? Let me remind you — you're at your son's baseball tournament. Our kid is here. What the hell is wrong with you?" Greg yanks me by the arm a tad too forcefully. The room is now on a tilt-a-whirl, and I have two livid husbands trying to extricate me from the bar. I try to focus on a spot on the floor, afraid if I look into Greg's eyes, I'll see the angry thoughts swirling through his head.

Lately, the way he stares at me with such heat and intensity, I wonder if he can see the thoughts swirling through mine.

I hear Susie's concerned voice asking if I'm okay, and my eyes find her face twisted like a funhouse mirror. It's as if I've drunkenly stumbled into the center ring of a circus. And then I'm staring at the back of her perfectly shaped head as she resumes flirting with Chip. Greg doesn't give me a chance to say goodbye and goodnight to my best friend.

"You're hurting me," I tell him as he pulls me out of the bar and through the lobby. He doesn't turn to look back at me. I think he's being a real asshole, but then I think my words might be stuck in my throat.

I have that familiar sensation again, where it feels like I could close my eyes and never open them again. My feet are like cinder blocks attached to tree trunks, and though I somehow manage to move one foot in front of the other, it's not as fluid as walking should be. The ground shifts beneath my feet, and I stumble on the flat wood floor.

"Seriously, Gabby. Were you actually going to go see your son in this condition? Have you lost your mind?"

I wonder if I have.

Then I wonder if he knows my secret.

ONE YEAR EARLIER
GABBY'S JOURNAL

Greg said that it's the final straw. I braced myself for the papers, for a soliloquy on why he couldn't stay married to me anymore. Things have been tense between us, to say the least. I keep replaying our conversation over and over, wondering if I could have said or done something differently.

"I'm worried about you, Gabby."

"There's nothing to worry about," I assured him. "Really, you're making a big deal out of nothing."

"Every day it's something, Gabby — your keys, your wallet, your phone. Now, this. Last time I checked, losing a chef's knife isn't nothing."

"Maybe it was the housekeeper?" I offered.

"We don't have a housekeeper, Gabby." My joke didn't land — Greg didn't smile.

I suppose he had a valid point.

I was slicing an orange when I realized I misplaced it. That was a week ago. I'd hoped he wouldn't notice its absence, but Greg notices whenever anything is out of place. 8,000 square feet is a heck of a lot of square footage to keep track of, yet somehow Greg manages to do it while holding down a full-time job. I can't get away with anything here. I looked everywhere for the knife — the dishwasher, sink, and garbage can. The trash outside. I even checked the freezer.

I should have just told him the truth — last I checked, it's not a felony to misplace something — but I chickened out, hoping it would somehow magically slip back into its place on the wooden chopping block and I'd be spared the third-degree by my husband.

But I'd been caught.

I sensed the conversation was ending when Greg handed me a business card — Dr. Green, Board Certified Psychiatrist.

"Really, Greg? Because I misplaced something?"

"It's not just the knife, Gabby. You need to talk to someone. This constant forgetfulness, confusion, and fatigue — I'm afraid it's not normal." I'm not sure if Greg was being kind, but he left out the paranoia. What a gentleman.

"Seriously, Greg. All because I misplaced one of our Henckels? It's not that serious. We can order a new one online. You can get anything on Amazon these days. It'll be back in the cutting block by tomorrow."

"Come on, Gabby," he said. "We both know it's more than that."

"Well, what if I don't want to go?"

"It's not a choice. I've already paid upfront in cash for the next few months."

So it's been decided, except I really don't want to go. Because since our conversation, all I can think about is my dead parents.

CHAPTER 9

GREG RIZZO

I want to crawl into a hole and die or bury my wife in it. Gabby can barely stand up straight, and I have to practically drag her through the lobby of our fancy hotel to get her to our room. We are pelted with stares and whispers, and I feel the heat rising from beneath my collared shirt up the back of my neck.

She's piss-ass drunk and, I remind myself, pregnant. Who does something like this — drinking like a fish when you have a life growing inside you? Apparently, Gabby does. Apparently, I don't know Gabby as well as I thought I did.

How manipulative is my wife?

I'd ask her, but based on how Gabby's feet and legs are functioning — or rather malfunctioning — I doubt I'd understand a word that came out of her mouth right now.

I feel the rage building inside me, a slow roll beginning to boil. I can't understand how Gabby would do this to herself, to me, to our son. And then I remind myself yet again that my wife likes to keep secrets, a fact I've only recently discovered.

Gabby leans her body against mine as I fumble in my pocket for the room key. A few torches have flickered out, and the hallway has grown darker as if a black cloud has settled over us.

I suppose it has.

I locate the keycard and press it against the magnetic strip. First comes the familiar beep, and then the light blinks green, and I turn the handle and push open the door. I'm half expecting to find a rat or something out of place, but the carpet is clean, and the room is warm and welcoming.

My eyes immediately travel to an ice bucket on the nightstand with a bottle of Prosecco peeking out, flanked by two champagne flutes, and a handwritten note propped against it — *Compliments of Foxcroft*. I wonder if all the guests receive this welcome gift or if it's a half-assed apology for the rat.

Since I never made it into our original room, I have no point of comparison.

I navigate my wife to the four-poster, king-sized bed and help her settle in. I untie her trainers, take off her socks and tuck her under the fluffy duvet, positioning her on her side in case she vomits again. Looking down at my shoes, I doubt she has anything left inside her, but still.

I would take off her makeup, but there are just a few stray flakes of mascara that she probably applied days ago. I wipe a hand across her face, and Gabby lets out a small snore. My wife rarely wears makeup these days. I get that she's not trying to impress me anymore. The honeymoon ended a long, long time ago.

I think a little effort would go a long way. But, unfortunately, that's not something you can just come out and say to a woman, to your wife, not without getting slapped across the face or served with divorce papers.

Hey honey, you could use a little mascara every once in a while. And while you're at it, maybe a touch of foundation. Look at Susie — do you see how she's always so put together? How about you try just a little harder? Maybe I'd stop fantasizing about your best friend.

Gabby might never speak to me again. I look at her lying pathetically in the bed, tongue hanging out of her wide-open mouth, and I think maybe that wouldn't be such a bad thing.

Still, given her current condition, I worry she will be in no shape to attend the doubleheader tomorrow. I know deep down that would shatter Cameron's heart into a million pieces. I might as well hit him in the chest with one of his composite baseball bats. I can't have my son go into the game tomorrow feeling distraught. Gabby's absence would be a distraction, and we must keep Cameron focused.

I find Gabby's purse by the foot of the bed, some knock-off she purchased on clearance at T.J. Maxx to piss me off. I've bought her Fendi, Chanel, and Birkin, but they sit unused in her closet, collecting dust next to the designer dresses I couldn't pay my wife to wear.

I unzip her off-brand purse — a two-tone black and blue, like a fresh bruise — to search for a bottle of Advil. If she pops two and chugs a glass of water, she might be in decent enough shape for tomorrow. No doubt she'll be hungover as hell but, hopefully, the medicine and hydration will give her enough strength to make it from the bed to the fields.

I'm not surprised to find Gabby's bag an absolute disaster, a microcosm of her current condition. I dig for the bottle of Advil, sifting through the random miscellanea. It must be here somewhere. My wife has everything — medications, Band-Aids, sunscreen, plastic cutlery, just in case — and . . .

I pull an envelope out of her purse, turning it over in my hands. It says *Gabby* in vaguely familiar handwriting on the front, but I can't place it. I should stuff it back in, find the Advil and call it a night. Except, I can't, considering.

I open the envelope flap, which has already been unsealed, and pull out the paper from inside. I make it through, *Let me just tell you how very lucky I am to know you,* before I'm interrupted by frantic banging at the door. I ignore the knocking and continue to read.

> *You are such a great mom, wife, and friend. Except, of course, for the fact that you have so many secrets.*

I wonder if your family knows who you really are.
Maybe someone should tell them.
Me, me, me!
Let's just say I'm thinking about it — long and hard.
I guess you'll have to wait to see what happens.
The suspense!!!
Good luck to your son Cameron at Startown. I bet this will be a weekend none of you will ever forget.
Xx

I slide down the edge of the bed to the carpet. The sweat from my hands blurs the words on the letter. I have my fingers wrapped so tightly around the sheet of paper it's beginning to disintegrate in my grasp. At first, I thought it was from Susie, but then it turned dark. Stalker dark. It couldn't be from Susie. Gabby would recognize her handwriting in a heartbeat. I flashback to the bar, and I'm sure I didn't detect an ounce of tension between them. I imagine such stress would be impossible to hide if the anonymous letter were from her best friend, even for Gabby, who is tops at hiding things.

My head is spinning, and now I'm the one who could use a few Advil. I continue fishing through her purse for the bottle of pills and swallow two with a gulp from the half-empty bottle of water I find buried beneath a tissue packet. *I bet this will be a weekend none of you will ever forget* runs through my head, and I fight a wave of nausea. It sounds like a threat. And then I think about the rat in our room, and panic tears through my veins. It *is* a threat.

Why would someone threaten my wife?

I can't hear my thoughts over the banging. It's become annoyingly incessant. It's as if whoever is out there is attempting to knock down the door to our room with their fists.

I throw the letter and envelope on top of my passed-out wife and hurry to the door. It's after nine now, and I can't imagine why someone would create such a stir in the hallway with kids asleep in adjacent rooms.

And then I remember how drunk we left Susie at the bar, and I think it must be her. I wish she would bother her husband, but then I remember that my son is in their adjoining room.

I swing open the door and am faced with a fist suspended in the air, ready to hammer again.

"*Matt*? What are *you* doing here?"

Matt's the last person I'd expect to find pounding on the wood like a maniac because he's always considerate and careful with the kids. He's probably looking for his wife. I don't have the heart to tell him we left her shit-faced at the bar throwing herself at the bartender, who is young enough to be her son if she were starring in an episode of teen mom.

In the light glow of the hallway, Matt's face looks green. I notice the beads of sweat gathering on his forehead.

"Thank God you opened the door." Matt is breathless, his voice infused with panic.

"Haven't seen her," I say, a half-truth. I haven't seen Susie, not in the past hour, anyhow. She could be anywhere by now, though I could make an educated guess as to where that somewhere may be. The hotel bar closed at nine. Last I saw, she was alone with the bartender, hands folded under her chin, breasts folded over the bar.

Poor, Matt — I genuinely feel sorry for him. I wouldn't want to trade places with him for a minute. Well, maybe just for a minute . . .

Matt shifts in place, trying to peer into our room over my shoulder. Does he think Susie is here? With me? I position my body so he can't see Gabby unconscious on the bed. I don't need anyone else to bear witness to my wife in her current condition.

"Is Cameron in there with you?"

"*Cameron*?" I'm completely caught off guard. "I thought you were looking for Susie. Why would Cameron be with me? Isn't he asleep with Jake in your room?"

"I don't know how to say this, but Cameron isn't in our room. I went to check on the boys before I turned in, and Jake was fast asleep, but Cameron wasn't there. I was hoping he had come here to see you. He's gone, Greg."

It's as if he's punctured my heart with a single word — one syllable.

Gone.

I grab Matt by the collar and slam him up against the wall. He lets out a gasp of shock. My fists are burning, and I remind myself that Matt is our friend, like an uncle to Cam. He would never, ever do anything to hurt him. He would sooner hurt himself. I release him from my grasp and pound a clenched fist into the wall instead.

"Greg, I'm so, so sorry. Please, let me help you find him. We'll go to the front desk, door to door. He couldn't have gotten very far."

"You better find my son," I say through gritted teeth. "If anything happens to him, I swear, Matt, I'll . . ."

Except, there's no need to finish the thought out loud.

CHAPTER 10

GABBY RIZZO

For the second time today, I'm jolted awake from a dreamless sleep. Only this time, by the baritone voices of Greg and Matt arguing in the doorway of our hotel room. My eyes struggle to adjust to the light, and it takes a minute to figure out where I am.

And then it all comes rushing back like a freight train — the rat, the bar, Susie, Greg . . .

I feel like I might be sick again. I swallow down the bile rising in my throat. My eyes catch sight of Greg's Golden Gooses tucked in the corner of the room, caked in my vomit, and I cringe.

Six-hundred-dollar sneakers ruined.

What the hell happened?

Two shots play on a loop in my head as my stomach roils.

I try to sit up in bed, but my body feels paralyzed, my arms and legs dead weight. I lift my head from the pillow, and the room spins. You'd think I was recovering from a horrific accident or a devastating infection. Or, a *really* good night.

Nope. None of the above. Two shots. I'm recovering from two shots of alcohol. I think about Dr. Green's warning,

"You shouldn't drink alcohol on these medications, Gabby," which I dismissed before he'd finished issuing it. Perhaps he was right. Maybe I shouldn't be drinking on my meds.

But still, the last time I felt this crappy, I was coming off a late-night revenge bender fueled by shot after shot, and Lord knows what else. It was the night after Greg cheated on me, and I was positive things were over between us. I mean, how could I possibly stay with a cheater? Trust him? Forgive him? There was no way I could do any of those things unless . . .

I evened the score.

Relax, relax.

That's what I should have done.

But no, I didn't do anything other than drink a shit ton of tequila, and boy, did I pay the price the next day. I felt even worse than I had in the morning when he stumbled through the door of our basement apartment, drenched in a mixture of another woman's sweat and cheap perfume.

Just not worse than I feel right now.

I'm thinking about how much I drank that night and the blaring contrast to this evening. I keep coming back to the fact that it was two measly shots. No more than eighty milliliters of alcohol at most. Medication or not, I didn't drink enough to warrant feeling like I'd been mowed down by a Mack Truck.

Which I realize means one of two things: either something is seriously, and I mean *seriously*, wrong with me, or someone must have slipped something into my drink. There's no other logical explanation for going from zero to fall-down drunk in a matter of minutes. At least, none I can come up with in my current condition.

Dr. Green has assured me there is nothing physically wrong with me. He has access to my medical records on My Chart. I'm sure he checks them regularly. If I'm to believe him, my theory about tonight must be the latter. Someone spiked my drink.

But who would spike my drink?

Chuckie? Or was it Chippy? Right, Chip. The bartender's name was Chip. What motive could the bartender possibly have for rendering me unconscious? Clearly, I wasn't there to stop Susie from making some horrible decision she'd live to regret. The only way she'd be more of a sure thing is if she were holding up a sign that said, hashtag sure thing.

If anything, drugging me would force Susie to leave her perch at the bar to take care of her best friend. Why would Chip be his own killjoy? The answer is he wouldn't. It wasn't him.

The bar was empty, bartender and present company aside. Taking that into consideration, who does that leave? It's a short suspect list consisting of my husband and best friend.

I can't think of a good reason they would want me incoherent the night before a major tournament. Or can I? I picture Susie's mouth pressed against Greg's ear in the hotel lobby, her hand draped over his shoulder, manicured fingers resting against his rock-hard pecs. Maybe I've chosen to ignore the signs there all along. Are my husband and best friend having an affair?

A fire ignites deep within my belly at the thought of two of the closest people in my life betraying me with each other. They wouldn't dare.

Would they?

Dr. Green chirps in my ear, *Stop catastrophizing, Gabby.* I take a long, deep breath and try to reset. It doesn't help. It never helps. Because this is what I do. I conjure worst-case scenarios and replay them repeatedly until I'm convinced they're real-time storylines. I tell myself lies and twist them into reality. In our last session, Dr. Green joked I could be a bestselling novelist or playwright with my vivid imagination.

But I am not imagining this. Greg and Matt are most definitely in the frame, arguing. I hope against hope it's something other than neighbor swapping they're carrying on about, something that won't reach into my chest and pull my heart out of my rib cage.

I quiet my breath and strain my ears to make out their conversation.

"Listen, man, you know I'm as concerned about Cam as you are," I overhear Matt telling Greg.

Cam? Why are they arguing about Cam? *Concerned* about Cam? Hearing my son's name in the middle of a strained conversation sends a jolt of superhuman strength through my body, a shock of energy that propels me upright. Mother's instinct tells me it's more than sour grapes that have Matt and Greg looking like the bell is about to ring for a boxing match.

Something is wrong.

I scramble from the bed to the door, my movements faster than I'd think feasible under even the best of conditions, which these are not. My head pounds with every motion, and my insides threaten to betray me again. It's no longer the alcohol having me feeling like I'm about to be sick. It's hearing Matt and Greg arguing about my son. I've never heard them argue about anything before. I won't deny there's an underlying tension between them when it comes to our boys, but nothing that's ever been voiced aloud.

Except now, Greg looks like he would've killed Matt had I not interrupted them. His hands are balled into fists, and he's breathing heavier than usual. It's as if it's taking all his strength and willpower to bottle the rage inside.

"What about Cam?" I manage, breathless, leaning against the doorframe for support. "Is he not feeling well? Matt, what are you doing here?"

Matt silently looks down at his shoes as if he might discover the answer to my question on the floor. I turn to my husband, but Greg won't meet my gaze either. My eyes slip down to the blood-red carpet.

Why won't they look at me?

I'm starting to panic. I search Greg's face, watching him closely as he runs a hand through his thick, sandy-blond hair. The vein on his temple throbs. I try to focus on the rhythm of that and not my own heart beating fanatically against my ribcage.

Then my gaze flicks back and forth between the two men who know something about my son that I do not. Someone had better answer me quickly.

"Matt? Greg? Please, will one of you say something?"

"He lost our son."

"Excuse me? What do you mean, he lost our son?"

"I didn't lose him," Matt corrects, standing taller. That's one thing I've always admired about our friend and neighbor — he's not afraid to stand his ground with Greg. Not many people have the chutzpah to stand up to my husband. Matt is one of the few in this world who doesn't bend his own position to placate Greg, though it's usually in the form of friendly banter.

Nothing about this conversation feels friendly.

I watch as Greg digs his nails into his palm, my heart beating faster with every passing second.

"I went to check on the boys before going to sleep, and Cam wasn't there."

"What do you mean he wasn't there? Where was he? Where *is* he?"

"That's the problem, Gabby. I have no idea where Cam is. He didn't tell me he was going anywhere. He just disappeared. And Jake is sound asleep."

This doesn't make sense, not just because I'm hungover.

I don't need to hear anymore. I'm already moving at full speed toward the elevator. My son didn't disappear. I think of all the reasons he could have been missing from his bed when Matt checked on them.

He went to the ice machine.

He went to talk to their coach.

He was in the goddamn bathroom.

Kids don't just disappear from hotel rooms.

As I frantically push the button to summon the lift, I think about the threatening, anonymous notes I've been receiving. I think about the rat. I think about how every single parent of every single child on this team wishes their son was as talented as Cam. I think about what's riding on this tournament.

And then I think, if someone wants them gone, maybe they *do* disappear.

CHAPTER 11

GREG RIZZO

I follow Gabby down the hallway and attempt to slip my hand into the elevator shaft to stop it, but it's too late. I pull back, and the door squeezes shut with my wife inside, nearly severing my fingers. I stand there, helpless, watching the lights above the frame crawl up painfully slowly.

I'm pretty sure I know where Gabby is going.

Coach Bob's room is on the fifth floor of the hotel. I imagine Gabby is going to check if Cam is there. Smart move. Cam absolutely idolizes his coach. I could tell my son, *"Choke up on your bat, get your glove dirty, follow through on your pitches,"* and he'll completely disregard me, but if Coach Bob says it, it's like fucking gospel. I think my son forgets that I've lived and breathed baseball my entire life.

I allow myself a glimmer of hope.

If Cam left on his own accord, of course, it was Coach Bob he'd be going to see. I'm confident we will find him there, scold him, and then one day recount with laughter how he single-handedly scared the living shit out of his parents.

This is all some silly mistake.

It has to be.

Other parents might worry in a situation like this that their child is up to no good. That's the last thing on my mind. My son knows better than to do anything stupid. He cares too much about baseball to risk losing it all. Despite how I tried to conceal it, he knows what happened to me. That's what has me the most concerned.

My insides squeeze with urgency. The only thing that matters is finding our son safe and sound, getting him into bed, and ready for his big start tomorrow.

The elevator is slower than a sloth rounding the bases. I can't stand around here waiting any longer. My eyes find the stairwell, and I sprint to it, ripping open the door. I hurdle two steps at a time, scaling floor after floor until I reach the fifth floor. Once there, I propel myself through the exit and take off down the hallway for his room.

I've never run so fast in my years of stealing bases. As I turn the corner, I catch sight of Gabby and Coach Bob standing in the hallway, the door to his room shut behind them.

"Is he here?" I'm slightly out of breath as the words pour out. My heart is beating frantically in my chest, not just from the exertion. Sheer panic runs through my veins like water bursting through a dam. I can barely contain it, though I know I risk pushing Gabby over the edge if I completely lose it. It's a minute until midnight on the Rizzo Doomsday clock.

"Wish he was here. Unfortunately, I haven't seen him." Coach Bob shakes his shiny bald head, and my stomach does a roller coaster dip. The alternative to Coach Bob not seeing Cam is someone else seeing him, having him.

"Did he seem overly nervous to you? Did he mention anything that might help us find him? You know Cam, Bob; he's a good boy. He wouldn't do something like this . . . disappearing without telling anyone where he was going."

I watch Gabby chew on a cuticle as she waits for his response. I hadn't noticed until now that her nails are chewed down to the finger pads.

Coach Bob scratches his chin full of days-old stubble. "You're absolutely right, Gabby. Cam is the best, on and off the field. But honestly, he seemed really excited for tomorrow. We talked about our strategy going into the game. He said he was feeling loose and ready to throw. I told him to get a good night's rest, and he promised he would."

My son is not perfect, but Cam always, and I mean *always*, listens to his coach. Bob is like a god to him. This is the worst news we could get. Only not, of course. Knowing he would never disobey his coach's orders tells us nothing about what's happened to him, only that he didn't leave here alone. Someone took him. I'm trying hard not to go to the dark places in my mind where the worst-case scenarios live, but it isn't easy.

Gabby turns to me. "Where is our son, Greg?"

I don't have the heart to admit I have no idea.

"We should split up," I tell her instead, aware that I might mean this in more ways than one. Because without Cam, what do Gabby and I have holding us together? "You go back to check their room. I'll check with the other parents. Coach Bob, can you stay here in case he comes to see you?"

I think *surely that won't be necessary*. Cam must be back in bed by now, where he belongs.

"Of course, I will, Greg. Anything you need. I'm a light sleeper. I'll hear him if he comes by the room. Not that I imagine I'll be able to relax until you find him. This is just unimaginable. I wish I could do more."

Coach Bob lets out a lion's yawn and stretches his arms overhead. "I'm sure you'll find him back in the room, out cold. He, out of all the kids, knows he needs to rest up, especially since we pulled the eight a.m. draw."

I glance down at the Rolex on my wrist. 10.00 p.m. A PSA flashes through my mind — it's 10 p.m.; do you know where your children are? It feels like a cruel joke that we don't.

Where is our son?

We promise Coach Bob to let him know just as soon as we locate Cam, and then we rip down the hallway like a tornado back to the elevator.

Gabby slips her fingers into mine as we wait. Her palms are sweaty. Her eyes look like melted chocolate chips. I squeeze her hand. "I'm sure he's back in their room, and this is all some big misunderstanding," I say, though I'm not sure I mean it.

"You think so?"

I nod my head and take a deep breath. I'm already thinking about what we'll do if he isn't there. Go door to door through the five-floor, hundred-room hotel? Call the police? We may be staying in a hoity-toity four-star resort, but we are also smack dab in the middle of nowhere. The nearest police station and hospital are a good forty-five minutes away. There are a few other motels and inns within a ten-mile radius, but other than that, there is nothing but fields and unforgiving, winding country roads, near impossible to navigate in the dark.

I drop Gabby off on the second floor on my way down to the lobby as an image of an injured Cameron on a lonely dirt road flits across my eyes. I blink ferociously because, no, it can't be.

No. No. No.

"Call me when you find him, okay?"

I try to keep my voice light, but even I can hear the strain. I'm not easily rattled, but I've never truly been faced with the prospect of losing my only child. Except for his first year of life, he's always been so easy. I guess we were kind of due for something.

As the elevator doors open, I push out into the lobby. It's after ten, and the lights are dimmed, the vast space cloaked in an eerie silence that sends a chill up my spine. My shoes echo in the vacant lobby as I approach the reception desk.

It's a ghost town at this time of night, so there's no one poised to help at the front desk. When I say we're in the middle of nowhere, I mean the middle of fucking nowhere. The next closest lodging is at least six, seven miles away. There's one mom-and-pop shop but no Krogers, Aldis, or any other major grocery chain. We passed a biker bar along that solo stretch of road, but I imagine even that has since closed. So we're here in this resort, where once the clock strikes nine, everything shuts down, and carriages turn to pumpkins. There's nowhere to go.

I ring the bell to solicit help. There's a shuffle behind the curtained door, and the man in the black suit emerges. There's something oddly familiar about his posture that I hadn't noticed earlier and can't seem to place.

"Sir?"

"Have we met before?" I ask him, suddenly convinced I know him from somewhere.

"Just this afternoon, sir."

The stress of the day has me imagining things, I guess. Although telling myself that doesn't dull my sense of déjà vu.

I refocus. "I need the room numbers of everyone staying here for the Startown tournament."

The manager cocks an eyebrow and shakes his head at me. "You know I can't do that, sir. Our room list is confidential."

"Look, Tomas," I say, reading off his nametag. "I get the whole discretion, anonymity thing you've got going on, but my son is missing. I need to check with the other parents to find out if anyone has seen him."

"Missing?" His eyebrows bend toward one another, making him look utterly confused, as if he's just learned that the earth is not flat.

"Look, he was supposed to be asleep, and he's not in his bed, and we can't find him anywhere. If you want to avoid a big scene with cops storming the place, I suggest you get me the room numbers. NOW. You'll have to hand them over to the police anyway. I'd think that you may lose a few stars over this and the rat in our room — which we have not told anyone about — if you know what I mean."

Tomas's lips pinch into a tight line, and his bushy black eyebrows bunch together again. I think he's about to tell me where I can stick my threat, but to my surprise, he pulls out a ledger from behind the desk. He opens the book and runs his fingers down the lined page.

"Here you go," he says, pointing to the guest list. "I hope this helps you locate your son. Please let me know if there is anything else I can do for you."

Invest in some fucking cameras.

I quickly jot down all the names and room numbers and rush back to the elevator. I'll swing by Matt's room first to see if he's heard anything. If he hasn't, Gabby and I can split the list. I'm sure Matt will not be in a hurry to leave Jake alone after this, and someone needs to be there if Cam comes back.

When.

When Cam comes back.

CHAPTER 12

GABBY RIZZO

I raise my fist to pound on Matt's door, but it swings open before I connect with the wood. Was he expecting someone? Rushing off somewhere?

"Have you found him?" he asks as I open my mouth to ask the same thing.

My heart sinks deep into my ankles because, *no*, I haven't found him, and it's clear he has not returned to the room.

"I was hoping he was here. Have you heard anything, Matt?"

"Not a word. I'm so sorry, Gabby. I feel absolutely horrible, like this is all my fault." I don't state the obvious. He was responsible for watching our boys; now, one of them is gone. My boy is gone. Not his, *mine.* I can't help but feel something like this would never have happened on my watch.

"I need to talk to Jake," I say, attempting to push past Matt to get into his room. He blocks me with his body. Matt is nowhere near as chiseled as Greg, but he's at least six feet tall and heavy enough to stop me. But as he moves to shut the door behind him, I wedge my foot between his open legs to stop it from closing.

"Why won't you let me in your room, Matt? Are you hiding something in there? *Someone?*" I shift my head around to peek behind him, but he moves with me as if we're playing the mirror game.

Finally, he shakes his head, ending our standoff. He steps to the side so I can look inside the room. I immediately catch sight of Cameron's empty bed and nearly collapse. On shaky feet I make my way into the room. I check the bathrooms and closets. I fall to my knees and check under the beds. Satisfied Cam is not in the room, I stumble into the hallway.

"See, I'm not hiding anything from you, Gabby. Jake is fast asleep, and he doesn't know anything. I've already woken and asked him. He's petrified. I had to give him two melatonin just to get him back to sleep, and I can't have you going in there and waking him up. Cameron didn't tell him anything. Jake didn't hear anything. I'm sorry to say this, but I think it's time you contact the police."

"The police? You don't actually think someone kidnapped him, do you?" I hadn't truly entertained this as a possibility, but as the minutes tick by, the reality of Cam's absence is sinking in. What if someone did kidnap him? What could they want with my thirteen-year-old boy?

I can't bear to answer my own questions.

"No, I mean, maybe. Gosh, I don't know. I was right next door, Gabby. Jake was no more than a foot away from him. We didn't hear a thing. I was completely shocked when he wasn't in bed. I can't for the life of me imagine where he might be."

Neither can I. I tell myself not knowing must be worse than knowing. Reality can't possibly be any direr than what my mind is conjuring.

Once the tears start coming, they won't stop. They're tears of frustration, panic, and loss — tears formed long before my son went missing. Matt pulls me into him, and I allow my body to relax slightly despite the clenching of my heart and roil in my stomach. He's trying to comfort me, though I don't feel comforted.

"I'm sorry, am I interrupting something? What the hell is going on here?"

Not surprisingly, I don't hear Greg approaching, but then I can't hear anything over the noise of the thoughts assaulting me. *What if someone kidnapped our son? What if he's in danger? Hurt? Dead?*

"He's not here," I say, pulling away from Matt.

"And your hands are on my wife because?"

"I was just comforting her, Greg." Matt holds his hands up in the air as if to show they meant no harm. Sometimes Greg forgets that we're all best friends. Matt is like a brother to me and an uncle to Cam. He's just about the last person I'd have an affair with on this planet.

Heat rises to my cheeks, and a shock of guilt shoots through my body. I need to get out of here now. I feel in my pocket for my cell phone and realize I left it behind in the room.

"I'm going to check our room," I say, walking away from them. "Maybe Cam's gone there looking for us," I throw over my shoulder as an afterthought.

Greg has his muscular arms folded across his chest. The veins lining his biceps and forearms bulge.

"I'll come with you."

"No," I say, a tad too forcefully. I temper my tone. "Why don't you check the other rooms, in case he went to see a friend? Let's meet up in the lobby in fifteen, okay?"

Greg seems to mull it over before shrugging his broad shoulders.

"Fine. Okay."

I can't get back to our room quickly enough. I need to check my messages. I think about all the texts I've ignored over the past few days.

I slip into our room and make a beeline for the bed. My purse is open, its contents splayed across the white duvet. My head whips around to make sure I'm alone. *Did someone break into our room* again*? Or did Greg ransack my purse?* Both scenarios fill me with dread. There's an envelope lying on the bed — the one I lifted off the dresser in our original room and stuffed into my bag before I saw the rat.

I read through it, and a chill scales up my spine. Someone knows my secret. Someone is threatening me and my family. Someone has taken my son.

I locate my phone in the rubble. There's an incoherent text from Susie from about an hour ago. I call her, but it goes straight to voicemail. She's probably passed out drunk.

There are seven other texts. From *him.*

My worst fears are confirmed.

We need to talk, Gabby.
I know you still love me.
We were meant to be together.
I know we can work this out.
I'm ready to tell Carla the truth.
You're not breaking up with me.
Either you tell Greg, or I will.

He wouldn't . . .

Or *would* he?

In addition to all the messages, I have five missed calls from Steven Miller over the course of the past hour. I wonder if he's heard something about Cameron. That's certainly one way to get me to talk to him. The other, of course, is him threatening to tell Greg.

I dial his number.

"Gabby? Oh, thank God it's you."

"What are you doing, Steven? You know you can't call me like this."

"I had to talk to you. It's important."

"You have my attention. What is it? Have you heard something about Cameron?"

"Not like this," he says. "I need to see you. Did you read my text? Carla didn't come to the tournament. You can come to my room."

"Seriously, Steven? My best friend is here. My husband. My son. The whole team. How will it look if someone sees me going into your hotel room?"

"I know, but trust me, it's important. I'm sorry I called so much, but you haven't returned any of my texts, and I was starting to worry about you. I thought maybe Greg found out about us, and he'd done something to hurt you. I don't know what I would do if someone hurt you, Gabby."

"No one found out about us, Steven. No one hurt me. There is no us. I meant it when I ended things. I can't do this anymore. My son is missing."

I hear a shuffle outside the door, and I scramble to end the conversation, to delete Steven's number from my call log. I know the drill. It's become second nature to me.

"I have to go," I whisper. "Please, leave me alone. I told you it's over."

"You don't get to decide when it's over . . ."

I hit the end button, and the line goes dead.

My hands are shaking, and the room suddenly feels like a sauna. I rip off my sweatshirt and wipe away the sweat from my forehead as the door swings open.

My husband has a haunted look in his eyes as if he's just seen a ghost.

I don't have to ask.

He hasn't found Cameron.

SIX MONTHS EARLIER
GABBY'S JOURNAL

I stick to myself at baseball practice.

Some days, I watch Cam through the window of the indoor facility. Most days, I read a book in the car. I spend an inordinate amount of time in my vehicle. None of the other moms come to practice — only the dads. I've begged Susie to go once in a while to keep me company, but she'd rather delegate that responsibility to Matt. The Futures practice at 6.30 every Tuesday and Thursday — the same time as Susie's Zumba class. Susie wouldn't dream of missing a Zumba class.

Just like I wouldn't dream of asking Greg to come home early every once in a while to help out by taking Cam to practice.

At least, that's how it was until last season when Colton Miller's dad knocked on my passenger-side window. The rattle against the glass made me jump, and the book I was reading flew from my hands into the back seat. Fifty Shades of Gray. *His eyes flicked to the soft cover before meeting mine. I rolled down the window, hoping the cool air from outside would help temper the color rising on my cheeks.*

"Want some company?" he asked as he leaned his body through the window.

"Um . . ."

"Steven." He extended a hand. "Steven Miller. My son Colton just joined the team, and I haven't met any other parents yet."

"Of course," I said, not wanting to be rude — simultaneously surprised and grateful for the company. I slipped my hand into his. "Gabby Rizzo."

A cool mist was forming outside, a precursor to a brewing storm. I unlocked the car doors, and Steven let himself in.

"Not to sound creepy," he said, turning to face me. "But, I've been watching you."

I laughed nervously, eyeing him with suspicion.

"I'm not sure how that could sound anything other than creepy."

"You look sad," he continued. "Lonely."

He was right, of course. I was sad. Lonely. But I couldn't tell him that. I couldn't tell anyone that. Not even Susie, to whom I told almost everything.

"What about you?" I asked, desperate to change the subject.

"Am I sad and lonely? Aren't we all?"

I felt guilty about this conversation and the dozens that followed, but I found it easier to talk to Steven than my husband. Tuesdays and Thursdays quickly became my favorite days of the week.

Steven was like a breath of fresh air. He was forgiving, charming, and incredibly handsome, and his face lit up like a Christmas tree when he saw me. He looked at me as more than a stay-at-home mom and wife.

It was the way my husband used to look at me.

It's as if I'd been sleepwalking through the past decade and suddenly woke up. Steven brought back to life a part of me that I hadn't even realized had died.

I tried to fight the magnetic pull between us. But one evening, as the sky blackened outside and we sat in the car, warmth spreading through our bodies from the heated seats, Steven asked, "Do you want to get out of here for a while? Come back when practice is almost over?"

"Sure," I said. "There's a diner down the block. We could go there."

"I have something else in mind, and I think you do too." He placed his hand on top of mine, and goosebumps lined my arms.

He was right. I did.

CHAPTER 13

GREG RIZZO

I'd momentarily forgotten about the pregnancy test, but finding Gabby wrapped up like a present in Matt's arms stirred something deep inside me. I wonder if it's his. Because it isn't mine. That's right, the baby my wife is carrying is one hundred percent unequivocally not mine.

Gabby isn't the only one in this relationship with secrets.

She doesn't know this, but I had a vasectomy a few weeks after Cam was born. I saw how our relationship shifted with the arrival of our son, and I couldn't stand it. Don't get me wrong, I loved Cam, but I also loved being the center of my wife's universe. From the moment our son entered this world, those days were over.

Gabby, who didn't want to have children in the first place, fell so deeply in love with Cameron that she wanted to create her own baseball team. I should have told her I couldn't imagine having another child. Instead, I did what I had to do and took matters into my own hands.

As the days, months, and eventually years crept by without her getting pregnant, the prospect of having another child became further removed from our equation. Life went on, and we fell into a routine. Gabby was incredibly busy and consumed with Cameron, who showed real signs of being a prodigy by age two. She talked about expanding our family less and less until the conversation was over.

Or so I thought.

But here we are, a decade later and, apparently, it was never over. Apparently, my wife found someone else to water her garden.

I ball my hands into fists so tight that my veins stretch out across the blanched skin of my knuckles. I still can't believe Gabby would do something like this to me. To our family.

I walk into our hotel room to find Gabby fidgeting on the bed. I eye her suspiciously as she stuffs her phone into her pocketbook along with the note I found earlier this evening. She looks guilty as fuck. I find it difficult to look her in the eyes, though I would if it meant I could read the thoughts going through her head.

"No one has seen him," I tell her.

"How is that even possible?"

"I don't know, but he's been missing for at least two hours now. It's time we call the police."

Gabby's face scrunches up, and I immediately recognize the expression. She's about to cry. I should go to her, comfort her, but I don't. I can't. I pull my phone from my pocket instead and dial 9-1-1.

* * *

Forty-five minutes later, two detectives walk through the looming archway of Foxcroft. A small crowd has gathered, concerned parents of Cam's teammates and random resort-goers who saw the lights or heard the sirens through their windows. I'm sure they've all checked on their kids, and after finding them fast asleep where they should be, they've come to offer support for the one who isn't where he should be. The one who is missing.

I still can't believe it's my son who is missing. But then, how can you ever prepare yourself for something like this? I mean, you hear on the evening news about kids getting kidnapped. You see their innocent, cherub faces on the sides of milk cartons beckoning, *"Have you seen me?"* but you never expect it to be your kid. Because your kid is untouchable. Bad things don't happen to you.

But they do, don't they?

It comes as a surprise that Matt's among the crowd, considering. I'm not sure I would have left Cam alone in a hotel room with his best friend missing. No less, in the very hotel room his best friend went missing from.

I'm not surprised by Susie's absence, though. Considering the condition we left her in, I'm sure she's sleeping it off somewhere, quite possibly in the bartender's bed.

I scan the crowd, spotting more familiar faces etched with sympathy and worry. Coach Bob is not one of them. He said he'd wait in his room should Cameron come to see him, but it's been hours. Considering Cam has not yet surfaced, I would expect to find Coach Bob among the crowd of concerned and interested observers. We haven't heard from him at all. Not so much as a text asking for an update. Or a kind, *"praying for you."*

It makes me wonder how well we know him, but it's a ridiculous thought, and I know I'm grasping at straws. Why would he, of all people, want Cameron gone? Cam is his ticket to winning the tournament.

I extricate myself from the crowd of people watching our lives unravel and cast a leery look in Gabby's direction. She's crumbled on a chair, elbows propped on her knees, head buried in her hands. I want to feel bad for her, but something has shifted between us, and at this moment, I highly doubt it will ever fall back into place.

"Excuse me, I'm looking for Greg Rizzo."

The voice of a female detective pulls me from my wife. She's tall and thin, clad in capri pants and a wrinkled white tee. Her hair is fire-engine red, with curls sticking out of her ponytail like hedgehog spikes. She's disheveled, looking as if she just rolled out of bed and threw on the first thing she could find. I imagine she's not woken up very often with missing person alerts that warrant investigation in the middle of the night.

The detective holds out her badge in one hand while the other rests on the holster peeking out from the waistband of her pants.

I think *surely that won't be necessary.* But then, I wonder, *what if it is?* We have no idea what has happened to Cam. I tell myself he's okay. Gabby and I might not be, but our boy is okay.

"I'm Greg Rizzo," I say, extending a hand. "I'm the one who called. It's my son who is missing." The detective engulfs my fingers in a surprisingly firm shake.

"Detective Leslie Grady," she says. "And this is my partner, Detective Randall Hawthorne." A stocky, balding man nods in my direction, and I return the gesture. He's about a foot shorter than his partner, though equally crumpled. Based on how the introductions have gone, it's safe to say Detective Grady is the one in charge.

My stomach rumbles. Here, I thought I was the one in charge, in control of our narrative, yet it seems we've veered entirely off course. This is not the way this trip was supposed to go.

A flash of light by the entrance interrupts my thoughts.

Detective Grady turns to her partner. "Am I imagining things, or are there news cameras out there? Looks like someone alerted the press." She quickly shifts her attention back to me. "Did you call the local news, Mr. Rizzo?"

"I didn't, but is this a bad thing?" I ask. "Maybe the coverage will help us find Cam?"

"It's not a bad thing per se, but it's a strange thing. We know nothing about Cameron's disappearance yet. So who would want the press here?"

"Someone who wants press coverage," says Detective Hawthorne knowingly.

"Look," I interject, "who cares who called the press? What matters is who took my son. Shouldn't we be focusing on finding Cameron?"

"In cases like these, Mr. Rizzo, the most important thing is establishing motive. Motive yields suspects. Clearly, someone wanted your son's disappearance to get media attention. We need to thoroughly examine every possible angle. I assure you, though, we will find him. I need you to come with me to answer some questions. I need you to tell me everything you know."

"Of course. I'll do anything to find my son."

I turn to take one last look at Gabby before I follow the detectives, but she's gone.

CHAPTER 14

GABBY RIZZO

There's something deeply unnerving about the police. As soon as the detectives walk through the entryway, I fill with a sense of dread, inflating me like a helium balloon. I get that they're here to help, and perhaps that's part of the problem — they're here to help because our son is missing. Therefore, their sheer presence is an exclamation point on our predicament.

I know deep down there's more to it than that, but I'm not about to start digging into the past. This has nothing to do with my past.

Greg took the lead, as he likes to, and I slipped out of the room under the cloak of invisibility I've come to wear so well. I suppose it is a blessing and a curse, depending on how you view it. Situational, like most things in life.

My insides feel like they're being torn apart, ravaged by a wild animal. It's only been a few hours, but I miss my son as if he's been missing for the past decade. He is my lifeline, my heartbeat, and I don't know how to breathe without him. The simple thought is enough to suck all the oxygen from the air. I am trying hard to block out the worst-case scenarios running through my brain, but they mull about like free-range chickens.

I'm still having a difficult time believing this is real. It's as if I've been unexpectedly dropped onto a horror movie set. I keep thinking, this can't be happening. Not to us. Not to me.

Yet, it is happening. It is real. This is not a hallucination. I'm not making up stories with my overactive imagination.

Take that, Dr. Green.

Cameron is missing.

Is my son out there somewhere wrapped in a carpet in the trunk of a car? Are his hands poking out of a shallow grave? Is his waterlogged body bobbing in the ocean?

Oh God.

I keep circling back to Steven. Was he desperate enough to do something like this? His words break through the terrifying images invading my brain —*you don't get to decide when it's over*— and a chill settles over me. I can't imagine the man who has had his hands all over my body with his hands on my son.

But then, he's broken every rule and promise we made to one another. *Rule 1: No phone calls. Rule 2: No contact outside of group chats and our Tuesday-Thursday rendezvous. Rule 3: No falling in love.* What we had was supposed to be an easygoing, good time. No strings attached, casual sex. Something to make us both feel good and escape the realities of our lives. He should never have crossed the line.

Carla may not be here, but my husband is here. Colton is here. *Cam.*

I round a corner toward the elevator, sliding my phone from my pocket. I pull up my call log and dial Steven back. He picks up after the first ring.

"Gabby," he breathes into the phone. "Ready to talk now?"

"I'm not thrilled about this, Steven, but I'll talk to you. And then you have to promise you'll leave it alone. Okay?"

"I promise, Gabby. All I want is to talk to you. Then I won't bother you anymore."

"What room are you in?"

"2012."

"Jesus, Steven, you're literally in the room next to us. We share a wall!"

The realization is greeted with silence. My gut tells me Steven somehow found out what room we'd been moved to, making me feel even sicker to my stomach, though I hadn't realized that was possible.

* * *

It feels like I'm making a terrible mistake. I attempt to talk myself out of going to see my married ex-lover. Unsuccessfully. I need to know what he knows.

I dart my eyes to the left and right to ensure no one in the hallway is watching before I knock on the door to room 2012.

My heart catches in my chest as I listen to the shuffle of familiar footsteps behind the door.

What am I doing?

The door opens, and I fight back a wave of nausea. Steven has positioned himself in the frame, clad in the hotel's complimentary fluffy white robe, his erect penis on full display. Does he think I've come here for sex? *Good luck with that one, buddy.* Sex is the last thing on my mind right now.

I push past him, hoping for him not to detect the color rising to my cheeks and mistake it for anything other than shame. And fear. I can't risk being seen here with him. This is all hitting too close to home.

"God, I've missed you," he whispers into my ear, sidling up behind me, pressing his erection into my backside. "You know I can't stay away from you, Gabby." His lips brush against the skin behind my ear, sending the hairs on my arms on end. His breath reeks of Jack Daniels, and I can tell by the rolling slur of his words that he's had more than he should have to drink.

I flip around, staring into the eyes of the married man I've been sleeping with for the past six months. I remind myself that my son is missing. That despite his adoring words and rock-hard abs, this mostly naked man standing before me may have had something to do with his disappearance.

"I shouldn't be here," I say, meaning it. "Did you do it, Steven? Did you send me those threatening notes? Leave a rat in our room? Kidnap my son? Where is he? Where is Cameron?" I slam my fists against his bare chest, sending him stumbling backward. "How could you, Steven? What the hell is wrong with you?"

"What the hell is wrong with *me*? What's wrong with *you*?" He backs further away from me as if I've just confessed I have herpes.

"As if you don't know. Cameron went missing earlier this evening. Matt Baker went to check on him, and he wasn't in bed. And then you send me these threatening texts. I just . . . I just don't know what to think. If you're trying to get me back, this is not the way to go about it."

A dark cloud passes over Steven's face, punctuated by an expression I don't recognize. He pulls the robe across his body and cinches the sash into a tight knot.

"Wait," he says, backing away, holding his hands out in front of him. "You actually think I had something to do with Cameron going missing? And a *rat?* Seriously? Have you lost your mind?"

"I told you, I don't know what to think. All I know is I need to find Cameron. Please, if you know anything, Steven . . ."

Steven points to the door. "Get out," he says, his voice suddenly stone-cold sober.

"What?"

"Get out."

"So you don't know anything?"

Tears drip down my face, slowly at first but then with an intensity that makes me fear once again that they may never stop falling.

"My God, Gabby, if you could think even for a second I would ever do anything to hurt you or your son, you don't know me at all. And to think I was falling in love with you."

"But I—"

"Don't," he says, holding up a hand to stop the words as I struggle to dislodge them from my throat. "Just leave it, Gabby. Don't worry; I'll do the same."

There's so much I want to say, but at the same time, there's nothing left to say.

I turn and walk from his room, my shoulders slumping under the weight of the night's events. The door slams shut angrily behind me. I pause in the hallway to process his words and reaction. I believe Steven was telling the truth. I'm no closer to finding Cameron now, and I'm even more alone than I was coming into this.

I head back toward the elevator to ride up to Coach Bob's room. Maybe Cam has stopped by since I was last there. Or perhaps Coach Bob knows something he hasn't told us that might help us locate him. I wonder for a moment why he wasn't downstairs with the rest of our team and all the harried spectators, and then thoughts start spraying me like the flames of a wildfire.

I think of the news media, with their cameras and live trucks spread out like a fan in front of the hotel entrance. I overheard the detectives tell my husband they were confused by the media presence. It didn't make sense for someone to contact them before the investigation had a chance to begin. Someone wanted them to know about our missing boy, which would make sense if it were Greg or me. But it wasn't either of us.

So who? And why?

It certainly wasn't hotel management. If there's such a thing as bad press, this is pretty much it. I can't imagine anyone wanting this type of attention.

Or can I?

What if this is all some stunt — a way to garner more attention for the games? So I ask myself who would benefit most from that attention outside our son, and I keep returning to Coach Bob. Is he satisfied with the career he's made out of coaching thirteen-year-olds? Or does he want something more out of his life?

Why didn't we insist on searching his room before?

With these thoughts comes an unlikely scenario and a glimmer of hope. Suppose Coach Bob has orchestrated some wild stunt to draw the media to the tournament and garner local and nationwide coverage. In that case, he'd want Cam there so he could show the world what a skilled coach he is. Perhaps he's sheltering Cam somewhere until he can find him before tomorrow's game. I could live with that. I could live with anything that ends with Cam alive.

I cling to the hope that this wild possibility allows for. It's the tiniest sliver of hope, but I grasp onto it tightly as if it's a solid reality. I could convince myself of just about anything right now if it meant Cameron would return unharmed.

Coach Bob's room is at the far end of the hotel, adjacent to a janitor's closet and emergency exit. I listen closely for the sounds of my son. But all I can make out is the persistent buzz of an ice machine down the hall and the electrical static accompanying the occasional flicker of a lightbulb.

I draw a deep breath and knock lightly on Coach Bob's door. I wait a minute, and when he doesn't answer, I bang harder. Louder. Insistently. He's probably asleep, but then, he said he was a light sleeper, didn't he? Besides, how can you sleep when your star player is missing? When any one of your players is missing?

Coach Bob is like a father to these boys. He married but never had children, and I suspect not for lack of trying. We've all marveled through the years at how expertly Coach Bob deals with his players as if he's got a baseball team worth of kids at home. He would never hurt Cameron. Parents don't do things to hurt their children — at least, good parents don't. I think about my own parents. *Who am I kidding?*

Despite my banging, Coach Bob doesn't answer the door. And last I checked, not too long ago, he also wasn't downstairs facilitating the search for my son.

So where is he?

I press my ear against the wood, listening for any signs of life — voices, a gentle snore, a breath. I can't hear a damn thing.

I need to get into his room.

Think, Gabby.

There's no way the hotel manager will just open the door to another paying guest's room, especially not with his unnatural obsession with privacy. I could request a well-check, considering the extenuating circumstances. The police are here if management refuses to comply. But then I will have to talk to the police. *Ugh*, I know it's only a matter of time before I have to speak to them.

My thoughts are running a mile a minute, and I need to slow them down to think rationally. Hysterical people do hysterical things; they make dangerous mistakes. Flames shoot behind my eyes, and I blink rapidly to rid myself of the images. I'm falling apart. I can't afford to let my emotions get the best of me. Not where my son is concerned.

I turn on my heels to head down to the lobby and run smack dab into Greg.

"Where did you come from?" I ask, completely startled. How many times can you have the same conversation with someone? My husband is so incredibly dense for an intelligent man, like an unmanicured yard filled with thistle.

"The police are interviewing all the guests now. They said I should check anywhere I think Cam could possibly be. I guess we had the same thought."

"I guess so," I say, loosening ever so slightly. "He's not here."

"Cam or Coach Bob?"

"Either."

"Jesus! Where is our son, Gabby?"

CHAPTER 15

GREG RIZZO

It's 2.30 a.m. Last night at this time, Gabby was waking me out of a deep sleep to tell me we shouldn't go on this trip. Did she sense something life-shattering like this was going to happen? Why didn't I listen?

Together, we go door to door, waking up hotel guest after guest in our search for Cameron. We're greeted mainly with concern, sprinkled with some minor irritation. We check all the stairwells, bathrooms, and pools. We look under tables in the restaurants and massage beds in the spa. We comb every last inch of the property that the dark will allow for, looking for signs of our son. The night is a thick ink, the only light coming from the speckling of stars in the jet-black sky.

And flashes. Goddamn camera flashes.

I don't tell Gabby this, but I'm starting to panic. We've looked everywhere and have come up completely empty-handed. Where else is there to look? I wonder if the police have checked the car trunks in the parking lot. I pray it doesn't come to that, but I suspect it's only a matter of time. Because our son is thus far nowhere to be found inside this hotel, which means he could be just about anywhere.

Anywhere but the one place he should be . . . with us.

We haven't been able to locate Coach Bob, either. I wonder what he will do if we don't find Cameron before their scheduled 8 a.m. game tomorrow. Will they cancel the game? Play without him? Just the thought of it stings like a knife twisting in my gut. No, they wouldn't do that. I keep telling myself we will find him before the game, but then I remind myself of something Gabby always tells me, *you're a terrible liar.*

We collapse on the stairs leading up to Foxcroft. The air is sticky and thick between us, not just from the crushing humidity. It's all that's unsaid hanging between us. Volumes of disappointment and hurt and suspicion and lies. We're sitting knee to knee, but the distance has grown exponentially since this morning, a giant chasm, and it feels like there's no bridging it.

"I have to tell you something," Gabby says as if reading my thoughts.

I take her hand in mine and stare deeply into her eyes. "Anything, Gabby. What is it?"

As I wait for her to answer, I wonder if this is it. Is this the moment she finally tells me the truth?

"I've been getting notes. I think it might have something to do with Cameron."

It's not the truth I was hoping for, but a step in the right direction.

"What kind of notes? What do they say?" I don't dare mention the note I discovered while rifling through her purse. Would she believe I was innocently searching for an Advil? And would I be forced to admit this isn't the first time I've looked through her things?

"It's the strangest thing, Greg — the notes are both complimentary and threatening, or maybe passive-aggressive and aggressive. I don't know. I've been getting them here and there for the past few months. In our mailbox, on the windshield of my car. There's at least a dozen or so of them."

"Okay . . ." I try to process what she's telling me, that the psychotic note I found this evening was not the first of its kind. How could she not mention this before? Seems like a pretty relevant thing to tell your husband. "Why wouldn't you tell me, Gabby? Do you have any idea at all who might be leaving them?"

"I honestly don't know, Greg. I guess I didn't really take them seriously enough. And we've been spending such little time together, I just . . ." She exhales a long breath before continuing. "I'm sorry; I should have told you."

"I'm not mad." *About this.* "Anyone at all you can think of?"

"I've tried to figure out who might want to hurt me and us, and I can't. We know everyone and their mother is jealous of Cam, but enough to . . ." Gabby pauses, seeming to choke on her words. "Threaten me? Kidnap him?"

"Some people will do anything to win, Gabby. You know that. I think you should tell the police about this. Maybe they can track the notes somehow? Why don't you show Detective Grady the one in your purse?"

I regret the words the moment they slip from my mouth. I wish I could push them back in. Swallow them. Digest them. But I can't take them back.

Gabby's anger is written all over her face as she yanks her hand away from mine. "How do you know about the note in my purse, Greg?"

"I can explain."

Her eyes burn with rage. Her jaw is clenched so tightly that tiny muscles twitch in her cheeks. I'm worried she might crack a tooth if she doesn't calm down. Although, that should be the least of my worries, considering. "You'd better start talking, Rizzo."

"I was looking for Advil, so you wouldn't be too hungover for the games tomorrow, and I saw the envelope in there."

"The envelope with my name on it? Is that what you're doing now, Greg? Going through my things? I suppose you look through my phone as well?"

I stare blankly into the distance, unable to meet her stare, and then I slowly nod. I sensed she's been hiding something, and confirming such as fact, well, I had no choice but to read that letter.

"I don't know, Gabby. Something told me I should open it. It's just this horrible feeling I've had since we got here like we are on the verge of some major catastrophe. I'm sorry I didn't tell you."

Her eyes glaze over. "I know the feeling. But still, there was a time when we used to tell each other everything, Greg . . ."

As Gabby's thought trails off, I wrap my fingers around the pregnancy test. There was never a time when she told me everything. There is so much I need to say to my wife. I've waited long enough. "There's something I need to ask you about, Gabby. I need you to be honest with me. Are you pre—"

"Mr. and Mrs. Rizzo, excuse me." I jerk my head at the sound of Detective Grady's voice. I wonder how long she's been standing there, how much she's heard. The last thing I want is for her to see the holes in our relationship. The focus must be on finding Cam, and our marital discord will only create an unnecessary distraction. So it suffices to say we both know we need to put on a united front, even if we've never been more divided in our lives.

"Have you found him?" I ask as my stomach clenches. I know we will find him. But will we find him unharmed? What ifs are worming their way in, and every breath I take is laced with panic and heartache. Because what if this doesn't have a happy ending? What if we don't find Cameron alive? We've built our lives around our only child. What do we have left if he's gone?

"We haven't found Cameron yet, but I think I may have a lead."

"A lead? What are you waiting for? Tell us, please." The desperation in my voice is almost tangible.

"How well do you know Cameron's coach?"

I flinch, surprised. "Coach Bob? Oh, I'd say pretty well. We've known him for a few years. He's great with the boys, like a father to them." I grit my teeth. More like a father to him than I am, apparently.

Gabby, meanwhile, is silent; her face has drained of all color as if she's gone into shock.

Detective Grady continues. "We can't seem to locate him, so I ran a background check. I can't say for sure this has anything to do with Cameron's disappearance. But, Bob Ryann has several priors for domestic disturbances, which indicates he may be capable of violence. Coupled with the fact that we can't locate him . . ."

"I don't understand," Gabby says, rising to her feet. "He should have been vetted."

"I'm sorry to say, people have been known to evade background checks before. And I have no idea how meticulous your organization is." Detective Grady shoots my wife a strange look, but just as soon as I notice it, it's gone. I must have imagined it. Gabby is really wearing off on me, not in a good way.

"Apparently not meticulous enough." I shake my head. "So what do we do now — wait?"

"I have an idea," Gabby says. "I'll call Meghan." She turns to Detective Grady. "Coach Bob's wife," she adds.

"That's a great idea," I agree. "I'm sure Meghan has heard from him, and this is all some big misunderstanding. I mean, he was acting completely normal when we went to his room. Wasn't he Gabby?"

Before I finish my thought, Gabby has already started dialing Meghan Ryann's number. My breath catches in my chest as I watch her face crumble. My wife is pale, to begin with — milky, with patches of red and a smattering of freckles across her cheekbones, shoulders, and body. But now, she's sheet white, like an angel or a recently deceased corpse. Her arm begins to fall, and I pull the phone from her hand before it slips from her fingers and crashes to the ground. My thumb finds the speaker button.

An automated message plays: "*The number you have reached is no longer in service. If you believe you've received this message in error, please check the number and dial again.*"

CHAPTER 16

GABBY RIZZO

It's official — Cameron *and* Coach Bob are missing. Meghan Ryann's phone is inexplicably out of service. All signs point in Coach Bob's direction, and it feels like the clock is ticking out of control.

Another hour has passed, and Foxcroft is now swarming with police, a pool of uniformed and plain-clothed officers canvassing the hotel. I'm grateful they called for backup. At least a hundred rooms here are occupied by people who need to be questioned. I'm sure Coach Bob is at the top of that list. But they can't question him until they find him.

According to the manager, no one unaccounted for has come or gone through the front entrance over the past six hours. However, that can't be verified because the hotel values the privacy of its patrons and therefore doesn't have camera footage like your typical twenty-first-century establishment. Ironic how badly that company's mission has backfired.

Assuming what the manager is telling the police is true, someone staying here must know something. My son didn't just vanish into thin air.

My only hope is that speaking with the media will get people talking. The press is still huddled outside the main entrance and has grown exponentially in number. Greg and I have mutually agreed to give a statement. We walk through the now ominous-looking archway, hand in hand, to face the news cameras. Greg's hand feels foreign in mine, as if it belongs to someone else other than my husband of the past decade.

For a moment, I think about Steven, wondering if he has told the police about our relationship. That information would not paint me in a favorable light. But then, what about this situation paints either of us in a favorable light? We've lost our only child. I shudder at the thought.

Detectives Grady and Hawthorne suggested we offer a reward. Perhaps that will be incentive enough to help someone remember something, *anything* to help us find Cam.

Greg and I walk together to the edge of the top stair, where the press has erected a makeshift podium. The lights are blinding, and I raise a hand to shield my eyes. I search the crowd for a familiar face. There are a few player parents, but most people have retired to their rooms, to the warmth and comfort of their children. I look for Susie in the sea of faces, but she isn't there. I haven't spoken to her since I got violently ill at the bar, and Greg dragged me like a ragdoll through the hotel lobby back to our room.

I think of the text she sent me earlier this evening — *need to talk,* followed by some gibberish I couldn't understand. I chalked it up to a drunk message from my wasted best friend, desperate to share details about the mind-blowing sex she had with the twenty-year-old bartender who is not her husband. Because even a blind umpire could have called that one.

I thought nothing of her phone going straight to voicemail when I tried her back.

But what if I was wrong? What if she knows something? And what if Cameron isn't the only one in danger? What if something happened to Susie after she sent me that text?

I wish she were here to answer my questions and figure out where we go from here. Susie would know what to do next. Despite her occasional wild displays of misjudgment (see extramarital sex with a twenty-year-old bartender), she's the most level-headed person I know. I think about how calmly she confronted my premature labor and all our emergencies since, and I crave that reassurance. The first thing I'll do after giving our statement is to find her and make sure she's okay. That's what Susie would do for me. Then I'll find out what she knows.

Susie loves Cameron almost as much as I do. She would do anything to help me find him. I'm certain of that. Even if it means . . . could it mean betraying her own husband? Matt was the last person to see Cam. Could he have had something to do with Cam's disappearance? Was that what she was trying to tell me?

I've entered full-blown panic mode. Sweat is dripping down my hairline, and my hands are trembling. My thoughts are all over the damn place.

Greg wraps his fingers around the microphone, brings it to his lips, and clears his throat. His other hand is still wrapped protectively around mine. I wonder if the faces intently watching us see a loyal, united couple desperate to find their missing son.

They'd have the desperate to find their missing son part right.

Still, I'm happy to put up appearances if it will help the investigation. And I hope Cameron is out there listening as Greg begins our desperate plea for his safe return. I hope he knows just how much we love him.

The mood is somber, and the crowd is silent as my husband speaks.

"Thank you all for coming out here tonight. Our thirteen-year-old son went to sleep in his hotel room earlier this evening and has not been seen since. We have searched every inch of this place but are no closer to finding him. We need your help. My wife Gabby and I are offering a fifty-thousand-dollar cash reward to anyone with information leading to the return of our son. No questions asked. Cameron is the light of our lives, and we beg whoever has him to please let him go, to bring him back to his mother and me. Cameron, if you're listening, your mother and I love you so much. We won't stop looking until we find you. That's all, thank you."

Questions shoot out from every direction while camera lights flash like laser beams. My knees buckle, and my legs threaten to pretzel beneath me. Greg wraps his hand around my elbow to stop me from collapsing.

A reporter shouts, "Where were you when your son disappeared?" And I swear, a part of me dies on the spot. Because we should have been with Cam. This would never have happened if we were with him.

Guilt pierces my insides as I recall how excited I was to spend the night alone with Greg. This trip was more to me than just a baseball tournament, regardless of who might be here watching Cam and what that might mean for his future. It was a chance to reconnect with my husband. It was a final shot at fixing things between Greg and me — either the beginning of a new game or our last inning as a team.

I said I would never leave my husband but, sometimes, relationships are fractured beyond repair. And the truth is, I was prepared to end things between us if it came to that. I just wasn't prepared to lose our son in the process. Not literally, anyway.

And look where we are now. Once again, the only thing fueling us is Cam, and he is gone.

"I need to get out of here," I whisper in Greg's ear as the questions continue to hit us like rapid fire.

Is it true Coach Bob Ryann is missing?

Do you think your son's disappearance has something to do with tomorrow's game?

What is the state of your relationship, Mr. and Mrs. Rizzo? Could this have something to do with Cameron's possible abduction?

Possible abduction? I slap a hand over my mouth to stop my insides from spilling out.

Greg once again addresses the crowd of a dozen or so hungry press, perched like wild animals ready to devour us. Our son is missing, yet it feels like they are the hunters, and we are their prey.

"Thank you again for taking the time to help us find our son. My wife and I will not be taking further questions at this time." Greg glances back over his shoulder and then retrains his eyes on the ravenous media. "I'm going to turn the microphone over to Detective Grady, who is leading the search for our son."

With that, Greg places a hand on the small of my back and steers me off the stage. My mouth is a strip of sandpaper, and I turn back to grab the water bottle I left on the podium but think better of it. Detective Grady has already traded places with us and is clearing her throat to address the press. I can't stand being assaulted with even one more question.

Thirst is the least of my problems, clearly.

Once inside, I collapse into a chair and try to catch my breath.

"How are they so well versed in this investigation already? And the part about our marriage?" I ask, shaking my head in disbelief.

"Honestly, someone here must be funneling information. Probably whoever contacted the press in the first place."

"Why in the world would someone do that? And who?"

Greg shrugs his shoulders. "Your guess is as good as mine."

I can't even begin to render a guess.

"This is all so messed up. Do you think Cameron is okay?"

Greg rests his hands on my shoulders, and I feel a momentary jolt of affection. But the movement is awkward, and the moment fleeting.

"We will find him, Gabby. I promise we will find him."

I should feel reassured, except I don't. How could Greg possibly know we'll find him? The only thing we both know is that my husband is a terrible liar.

CHAPTER 17

GREG RIZZO

I leave Gabby crumpled in a red velvet bucket chair and drag myself to the front desk to wait for Detective Grady to finish her session with the press. I watch the manager robotically busying himself behind the desk. I bet he's operating on autopilot and has no idea what to do with himself. I'd bet when he woke up this morning and drove to work, he was expecting an average day, not the complete shitshow it turned out to be.

Unless he wasn't?

The creepy sensation crawls up my spine again as I wonder if he knows something he's not telling us. The rat, the disappearance . . . could he possibly have seen nothing? Paranoia is getting the best of me. Surely the police are asking the same questions. I have to trust that they are doing their jobs.

Detective Grady finds me at the front desk, lost in a storm cloud of suspicion.

"Damn scavengers," she says, shaking her head at the mob outside.

"What do you think?" I ask as she closes the space between us. "Will it help?"

"Well, it certainly can't hurt. I've released the picture you provided of Cameron. The story will be airing all over the local news and in the surrounding areas. We both know your son didn't just disappear without a trace, Mr. Rizzo. Someone had to have seen him. Someone has to know something."

Static from the detective's walkie-talkie interrupts our conversation, followed by Detective Hawthorne's husky voice on the other end. "We found him, partner. We found him."

I grab Detective Grady by her slender wrist. "They found Cameron? Where is he? Where is my son?"

She immediately pulls back, and I know I've made a mistake. Her hand finds the gun handle settled in the holster on her pants, and my heart jumps in my chest.

"I'm sorry," I say, holding out my hands. "It's just. My son . . . I need to see him, to know he's okay."

"You need to stay calm," she warns, shaking her head in disapproval before speaking into the walkie-talkie. "You have the boy, Hawthorne?"

"No, not the boy. We have the coach."

My heart does a weird flappy thing in my chest. It's an irreconcilable movement of hopefulness and dread. The police have Coach Bob, but they don't have Cam. Then the thought too tragic to contemplate follows: has Coach Bob done something terrible to Cam? Is that something you don't mention over a walkie-talkie in the event some poor parent is listening? In this case, that poor parent being me?

"Text me your location. I'm on my way." Detective Grady clicks off the walkie-talkie and affixes it back to the waistband of her pants, adjacent to her gun.

"Where is he?" I ask. "Where are we going?"

"We are not going anywhere, Mr. Rizzo. I am going to question Bob Ryann. You are going to stay close by where I can find you."

I shake my head in disbelief. "No way, I'm coming with you. What if that son of a bitch has done something to my son?"

"This is precisely why you're not coming with me. You're too emotional to act rationally. Bob Ryann is a potential suspect, but that does not make him guilty of anything other than being difficult to track down. I can't chance you doing something rash and blowing up this investigation. There's a good reason why they say you shouldn't take the law into your own hands. Do you understand what I'm saying?"

"You think I'm a liability."

"No, Mr. Rizzo, I think you are a desperate father looking for his missing son. Go comfort your wife. I promise I will do everything I can to help you find him. I'll be in touch as soon as I have any information."

I nod my head, defeated, and watch helplessly as Detective Grady walks away, her back disappearing into the grand lobby. I debate following her, staying close enough that I can see where she's going but distant enough that she doesn't notice me there. Ultimately, I opt against it because I know she's right. I can't control my emotions right now. If I saw Bob, knowing he might have done something to Cam, I could kill him with my own two hands.

I reach into my back pocket, pulling out the lineup for tomorrow's game. Coach Bob slipped it to me when we first arrived at the hotel. I'm not sure what I'm looking for, but this piece of paper might explain Coach Bob's state of mind coming into this tournament. It might also indicate the presence of a disgruntled family that would like nothing more than to have Cameron sit out of the game tomorrow.

Impossible to play when you're missing, right?

I unfold the lineup and draw a breath. I see my son's name penciled in on the mound and listed first in the batting order. Cameron always bats first in the lineup because he's sure to get on base, whether it's a walk, a line drive, or a solo home run. And once he's there, the boy runs like a gazelle. Plus, Cam wears it better than anyone I've seen, not so much as flinching when he's hit by a wild pitch. Of course, by the end of the game, all he gets are intentional walks, but Cam steals bases like they're giving them away for free.

I look for Jake on the roster and find him in left field. Matt and Susie like him in center field, so I imagine they're not too thrilled about that. He's batting sixth, which isn't terrible, considering the slump he's been in for the past month. I'm sure *they're* unhappy — because people like them are never happy — but their issue is with Coach Bob, not Gabby and me. Certainly not with Cameron.

I wouldn't expect to find Matt and Susie to shed any tears if Levi Hertz were to wake up with a severe case of food poisoning or a pulled Achilles tendon. Still, I really can't imagine them wishing any harm on Cam. We're like a family. One great big dysfunctional family.

Everything else checks out. The roster is the same as it's been all season. The dominant bats are at the top of the order, and the weakest hitters are at the bottom. The same three guys are riding the bench, serving as pinch runners and the occasional designated hitter. Nothing has changed here. Nothing would merit another parent from our team taking such drastic measures to prevent Cameron from playing tomorrow.

Of course, there's a possibility I hadn't considered that one of the other teams is attempting to sabotage us for tomorrow. Except, none of the other teams are staying at this hotel. I'd think the manager would have mentioned a minor detail, like someone coming here looking for my son, especially in light of our current predicament.

My head is spinning like a toy top. I can't wrap my head around why anyone would do something like this. Cam is thirteen years old. He's a good kid. He doesn't deserve whatever might be happening to him right now. The thought of my boy alone and afraid somewhere in the night tugs at my chest.

I take the bucket seat next to Gabby. I examine my wife's face — it's red and blotchy, puffy from all the tears she has shed. Her eyes are clouded over, dazed, focused on some invisible spot in the distance. She looks as though she's in another world, a world I presume where her only son didn't vanish from plain sight.

"Gabby," I say gently, not wanting to startle her.

"Any news?"

"They located Coach Bob."

"And Cameron?"

I shake my head, finding myself unable to meet her gaze.

"Cameron isn't with him? Do they know where he is?"

"Detective Grady told me to wait here while they interrogate him. We should hopefully have some answers soon. In the meantime, I'm going to camp out here, just in case . . ."

"Just in case what, Greg? He miraculously walks through the door?"

I force a small smile. "Remember the time when Cam said he was running away from home?"

Gabby's lips give the slightest hint of a curl. "How could I forget? He packed a duffel bag full of Oreos and baseball gear and camped out on the corner of our street. We watched him for hours from our bedroom window."

"Came home when he had to use the bathroom after eating all those Oreos," I add, and we both lightly chuckle. The laughter is as strained as our marriage. "He was okay then, Gabby, and I feel it in my gut that he is okay now. He has to be. Do you feel it?"

"I'm not sure what I feel other than a giant gaping hole where my son should be. I can't just sit here any longer, Greg. Sit here and wait and do nothing. I need to do something."

"We have to trust that the police will find him."

"We're his parents, Greg. We're the ones who are supposed to protect him. And we didn't. We've completely failed him as parents."

I can't argue with her because she's right. We have failed Cameron. I promise myself that if — no, when — Cam comes back, we will never fail him again. We will keep him safe for as long as we both shall live. That's the unspoken oath you take when you bring a child into the world. And despite what's happened, I take that oath seriously. I only wish Gabby took our vows half as seriously.

There it is again — the anger simmering below the surface, beginning its boil. Maintaining your composure is challenging when you know someone you love and, once trusted, is lying to you. I've done my best so far, but I'm not sure how much more I can take before I explode and it all comes rushing out.

"What do you suggest we do, Gabby?"

"I'm going to find Susie, and then—"

"Of course you are."

"What the hell is that supposed to mean?"

"It means exactly what I said. You always turn to her. Susie this and Susie that. I'm sick and tired of your obsession with this woman." My hand flies to my mouth as if I could physically stuff the words back in. I wish I could.

Though I've thought this since Susie came into our lives, I didn't mean to say it out loud. It was a mistake. I've taken it too far. I see it in how Gabby's face has fallen, and her jaw has tightened as if she's a wild animal backed into a corner. She jumps to her feet and begins to walk away but then swivels back to face me.

"You just sit here and do you, like you always have, Greg. Leave me to pick up the pieces. I'll take care of this like I always do. Because I'm not leaving this place with or without you until I find our son."

CHAPTER 18

GABBY RIZZO

I storm through the lobby of Foxcroft, my flip-flops flopping loudly against the wood floor, echoing through the massive space. I feel Greg's eyes on me, but I don't look back at him. I can't look at him right now.

As the distance grows between us, I unclench my fists and allow myself to breathe again. My heart is racing a mile a minute. It's the urgency of our situation and my anger toward my husband.

He has some nerve, considering. I think of all the things I should have said. *Maybe I'm always looking for Susie because you're never around. Perhaps if you'd been there for me, I wouldn't have looked elsewhere. Maybe if you cared about our son more than yourself and about baseball . . .*

It's too late now.

I have never wanted to see my best friend more than I do now. The nerve of my husband calling me obsessed. Greg's problem is he doesn't understand unconditional relationships. One of his many problems.

I imagine Susie is back in her room by now, snuggled up with Matt. He's probably rubbing her feet or stroking her hair while pretending not to notice the odor of Calvin Klein for Men that she brought back from the bartender. I guess sometimes you accept the things you hate about a person you love to keep from losing them. I've become quite the expert on that.

I crave the warm reassurance of my best friend. But it's not just Susie I want to see. It's Jake.

Matt claimed Jake didn't know anything about Cam's whereabouts. But if something were going on, who would he tell — the dad or the cool aunt? I've known Jake since he was a baby, and Jake knows he can trust me. He's a good kid, like Cam, and I'm counting on him telling me the truth. Because could he really have slept through his best friend getting snatched in the night from the bed adjacent to his? Jake never was a good sleeper.

I pound my clenched fist on the door to their room repeatedly. I press my face against the peephole but can't make out anything of substance. It's like I'm opening my eyes in pitch-black water. Then, as I'm about to turn to leave, I hear the shuffle of feet and jump back as the knob turns.

My heart is hammering in my chest. It's a sensation I've grown accustomed to this evening — the rhythmic thud quickening in pace each time I think about what may have happened to my son.

Matt opens the door, rubbing his eyes as if I've just woken him. Seriously, how could anyone sleep at a time like this? I guess it's easier to do when it's not your kid who's missing.

"Sorry, I must have nodded off. I was waiting, hoping to hear something."

"Is Susie here?" I'm already looking past him, straining to see movement or bodies in the room. The answer to my question is written all over Matt's face. His eyes are swollen, blackish-blue shadows circling out, and red-rimmed as if he's been crying. He looks disheveled, and not just from having been woken up.

Matt purses his lips into a tight line. "I haven't heard from her all night."

"That's not good. It's almost morning, Matt. Have you looked for her?"

"Where am I going to look? Are you that dense, Gabby? This is what Susie does. She disappears. Use your imagination. I'm sure you can figure out where she is."

"I'm so sorry, Matt." I lower my eyes to the floor, unable to meet his gaze.

He shakes his head. "Don't act surprised, Gabby. I would think you, of all people, know how Susie is."

"I need to talk to Jake," I say, choosing not to acknowledge the obvious — Susie has gone to bed with another man. I mean, at least I know it isn't my husband. At least, this time, I know it isn't my husband.

Matt steps aside so I can enter their room. It takes a moment for my eyes to adjust to the darkness. I feel a flicker of hope. There's a light on in the adjoining room. It was pitch black when I checked for Cam earlier in the night. Maybe Cameron came back while Matt was dozed off. "Have you checked the room, Matt? The light is on . . ." I let the possibility hang in the air — our boys back in the room together.

I don't wait for him to answer. Instead, I push the partially ajar door fully open, filled with optimistic caution. I step into the adjacent room, and my heart drops to my feet. Jake is sitting in bed, staring out the window into the blackened night. It takes a split second to register that Cam is not with him.

"Jake," I say, moving slowly toward his back. The stillness of his body, the way he's leaned in toward the window, it looks like he's watching something. My eyes dart to the window, but all I see is the darkness of a brutal night that has my son.

Jake doesn't turn around or answer me.

"Jake," I repeat, louder this time.

He doesn't move at all.

An overwhelming sensation of fear unfurls in my abdomen. Why won't Jake look at me? Why won't he say something?

I place a hand on his shoulder, and he whips around as if I'm about to attack him. "It's just me," I say, staring into a set of familiar eyes that suddenly look foreign.

He registers my face and then turns back to resume staring at nothing. Or something? Jake knows something. He definitely knows something.

"Talk to me, Jake, please. I promise no one will be in trouble. Where is Cam?"

Not a word.

"I'm begging you, please, Jake, tell me something, *anything*. He's your best friend. If you can help him, you have to help him—"

"Enough, Gabby. Leave him alone," Matt calls from the doorway separating the rooms. His hands are on his hips, and he doesn't look pleased.

I back away from Jake and turn to Matt. "What's going on with him?"

"His best friend is missing, and his mom has disappeared to who knows where. Where do I even start?"

"Has he said anything?"

"He's not talking, Gabby. I found him here staring out the window, as you see him now, in this almost catatonic state. I can't get a word out of him."

"Something obviously happened, Matt."

"Obviously."

"My God, Matt, you don't think he's done something to Cam, do you?" The thought is impossible, but nothing about this situation is possible. Cameron couldn't possibly be missing. No one could have possibly taken him. But yet, he is. And someone has.

And the fact of the matter is — his thirteen-year-old best friend seems to know something he's not telling us. Why? Why wouldn't Jake try to help Cam if he could?

"You actually think Jake had something to do with this?" There's a fire in Matt's eyes I never noticed before. He looks dangerous, like a man capable of anything. Including doing something to my son? I take a step back from him to put some space between us.

Someone clears their throat, interrupting our standoff. "Sorry to interrupt." I jerk at the sound of Detective Grady's voice. "I knocked, but no one came to the door. The manager let me in. There's been a development, and I need to ask Jake a few questions if that's alright with you."

Matt runs a hand through his messy dark hair. "Be my guest. He told me he didn't know anything — that is, when he was still speaking."

"If you don't mind, I'd like to speak with him alone."

Matt throws his hands up and storms out of the room. I follow him, wondering if something other than the obvious has him so worked up. Does he suspect Jake may have done something? Or does he know as much? Is he covering up for his son?

"Matt, please, if you know anything . . . Imagine if it was Jake missing. I'm dying here."

Matt looks at me, and I think he's going to say something, to offer me words or a hug or some other gesture to stop my insides from crawling out of my skin, but he walks back into the room and slams the door in my face.

CHAPTER 19

GREG RIZZO

Coach Bob is the last person I expect to find strolling into the hotel lobby. *Strolling*. As opposed to being escorted with his hands snuggly secured behind his back in cuffs. I convinced myself he was behind this, and now it looks like we are back to square one.

So who the hell has my son?

My muscles stiffen as Bob approaches. I don't know what to say to him. I don't know what to ask. I'm filled with an indescribable sense of urgency that makes me want to either run away or vomit.

"Greg," he says, placing a hand on my shoulder. "I'm so sorry. It's quite the shitshow here. Any word?"

"We've heard absolutely nothing. It's as if Cameron just vanished into thin air."

The corners of Bob's mouth dip down. "Yeah, well, the police questioned me for a good hour. I can't believe anyone would believe I'd have anything to do with this. Thank goodness I had an alibi, or they'd probably still be questioning me when they should be looking for an actual suspect. Believe me, Greg, I'm just as concerned as everyone else."

Do I believe him?

"Yeah, well, no one seems to know anything. Where were you, anyhow?"

Bob's face reddens, and he clears his throat loudly. He stammers, "Listen, Meghan and I are having some issues. Let's just say I wasn't in my room." *I'm sorry I asked.* "Uh, maybe we'll hear something at the game," he adds as an afterthought. As if my son is an afterthought.

"The game? Why are you going to the game? You can't tell me you're actually going to play?"

My mouth feels like it's fallen to the floor. My son is missing, and they're going to play a baseball game. A freaking baseball game.

The sun is rising outside, casting its hazy glow through the entryway. I glance down at my watch — 5 a.m.

Coach Bob didn't come down here to find me or to help with our search for Cameron. He came down to the lobby to rally his troops for the baseball game that will now have more media attention than the Kentucky Derby, thanks to their star player's disappearance. Dumb luck — that's what has me sitting here, pathetically waiting for Cam to reappear. All I am to Coach Bob is an obstacle to the door.

He clears his throat again. It's a tell that he doesn't believe what he's about to say. We all have tells when we're lying. Take Gabby, for instance; her right eye twitches uncontrollably when she's hiding something. Like, when I walked into the hotel room and found her stuffing her phone into her purse. I can tell when she's being untruthful about something, which, if the pregnancy test is any indication, is pretty much all the time. I've never told her this because she doesn't need to know I can detect her deceptions.

"Look," Bob says, "I can't imagine what you're going through right now. These boys are like children to me, but I know it's your flesh and blood missing. Whatever happens, this will traumatize everyone here. I can't pile on not allowing the boys to play in this game on top of that. They've been counting down the days for the past year. We don't know that anything bad has happened to him, Greg. We have to believe he's okay."

I shake my head, unable to believe what I'm hearing. The casualness in which Bob is handling my son's disappearance like it's a routine ground ball a shortstop could field with his eyes closed.

"Good luck with your game," I say through gritted teeth, but I don't mean it. I hope the Futures lose and are eliminated after the first game and each and every one of them sits miserably in their SUVs on their nine-hour car rides home, which stretches to twelve because of an accident on I-87 North and bottleneck traffic. I hope they ruminate on how different the outcome would have been if Cam had been there.

Coach Bob is a damn fool for playing this game. These parents allowing their children to play when their teammate and friend is missing are idiots.

Who am I kidding?

I'd like to think I'd choose differently if this were happening to another family, but maybe I wouldn't. Perhaps I'm just as selfish as the rest of them. Maybe it took losing the only things that mattered to me to realize it.

Footsteps and the low hum of conversation as the parents and players trickle into the lobby are disorientating. Heat crawls up the back of my neck. I'm inundated with awkward half-waves and head nods. It's as if I have some fatal disease, and they're afraid of getting too close, as if losing your child might be contagious. It's a team no parent wants to be a part of. Still, I thought some of these people were our friends, Cam's friends. They should be offering to set up search parties, hang fliers, and go door to door in the nearest towns, not shuffling to their cars to drive to the baseball fields.

I swivel my head around, searching for the Bakers. They haven't come down yet. I imagine Susie is sleeping it off after the bender she pulled last night. I've never seen another person throw back shots like she did. All 105 pounds of her. Susie wasn't back in the room when we checked there earlier, at least not that I could tell from the hallway. Did she *actually* go home with the bartender? Classy move to pull at your son's 13U baseball tournament. Then again, class is probably one of the only things Susie doesn't have going for her. I think even Gabby would agree.

My limbs feel like they're submerged in thick mud. It's as if I've been sitting here for days and am going into atrophy. I rise to my feet, stretching my arms overhead. My body cracks in protest. Gabby hit the ball on the barrel — we can't just sit around doing nothing. Cameron is not going to simply walk through that door. We need to find him.

It occurs to me that one of us needs to go to that game — talk to all the parents and players, observe the other team, and figure out if one of them could have done something to our son. My feet carry me to the front of the hotel because I know that person is me.

I pause momentarily. On second thought, if I have to listen to even one parent scream from their lawn chair or bleachers for their kid to have fun while my son is missing, I might wind up the one in cuffs for inciting a disturbance. But you know what? I'm sick and tired of playing by the rules. Because look where that's gotten me.

I'm halfway into the open air, the hot breath of a Georgia summer morning slapping me across the face, when I feel a hand dig into my shoulder. I swing around and find myself face to face with Detective Hawthorne.

"Where are you going, Mr. Rizzo?" He's got one hand on his hip, inches from his holster, the other barely hovering above my arm's flesh.

There's something I don't like about his tone. I can't put my finger on it, but it feels like he's a breath away from — *you're not going anywhere.* I'm not used to being treated like this. I didn't realize how much of my confidence and clout were tied up in having a star for a son like Cam. Are tied up.

Are.

"I'm headed to the game to see if I can find anything out there since we aren't having any success here." *Since* you *aren't having any success here.*

"Yeah, well, actually, I'm going to need you to stick around." And there it is. I'm not allowed to leave.

"Is that a request or an order?"

"Right now, it's a request. But if I have to, I suppose I could make it an order. Will that be necessary?"

"It won't."

"I just need to ask you a few more questions, Mr. Rizzo. We have some new information. I'm following up on a possible angle. Shall we?"

Detective Hawthorne motions inside the hotel. I trail him through the lobby to the bar, which was hopping with life just hours ago — with shots, flirting, and the wholeness of not having a kidnapped child.

Detective Hawthorne signals for me to have a seat in one of the round booth tables tucked into a corner overlooking the parking lot. I watch as a line of cars pulls out of the gravel lot and down the rocky lane that leads to the main road. I wonder why he's not making any of these other families stay — keeping them close by for questioning. How is *anyone* allowed to leave this place until we've located my son? I assume the police have done their due diligence, but who knows what these people, the ones I thought I knew, are hiding.

We all have something to hide.

I want to get this over with as quickly as possible, so I can leave the hotel and go to the baseball game.

"So what do you want to speak with me about, Detective?"

"I'd like to speak with you about your wife."

CHAPTER 20

GABBY RIZZO

I wait in the hallway for Detective Grady to emerge from Matt's room. I wonder if Jake is speaking and if he's told her anything. I wonder if he knows what's happened to Cameron. I wonder if he's hiding something from us. Lastly, a part of me wonders if Jake had something to do with this. It's an impossibly horrible thought that physically pains me to contemplate, but I'm out of theories about what has happened to my son.

Someone. Did. Something.

Besides, there's no denying Jake's behavior was strange and completely out of character. He's known me forever, almost as long as he's known his own parents. I've babysat him, cooked for him, and rubbed his back as he fell asleep on Cameron's trundle bed. I cared for him when he was sick and welcomed him into our home whenever his parents were out to dinner or out of town. Jake is practically a part of my family, as I am his. He calls me Auntie Gabby, for goodness sake.

But the way Jake was looking at me — there was a vacancy, a darkness in his eyes that I didn't recognize. It was as if he'd seen something too horrible to unsee, something impossible to put into words. And the only thing I can think right now is that that something was my son.

I pace back and forth in front of the door to their room. I notice a chip of paint on the wall and start peeling it, mildly comforted by the fact that no cameras are watching me destroy hotel property. What about what this hotel has done to me? To my family?

When the pacing and peeling grow old, I rise up on the balls of my feet, testing how long I can hold my weight before my heels slip down to the ground. Anything to distract me from frantically panicking about my son.

Finally, there's a creak, and the door to Matt's room slowly begins to open.

"Jake?"

I'm shocked to see Jake walking out of the room, fully decked out in his Futures uniform. His gaze meets mine for just a second, then skirts away. Why won't he look at me? And why is he dressed as if he's going to play?

Detective Grady follows a few steps behind. She stops short when she sees me standing in front of the door, then motions for Jake to continue to the elevator. She steps to the side and Matt emerges, his red pulley wagon filled with chairs and a cooler in tow. My God, he *is* going to play.

I'm suddenly hot and dizzy, and I have to lean against the wall to stop myself from falling down. It's been less than twelve hours since my son disappeared without a trace, and they will go ahead and play in the tournament he was to star in. Talk about defensive indifference.

"Mrs. Rizzo." Detective Grady's voice sounds harder than it did an hour ago as if she's misplaced her empathy chip. "You are just the person I was about to look for."

Now that's not something you ever want to hear from a detective.

"I am? What is it?" I ask. "Did Jake tell you something about Cameron? Do you know where he is?"

"Unfortunately, he doesn't have any knowledge as to Cam's whereabouts. Whatever happened, Jake wasn't awake for it."

"So why wouldn't he just say that when I asked him? Why does he look like he killed someone?" I nearly choke on my words.

"I'm going to be blunt, Mrs. Rizzo. He felt threatened by the aggressive way you were questioning him."

"He felt threatened? By *me*? I didn't realize asking Jake if he knew what happened to his best friend was aggressive." A chortle escapes from my mouth. "This is seriously the most ridiculous thing I've ever heard. I can't imagine where he got that from, why he would think, let alone say something crazy like that."

Detective Grady's eyebrows turn in, highlighting a deep crease between her light eyes. "Look, Mrs. Rizzo. We are exploring all possibilities, but you can't strong-arm a child into telling you what you want to hear. He clammed up because he was scared."

"But . . . but . . . Matt said he wasn't talking before I came in there. Do you actually think I wanted to hear Jake say he did something to Cam? I just want my son back. And clearly, you're not doing enough to find him."

"I assure you we are doing everything we can to find your son. Unfortunately, we haven't been able to locate him yet, but we will. In order to do that, we need to cover all our bases and rule out any possible suspects."

"So stop wasting time here and do it. That boy knows something."

"I'll need you to detail your whereabouts beginning when you first arrived at the hotel." Detective Grady pulls a notebook and pen from her pocket and flips to an open page. She's wholly disregarded my observation about Jake, and it's obviously because she has a different theory about what happened to my son. One that involves me.

"You can't be serious. Do you think *I* had something to do with Cameron's disappearance?"

"As I said, we're not ruling anything out. However, I don't think you've been completely forthcoming, Mrs. Rizzo. And if you want to help us find your son, it's time you start talking."

She can't possibly know who I am. She can't possibly know who I am. I repeat this mantra over and over again in my mind until I almost believe it. Because the paranoia coursing through my body and the way she's looking at me speaks otherwise.

But how could a small-town detective in a desolate area like this know anything about my past? Unless the same person who contacted the news media, who leaked information from the investigation, who left threatening notes, who killed the rat I found in our hotel room, who kidnapped my son is setting me up to take the fall for whatever this is.

"Tell me you think I had something to do with Cam's disappearance. Tell me. Do I need to get a lawyer?"

She glances down at her watch as if there is somewhere she needs to be. Or to tell me my time is running out.

And I realize I am being set up.

And I might actually need a lawyer.

CHAPTER 21

GREG RIZZO

Detective Hawthorne has completely caught me off guard. He wants to talk about my wife. Gabby is just about the last person I'd expect to be questioned about in Cam's disappearance. But then, for the hundredth time today alone, I remind myself Gabby is not who she seems to be, and the surprise dissipates, much like the trust in our marriage.

The positive pregnancy test is proof of that. Not to mention the secrets Gabby has kept from me since we met. Sometimes I think I don't know Gabby Rizzo at all. And then, I realize that's because I don't. Gabby Rizzo doesn't exist.

I've strongly suspected that my wife was up to something for some time. Now I know. Suspecting and knowing are two entirely different things. And holding the evidence of your wife's betrayal in your pocket is in a universe of its own.

Detective Hawthorne studies me as if he can read the thoughts going through my head. God, let's hope not. I try to stop my eyes from traveling to my pocket, lest he also sees what's in there.

I'm angry at my wife for lying to me, but the last thing I want is for the police to start scrutinizing our lives. Nothing good will come of that. All I want at this point is to find my son. I'll sort out this mess with Gabby later. Right now, the only thing that matters is finding Cameron.

We sit awkwardly for a few minutes, the silence stretching like an endless ball of yarn. I don't want to be the first to speak, but I also realize time is not on my side. The longer Cam goes missing, the less likely we will find him alive. The first twenty-four to forty-eight hours are the most critical in a missing person investigation. Less when it comes to a missing child.

Our window for a happy ending is rapidly closing.

"What is it you want to ask me?" I set my hands on the table between us, one draped tightly over the other to hold them steady. Inside I'm shaking like a 7.2 magnitude earthquake, but I'm determined to project calm. Fidgeting projects guilt. I'm not guilty of anything.

Other than not being the best husband or father, apparently.

"Here's the thing, Mr. Rizzo. We ran a background check on both you and Mrs. Rizzo. Complete protocol. When it comes to a missing child, we always check out those closest first. You'd be surprised how often the parents have something to do with it." Detective Grady taps his pen on the table. Tap. Tap. Tap. "Except for an unpaid parking ticket, you're clean, but your wife . . ." Tap, tap, tap.

I wait for it, for the ceiling to crash down.

He pauses, glancing down at his notes. Then he looks me dead in the eyes.

"We couldn't seem to find a record of Gabby Rizzo, formerly known as Gabby Reynolds, before 2005. It's as if she just dropped into the world as an eighteen-year-old. And you know what?"

I shake my head, unable to meet Detective Hawthorne's stony gaze.

"In my experience, people don't just drop into the world as eighteen-year-olds. They come from somewhere. Everyone comes from somewhere. So perhaps you could shed some light on where your wife, Gabby Rizzo, came from."

I hold up my hands as if I've nothing to hide. "Listen, I'm happy to tell you everything I know. But I sincerely hope you're not implying my wife had anything to do with our son's disappearance. She loves our son more than life itself. And I don't see what this has to do with finding Cameron."

"I'm not ruling out anything at this point, Mr. Rizzo. Including entertaining the possibility that either your wife had something to do with his disappearance or someone from her past has returned to hurt her. I mean, what better way to hurt a woman than by kidnapping her child?"

The knife twists in my side. *Kidnapped.* The detective believes someone kidnapped our son. I think again about the note I found in Gabby's purse, and I wonder if he's right, if someone from her past has returned to hurt her.

"My wife had a rough childhood, Detective. She was an orphan and spent her teenage years hopping from home to home in the foster system. She worked her ass off to earn a college scholarship, to turn her life around. We met at orientation, and I instantly fell head over heels for her. I wanted to make her life better — to be the family Gabby deserved. She told me everything about her past."

Nothing. Gabby told me nothing.

"And you believed her story?"

I don't like his tone. I don't like where this is going.

"What reason would I have not to believe her?"

I now have every reason not to believe her.

"We ran prints on her, Mr. Rizzo. Wanna know what came back? Or maybe you already know? Does the name Brittany Stone sound familiar to you?"

I shake my head. "Prints? When did you take her prints?"

"Water bottle," he says matter-of-factly. "My partner grabbed her water bottle from the podium after you addressed the press."

I'm no less confused. It feels as if everything is moving at hyper speed, but I'm stuck in place, watching the scenery whirl by in a dizzy blur.

"But, but . . . you just arrived last night. How is that even possible?"

"I realize this resort is secluded, Mr. Rizzo, but we are right outside of Atlanta. We've got some of the best forensic labs in the country in our not-so-little state at our disposal. And, I called in a favor." He pauses for good measure. "Sorry to be the bearer of bad news but, well, here, you can see for yourself." Detective Hawthorne pulls out his phone, types something into the search bar, and slides it across the table so I'm staring at a small-town news article from 2003.

LOCAL PSYCHIATRISTS DIE IN A FIERY CRASH WHILE PURSUING THEIR SIXTEEN-YEAR-OLD DAUGHTER.

I quickly scan through the article, with a picture of a much younger Gabby posing happily in a portrait with her parents.

Two prominent local psychiatrists have perished in a fiery crash, devastating the tight knit community they called home. The husband and wife were inside their vehicle when they lost control and wrapped around an oncoming SUV, instantly killing them both. The driver of the SUV remains in serious condition, with burns covering over forty percent of her body, but is expected to survive. Her family has asked that her identity not be released. Authorities have ruled this tragedy an accident, clearing both drivers and the deceased victims' underage daughter, who purportedly fled the scene, from any criminal responsibility for the crash.

I try to feign surprise, but the truth is, I knew this already. Gabby's grandmother contacted me a month ago, attempting to connect with our family. Ever since that day, I've read this article and a dozen or so like it hundreds, if not thousands, of times. I've agonized over how to confront her with this information. Could I stay married to a woman who is as authentic as an illusion? The pregnancy test is just icing, really. The affair, sprinkles.

After fourteen years together, Gabby hasn't told me the truth. She was never going to tell me the truth if I hadn't found out for myself.

"I, I, I don't know what to say." I push his phone back across the table, unable to look for another second at the smiling image of my deceitful wife.

"So you had no idea?"

I inhale until my lungs burn in protest and can't stand another sip of air. I exhale it out slowly, willing my pulse to follow. "I had no idea until recently."

"Until recently? Care to elaborate?"

"Her grandmother reached out to me about a month or so ago. I was confused because I believed she had no family. She said they were desperate to have her back in their lives again. She told me what Gabby hadn't."

I drop my head into my hands.

"I still can't believe she lied about her grandparents, foster homes, neglect, and abuse. It was all a big lie. My marriage is a big lie."

"Mr. Rizzo." I lift my head slowly to meet Detective Hawthorne's gaze. His brown eyes are a mixture of empathy and confusion. "I'm not sure the best way to break this to you, so I'll just come out and say it. Your wife's grandparents are dead."

CHAPTER 22

GABBY RIZZO

"Am I in some sort of trouble here?" I ask as Detective Grady continues challenging me to a staring contest with her arms folded across her chest. I'm not going to win this one; that much is obvious.

I look away.

"Is there a reason you think you should be in trouble?"

"My son is missing, yet it feels like I'm the one under attack here. Like I'm on trial for a crime I didn't commit. If it takes me getting a lawyer for you to do your job and find Cameron, I'll make the call right now."

She unfolds her arms and reaches into the pocket of her floral capris, emerging with her phone. My heart drops to my feet. She thinks I've done something. And she's right. Only not in the way she thinks she is.

"Are you seriously going to arrest me for trying to find out if anyone knows what happened to Cameron?" The question is bitter in my mouth, as if I'm sucking on a roll of pennies. The one time I'm not carrying any Tic Tacs. Go figure.

"You're not under arrest, Mrs. Rizzo. Not yet. We are just trying to work some things out. If you want us to find your son, you must be as cooperative and forthcoming as possible. That starts with answering my questions as honestly as you can. You may know something you don't realize you know."

"I come from a family of mental health professionals, Detective Grady. Reverse psychology doesn't work on me. But I will answer your questions after I call my husband." I try to keep a neutral expression, though I know I've already said too much.

She nods, and I walk a few doors down where she can't hear me dial Greg. It rings half a ring, then goes to voicemail. So I try again, and the same thing happens. A third time and I'm convinced he's silencing my calls.

My body stiffens as I think about why he would send me to voicemail. It has me wondering what my husband knows and, in turn, what the detectives know.

I take a deep breath, count to ten, then slowly release the air from my lungs.

"Ask away," I say as I approach Detective Grady. "I have nothing to hide." I have *everything* to hide.

"Not here," she responds with an arm wave for me to follow her. I do as I'm told. I'm filled with an overwhelming sense of unbidden déjà vu. I don't want to remember. All I've ever wanted was to forget. All I've tried to do is build a better life for myself and my child. Is that a crime — wanting better for your child?

We walk down the hallway to the elevator. Detective Grady presses the down arrow, and we wait silently for the lift to arrive. Since we arrived here yesterday, there's been a lot of uncomfortable silence. I hated the silence after my parents died, and I hate the silence even more now that my son is missing. Because it's in the silence where the dark thoughts come. I need noise to drown out the chatter — especially now — because it's a free for all in my head.

It's hot inside the elevator, and I feel the beads of perspiration collecting along my hairline. What a great place Susie picked for us to stay at . . . no CCTV and faulty AC. No wonder she got such a ridiculously low rate.

It feels like the walls are closing in, in more ways than one. The moment the elevator doors open, I lunge through them, desperate for air.

I swallow the lump in my throat as Detective Grady leads me to a conference room off the main lobby. It's as if we're strolling into a board meeting instead of an interrogation with higher stakes than any business meeting I could conjure. It's my son at stake. My pride and joy. My heartbeat. My breath.

And though I'm trying not to think about it, and I can't fully articulate why — I sense it's also my freedom.

We sit caddy-cornered at the edge of a long rectangular table designed to seat up to fourteen. The chairs are surprisingly comfortable, red velvet, which falls in line with the rest of this place. The walls are brighter, though, and a television hangs in the room's far corner.

"When did you last see your son, Mrs. Rizzo?"

And so it begins. I'm asked about our activities since we arrived at the hotel, Cam's mood yesterday, and the state of my marriage. I should feel violated, but instead, I'm starting to relax as I realize Detective Grady has no clue who I am. Because the reality is the truth will only complicate things exponentially. And chances are, my past has absolutely nothing to do with my current predicament.

I mean — why would my grandparents resurface after all this time? Why would they do something to harm their own great-grandchild? They may hate me, but Cam? Cam could never hurt anyone.

I wasn't that much older than him when my world was flipped upside down. Sixteen — still a child, really. The human brain takes a good twenty-five years to develop. Thanks, Mom and Dad, for that fact. But would Greg see that? This is why I never shared with him the truth about where I came from. I may have meant no harm, but what do intentions matter when the result is death? Not intending for my parents to die doesn't make them any less dead. Telling Greg the truth wouldn't do anything to bring them back. All it would do is make him look at me differently. I love the way he looks at me. *Looked.* The way he used to look at me.

I've waited too long. How could I come clean over a decade after the lies started pouring from my mouth? After I fabricated a past that didn't exist? He would never forgive me. He would certainly never trust me again.

Not that he trusts me now. I think about Greg reading the note in my purse, secretly checking my phone.

Still, telling him the unedited truth would only hurt us and, more importantly, Cameron. My stomach clenches into a closed fist at the thought of my son.

I sense the questioning is coming to a close. Detective Grady shuts the notebook she's been scribbling on throughout our conversation. I push out of my chair to rise to my feet. I need to find Susie. She will know what to do. She will talk me off the inch-thin ledge I'm dangerously teetering on.

I'm beginning to walk away, when she adds, "Just one more thing, Mrs. Rizzo."

I swivel back to face her. "Yes?"

"What can you tell me about Brittany Stone?"

My breath catches in my chest as my hand finds the edge of the chair's back. The room is spinning like a tilt-a-whirl, but I feel oddly tethered in place by the motion. Everything in the room has shifted. Detective Grady knows *exactly* who I am.

My heart starts beating a mile a minute, but I force myself to talk.

"I was born Brittany Stone," I admit. "I grew up in a small town outside of Johnstown, Pennsylvania. I was an only child. My parents were both psychiatrists. They ran their own practice together — Stone Therapeutics."

The irony of the name strikes me as hard today as it had so many times growing up. Stones have a unique duality — cold, yet smooth — like my parents. They were miracle workers for their patients because of the professional detachment with which they were able to treat them. But I wasn't one of their patients; I was their daughter.

"How would you describe your relationship with your parents?"

I chew on a nail as Detective Grady opens her notebook and jots down something I can't see.

"I loved them, I suppose. I guess they loved me, just not in an outwardly affectionate way. Listen, I appreciate the therapy session, but I don't see what this has to do with my son."

"Tell me, where did you go after your parents died?"

"I went to live with my grandparents."

"And what was your relationship like with them?"

"It was great, really great — until I left for college. My grandfather wanted me to stay after graduation and help out with the farm. But I needed to move on with my life. So I left. They stopped returning my calls, even when I called to tell them I was pregnant with Cam. Eventually I gave up. I moved on."

"When was the last time you spoke with them?"

"I don't know. Thirteen years maybe?"

"Are you aware, Mrs. Rizzo, that you are wanted in Pennsylvania for questioning in connection with their double murders?"

"Double murders? My grandparents are *dead?*"

This is the last thing to come out of my mouth before I faint, and my head hits the conference room floor.

CHAPTER 23

GREG RIZZO

"Dead? That's impossible. They can't be dead. I just spoke with her grandmother a few days ago."

"Did you ever meet them in person?"

"Well, no, but . . ."

"But you're certain it was them?"

"I mean, I was, but now, I have no idea. When? How did they die?"

"They were murdered in their home six months ago. It was pretty vicious, which usually indicates it was personal. I'll spare you the gruesome details. All you need to know is that your wife is wanted for questioning in connection with their deaths. The Johnstown police have reason to believe she may have had something to do with their brutal murders."

My wife?

I run a hand through my hair, now matted with sweat. Gabby, the mother of my child, my missing child, is wanted for questioning in her grandparents' deaths. Murders. Her grandparents' murders. The grandparents she never told me about. The ones I hadn't known existed until that letter showed up in our mailbox.

My head is spinning, blips of light dancing before my eyes. My wife is a lot of things — a liar for one and an adulteress for another — but a murderer? She hasn't spoken to her grandparents in well over a decade, or so they said, so what reason could my docile stay-at-home wife have to slaughter an elderly couple?

And I realize it couldn't have been them trying to connect with my wife if they'd been dead for half a year. Not unless there's some postal service I'm unaware of from beyond the grave.

Who sent me that letter? And if it wasn't her grandmother, who have I been talking to?

I bring a hand to my mouth to push back the rising bile.

Then, a comforting thought.

"Gabby couldn't have had anything to do with their deaths. My wife is deathly afraid of blood. You should have seen her face when she found the dead rat's bloody carcass in our room."

"You're referring to the rat that we've been unable to verify the existence of? The hotel has denied any knowledge of such a discovery. Did you personally see the rat, Mr. Rizzo?"

I shake my head. I never saw the rat. I saw a group of hotel employees standing around the hallway outside our door. I saw Gabby waiting outside of the elevator, a look of terror on her face. "But the manager — Gabby spoke to him about it. I heard her."

"The manager claims Mrs. Rizzo was mistaken, and he was being gentle with her. Housekeeping reported finding Mrs. Rizzo standing in the middle of your room, talking to herself and screaming. Mr. Rizzo, I have to ask, how would you describe your wife's current state of mind?"

I think about the vials of pills lining our medicine cabinet. I think about how Gabby is always tired and confused. I think about the positive pregnancy test. I think about the murdered rat that may never have existed other than in Gabby's mind. I think about the mountains of lies she's told.

And then I think, I don't know my wife's state of mind very well.

"Please, all I care about right now is finding my son. We can sort this mess out with Gabby later. She would never do anything to hurt Cam. I know her well enough to say that with one hundred percent certainty. She loves our son. We both love our son."

"We will continue to look for Cameron, but we can't just sort this mess out with Mrs. Rizzo later. I must inform you we are taking your wife into custody. I recommend you contact a lawyer. She will most likely be extradited to Pennsylvania. Although, we are working on having a detective come down here to interview her, given the current circumstances."

How very considerate of you, I think, suddenly glad Coach Bob decided to go ahead and play the game. The kids and parents are all at the fields, warming up, instead of at Foxcroft watching my wife get hauled away by the police.

Because that's where this is going, clearly.

"Where is Gabby now? Can I speak with her?"

"I don't see why that would be a problem if they haven't left for the station yet."

Detective Hawthorne pulls his walkie-talkie from his pants and holds down the button on the side. "Grady," he says.

There are a few moments of static silence, and I swear, my heart has stopped beating.

"Yup."

"Is Mrs. Rizzo still with you?"

"She is. We're in the conference room. She's being evaluated by a medic."

"A medic? Why is my wife being evaluated by a medic? What the hell happened to her?"

Detective Hawthorne raises a hand to stop me as I jump to my feet. His eyes narrow as he mouths, "Wait."

"She fainted, but her vitals appear normal." Detective Grady's voice is calm and steady, incongruous with the blood fiercely pumping through my veins.

"Roger that. We're on our way. Mr. Rizzo would like to speak to his wife before we bring her to the station."

As I follow Detective Hawthorne to the conference room, I'm a kaleidoscope of emotions. Worried. Hurt. Angry. To name a few.

A part of me — a small part at the moment, but growing by the second — wonders if Gabby is somehow connected to Cameron's disappearance.

* * *

My wife is slumped over her knees on the floor, her lower back pressed against the wall. Two medics are crouched beside her, one manning a blood pressure cuff hugging her arm, the other jotting down notes on a clipboard. Detective Grady is blocking the doorway to the conference room as if my wife is a flight risk.

Which I suppose, if history is any indication, she is. I've learned much about Gabby over the past month from her quote-unquote grandparents. From the people I thought were her grandparents. And now, I may have learned even more from Detective Hawthorne.

I push past Detective Grady and drop to Gabby's side. She looks fragile, and I'm torn between the desire for comfort and confrontation.

"What have you done?" The question comes out louder than I expected or intended. The room grows silent. I feel the detectives zoning in on our conversation. Gabby widens her big, brown eyes, and I ask her more quietly this time, "Tell me, Gabby, what have you done?"

CHAPTER 24

GABBY RIZZO

What have I done?

A police officer helps me to my feet.

"It's time to go," he says.

"Could I have one more minute with my wife?" Greg asks. I'm surprised my husband still wants to speak with me after learning our marriage was built on a bed of lies.

The officer nods, but his grip remains tight around my elbow.

"I've contacted Rick, Gabby. He is going to meet you at the police station." Greg doesn't look at me as he says this.

"The police station? Rick Prendergast? What is Rick going to do?"

Rick is Greg's corporate attorney, well versed in business and finance laws, but this is not a white-collar crime we are talking about. I'm being taken in for questioning about a double murder. I am a person of interest in a double fucking murder. I'm not sure what Rick is going to do.

"Not a word, Gabby."

"But I didn't do anything, Greg."

"They seem to think you did."

"And you?"

He won't meet my gaze, which is answer enough.

"What am I supposed to think, Gabby? I didn't know you had grandparents, and now I find out you lived with them, and they were murdered. What else haven't you told me?"

Too much, I realize.

"You think I killed my grandparents? You actually think I'm capable of murdering my own flesh and blood? Why, Greg? Why would I do something like that?"

"Of course I don't think that." Greg runs a hand across his forehead, wiping away the sweat beads forming along his hairline.

I don't believe him. My husband is a terrible liar.

I hear the shuffle of flats and my head turns toward Detective Grady, watching as she approaches. She's a surprisingly welcome distraction. It's too painful to look at Greg. My husband. The father of my child. The man who thinks I murdered my grandparents. Does he believe I could have done something to our son? My heart beats rapidly in my chest, threatening to explode from my rib cage as it sinks in that the last of my birth family is dead; that my only child is still missing; that my husband no longer loves me.

Why would someone murder my grandparents? There's only one reason I can think of — to bury me for a crime I didn't commit.

SIX MONTHS EARLIER
GABBY'S JOURNAL

There are some things other people could never understand.

For one, how it felt growing up in a house with two overachieving, overly analytic psychiatrists for parents. A frigid place where nothing was ever good enough. A clinically cold house where you are a comment or behavior away from being diagnosed with this mental illness or that. I was well versed in bipolar disorder and multiple personalities by age six. Treated for anxiety and suicidal thoughts I didn't know I had at ten. Diagnosed with an antisocial personality disorder at twelve.

I was essentially a lab rat, and my parents were mad scientists. I had a childhood I wouldn't wish upon my worst enemy. Certainly, not my own son.

I made mistakes, just like every teenager does. We all make mistakes. Though I try not to, I think about that night often.

It was just a fight.

I shouldn't have stormed out of the house. I should have taken deep breaths, popped a Xanax — yes, my parents prescribed me Xanax — stomped up to my room, slammed my bedroom door, and drowned myself in loud music that would annoy, not kill them.

But I'd had it. I needed to get out of the psychiatric ward we called home. I grabbed the keys off the mantel and ran out into the night. I swung open the car door, fighting against the wind. Then I shifted my mother's Honda Civic into reverse, leaving a cloud of dust and gravel in my wake as I hightailed it out of our driveway.

I had no idea where I was going, only that I needed to be gone.

The lights were blinding in the rearview mirror. My parents were trailing me. My foot sat like a lead weight on the pedal. I pushed the gas further down until it hit the floor mat. The car began to shake, but I wouldn't let up. I couldn't let up.

We drove like this for a while, dangerously hugging the endless curves of our winding streets.

I didn't see the headlights of the oncoming car until it was too late. I swerved right, sending my car into a tailspin that seemed to last for an eternity. It was only a matter of seconds though before the car righted itself, screeching to a halt on the side of the road, nearly tipping on its side.

From there, I watched the crash in slow motion, pinned by my seat-belt, with my breath caught in my chest. The impact boomed like thunder as my parents collided with the oncoming car I had narrowly avoided. And then came the lightning, as both vehicles burst into angry flames.

It was an accident. At that moment, I couldn't have known a car was traveling on the same road, going in the opposite direction. We lived in the middle of nowhere, in a town with a population of 2,500. I'd never seen another car on the road at this time of the night.

Until now.

I should have gotten out of the car. I should have checked to see if I could help, though I came to learn from the news articles that my parents died instantly. Still, I should have at least tried to save them. Done something other than fleeing the scene of the accident. I'd like to think I was in shock. But the truth is, at that moment, I was driven by the instinct of self-preservation.

I stabbed at the ignition a few times before I was able to start the car. My fingers trembled as I shifted the car back into drive. Somehow I found my way through the night back to my childhood home. The police showed up a few hours later to question me. The reporters soon after that. There were talks of juvenile detention, foster families, and group homes. There were psychiatric evaluations by state-appointed doctors who were easier to manipulate than a blind mouse. There were rumors

— wild, fabricated stories — that my friends and neighbors offered up and devoured like Halloween candy. And there were death threats. So many death threats.

Days into the chaos that ensued, my maternal grandparents showed up in their Cadillac DeVille to claim me as if I were some abandoned puppy needing to be rehomed. They brought me to live with them in an even more rural part of Pennsylvania, where extracurricular activities consisted of tipping cows for fun. Sounds great, right? Except, that's when the nightmare truly began. There are some people you look at, and you can't imagine why they ever had kids. My grandparents were those people.

Why had they taken me in?

Hindsight has allowed me to recognize it for what it was. My grandparents took me in to punish me for killing their daughter, my mother.

Punish me, they did.

I try not to think about those two years of hell — when my grandmother starved me and my grandfather beat me senseless. They reminded me every day with their words and fists of what my teenage rebellion had caused.

I feared if I didn't get away, they might try to kill me one day.

CHAPTER 25

GREG RIZZO

Rick is no criminal lawyer, but he tells me that in the absence of physical evidence tying Gabby to her grandparents at the time of their deaths, all they've got are theories and speculation. You can't convict on theories and speculation. At least not in a court of law. The court of public opinion is another story, but I can't control that. There's no spinning this in a way that will make Gabby look anything other than evil. Anything other than guilty.

Did she kill her grandparents? The jury is out on what I believe. Because if she lied about something as significant as this, who's to say what else she's lied about? When it comes to my wife, I can no longer separate fact from fiction.

The police must have some reason to be hauling her into the station for questioning. Whatever cards they have, though, for now they are holding them close to their chests. I should look into a criminal attorney, and if the situation escalates, my God — if they place Gabby under arrest, I will. Despite everything that's happened, I still love my wife.

But it's 7.50 a.m. and the game will be starting soon. Right now, that's where I need to be. It's where Cam needs to be.

I'm once again paralyzed by the thought that we may never see our son again. The clock is ticking away, each second further removing us from our son, each minute generating worse case scenarios.

As soon as Detective Hawthorne lets me out of the car, I dash through the parking lot, where I left our Escalade the day before when we arrived. I wish I had confronted Gabby about the pregnancy test then. I wonder if things would have played out differently, at least between us. Perhaps we would have both come clean and come to terms with the lies we've been living with.

But therein lies the problem with hindsight. You never know what might have happened.

They will hold Gabby for questioning until the Pennsylvania detectives arrive at the precinct. Detective Grady informed me that it is highly unorthodox for detectives from a jurisdiction states away to travel to their precinct to interview a person of interest in a double homicide. And by highly unorthodox, she means it's never, ever happened.

But obviously, these are unique circumstances. We are dealing with a missing child, with *our* missing child, and time is of the essence.

After the interrogation, they will either arrest Gabby and transport her to a jail in Pennsylvania or let her go. Only God knows what happens with my wife after that. What happens with us . . .

I slip into the car, the trapped heat choking me as it pushes into the equally stagnant air outside. I half expect to find Cameron watching baseball videos in the backseat just as he did on the drive down. But the backseat is empty. My heart is empty. I've lost my son and wife in a matter of hours.

Everything left that matters.

I turn the key in the ignition and slam my foot down on the pedal. I pull onto the gravel road that leads down to the only street in and out of town, spraying a dust cloud of rocks and debris. I glance at the clock on the dash. 7.53 a.m. The game starts in seven minutes. I'm ten minutes away.

I press down harder on the pedal, determined to make it to the fields on time. I must observe the coaches' body language, the players, and the parents. I need to watch their faces as they sing along to the national anthem. I need to talk to someone, to everyone. I need to do whatever I need to do to find my son. And I will.

I rip into the parking lot at 8.01, swerving onto a curb and nearly flipping my SUV. I abandon it there and sprint toward the field. The players and coaches are lined up outside their respective dugouts, spectators on their feet in the stands with baseball hats pressed firmly against their chests.

O'er the land of the free
and the home of the brave.

The crowd applauds, and I watch as the Futures jog to their respective spots on the field. Home team. I should be happy that Cam's teammates have a home-field advantage, but I'm numb.

And then my stomach drops into my shoes. There's Jake, settling in onto the mound, adjusting his baseball hat, throwing warmup pitches, and tossing around with his teammates. With Cam's teammates. He looks good out there, especially considering how torn up he supposedly was about Cam's disappearance. I'm pretty sure I heard the word catatonic being thrown around. He certainly doesn't look torn up. He certainly doesn't look catatonic.

It should be Cam out there on the mound. I crumble the lineup in my pocket. And then I search the stands to find Matt beaming, a stupid grin plastered across his face.

He got his wish, didn't he? His son starting as pitcher over mine.

I press my nails into the palms of my hands, squeezing. I'll wipe that cocky expression off Matt's face. I swear if that son of a bitch laid a hand on my boy . . .

Strike three, and you're out!

My muscles seize as another round of applause echoes through the stadium.

Jake struck out the first batter.

I grit my teeth and make my way across the bleachers toward Matt. His gaze meets mine, and something unfamiliar flashes across his face. The concern he wore earlier is all but gone. I try to process what I'm seeing and realize Matt looks smug.

I draw a deep breath and count to ten as my legs propel me forward. It's as if some invisible magnetic force is pulling me toward him. He rises to his feet, eyes fixed on mine. I look him over, noticing how his fingers are curled into fists as if he's ready to fight.

"Where is he?" I ask, my question barely audible over the crowd of cheering fans.

Matt shakes his head and raises his shoulders as if he has no clue what I'm talking about. His body language says otherwise.

"I said, where is he?" I shout this time, and the spectators surrounding him suddenly go silent.

"You better check yourself, Greg," he warns, holding up a hand to stop me from coming any closer. "The kids are all down there watching this. There's no need to make a scene."

"Yeah, I bet. Your kid. The other kids. What about my kid, Matt?"

I close the space between us, but a hand on my elbow momentarily pulls me back. "Come on, man, don't do this."

I look over my shoulder at James Hertz incredulously. If he only knew half the things Matt's family has said about him, his wife, Sandy, and his son, Levi. Gabby told me Susie tried to get signatures for a petition to get him kicked off the team. And he's what — defending him?

"Don't do what?" I ask defensively. "Find out what's happened to my son?"

"Look, we're all worried sick, Greg. Levi didn't even want to play today. But Coach Bob felt it was important to the kids to carry on some semblance of normalcy. I know you're worried. We all are. But you can't actually believe Matt had anything to do with this."

Didn't he?

"Trust me, James. You don't know Matt at all." Apparently, neither do I.

"Let the boys finish their game, and then we will set up search parties to look for Cam. We will help you find him, Greg. Believe me, you're not alone in this."

"Funny because that's exactly how I feel."

My gaze travels down to the field, to the sea of thirteen-year-old eyes watching nervously to see what I'm going to do next. The boys I once coached in little league, Cam's friends, and teammates look up to me. I watch as Jake chews the strings of his leather glove, a nervous habit he's had for as long as I can remember.

I can't very well beat down his father in front of him, can I? In front of them?

I can't very well stop myself, either.

I rip my arm from James's grasp, clench my hand into a fist and turn toward Matt. I'm halfway to connecting with his face when my phone buzzes in my pocket, and I freeze in place.

Suddenly all I can think of is Gabby and Cam. Have they released her? Have they found him?

I grit my teeth and pull the phone from my shorts. As I read the text — *I'm ready to talk* — the fire burns out, and my blood turns to ice.

CHAPTER 26

GABBY RIZZO

Three hours later, Rick barges into the interrogation room they've been holding me in. I've had nothing to eat or drink, and only once did Detective Grady poke her head to ask if I needed to use the restroom. I breathed a heavy sigh of relief, and then my mind raced with all the possibilities of where Cam might be.

As Detective Grady stood in the doorway, waiting for me to say something, I contemplated pointing out the obvious — hydration is a precursor to urination — but thought better of it.

I hear Rick speaking with the detectives in the hallway before he enters the room.

"I'd like a few minutes alone with my client before you question her."

I've known Rick for almost as long as I've known Greg. In all that time, I never expected to be referred to as his "client."

Yet, here we are.

In a matter of twenty-four hours, my entire world has been turned upside down. I told myself things could never get worse after I had put my past behind me. Maybe I'm just as bad a liar as Greg.

"Gabby," he says, leaning down to kiss my cheek. His hand lingers on my shoulder as he looks at me over, his face etched with concern. "Have they treated you okay in here?"

I roll my eyes. "Well, if no food or water is being treated okay, then I suppose you could say they have."

Rick shakes his closely cropped head and pulls out a chair next to me. The metal legs screech across the epoxied concrete, spiking the hairs lining my arms. He sits down, fetches a legal pad from his briefcase, jots down a note, and then turns to me.

"Do you need anything before this begins?"

"I need you to get me out of here, Rick. I need to find my son."

Rick nods sympathetically. "Yes, Greg told me Cameron is missing. I'm so sorry. I'll get you out of here, Gabby. But I need you to tell me everything. And I mean everything."

I know what he means. And I also understand what telling him everything means. What I stand to lose. But I need to get out of here. There can't be anything worse than losing my son. Not even my freedom.

"Rick, you have to promise me that nothing I tell you leaves this room."

"Look, Gabby, I know Greg writes my paychecks, but you've always been like a younger sister to me. I want to protect you. I want to get you out of here and back to your husband. I want to help you find Cam. Anything you tell me is between us. But I can't defend you if I don't know what I'm up against. Does that make sense?"

It does.

I have to trust Rick because I don't have any other options. Not if I want to get out of here sometime today. And there was also that one time I caught him sneaking out of Susie's house at 6 a.m. when Matt was away for work. I doubt his wife, Keri, would believe they were discussing governance issues. Not that I've ever so much as hinted at betraying his secret, but I'm sure that's a possibility he's never entirely dismissed.

And so, I begin.

I bring Rick up to speed on everything I've never told anyone in my entire life. My entire marriage. I spare no details about my parents, grandparents, husband, and affair. By the time I finish, tears are streaming down my face, and Rick's complexion has blanched white.

"Say something . . ." I plead. "You believe me, don't you? I'd never intentionally hurt anyone, let alone kill my own flesh and blood."

Rick rubs a hand across his clean-shaven face. He's scooched his seat away from me, but I can still smell his after-shave — a mixture of bergamot and amberwood. Dior, I'm certain. I wonder if he's inching away because I reek of booze and sweat or if it's disgust with all I've admitted to.

I don't suppose it matters.

Rick fidgets nervously with his tie — a red checkered print, bold crimson boxes with white specks inside. It was Greg who taught me red is the color of power. I've always found that fact interesting, especially now, since it's also the color of blood.

"Of course, I believe you, Gabby. This must be some silly mistake. You haven't seen your grandparents in fourteen years. You live in a different state — five hours away. They can't have anything tying you to the murders if you didn't do it. We should be out of here within the hour — I suspect with a lawsuit against the police department in our back pocket."

I exhale all the air I am holding. My lungs feel like they've been set on fire.

"I didn't do it, Rick."

"Exactly."

Rick rises to his feet and opens the door so Detective Grady can enter the room. She's flanked by a man and woman, both dressed in sensible pants suits, with no-nonsense expressions on their faces. I shiver, though even the paint on the walls is sweating.

"This is Detective Nick Wren and Detective Rhonda Marx from Johnstown, Pennsylvania P.D."

I stare straight ahead, wondering if this is all some horrific hallucination. Dr. Green said hallucinations were a possible side effect of my medications. Didn't he? I remember him telling me as much. But then, my memory has been spotty as of late. It was supposed to get better, not worse.

Rick signals for the detectives to have a seat while I remain silent.

Detective Wren reaches out a hand while his partner sits in the metal chair next to him, folding her arms across her chest. I've seen this play out on the big screen more times than I can count. Good cop, bad cop. I look to Rick for direction, and he nods his head, so I extend my hand and shake that of the detective who might very well arrest me for murder. Sorry, double murder.

How did I get here?

Detective Marx reaches into her briefcase and pulls out a handheld recording device, which she slides across the table so it's sitting between us.

"I am informing you that this interview will be recorded. Do you acknowledge this?"

Again I look at Rick before nodding my assent. The thought passes that my life is in the hands of a corporate tax attorney, but Rick is all I've got right now. They've got nothing on me, no reason to hold me here, but it's almost as if my husband wants me to go to jail.

Detective Marx presses the record button, and a light flashes red. I take a deep breath.

Detective Wren states the date and time.

Then his gaze meets mine. "Please state your name for the record."

"Gabriella Ann Rizzo."

"Is that your birth name, ma'am?"

"No, sir."

"Could you please state your birth name for the record?"

I struggle to speak. "Brittany Stone."

"We need you to speak up."

"Brittany Stone," I repeat, louder this time. "I was born Brittany Stone."

"I understand you were orphaned at sixteen and then went on to live with your grandparents, John and Edna Smith. Is that accurate?"

"It is."

"What is the nature of your relationship with John and Edna Smith?"

"I loved my grandparents." *Lie.* "But we are estranged."

"And when did this estrangement occur?"

"When I turned eighteen and left for college."

"So are you saying you've had no contact with John or Edna Smith since you were eighteen? Is that correct?"

"Yes."

"Are you aware that your grandparents were brutally murdered six months ago, and you are a suspect in their double murder?"

My head is spinning.

Detective Wren slides a folder across the table and opens it up, exposing a set of pictures from the crime scene. John and Edna Smith, my grandparents — stabbed to death. My grandmother's favorite paisley scarf cinched around her neck. My grandfather, face down in a pool of his own blood.

I think I may be sick. I swallow the lump in my throat and try to breathe away the panic building within me. Somehow, I pull myself together enough to answer the detective's question. It isn't easy.

"Yes, I have recently been made aware of this. Today, in fact."

"Do you deny having any involvement in their murders?"

Rick interrupts. "I think we've established that my client has not had any contact with her estranged grandparents in the past fourteen years, let alone six months ago. We are all well aware the Smiths were murdered. And my client is not contesting the fact that she was estranged from them. I'm not sure where you're trying to get with this line of questioning.

We will have to cut this chat short unless you have something concrete other than speculation. My client's son is missing."

I feel a swell of affection for Rick, and my eyes swim. Sure, he's probably only here because he's afraid of me exposing him for the cheating husband he is, but still . . . He's the only one here for me.

"I'll take this one, partner." Detective Marx leans across the table, close enough that I can smell the coffee on her breath. She's baring her teeth like a pit bull ready to attack, and I involuntarily shift in my chair.

"Please answer the question, Mrs. Rizzo."

"You are correct. I have not had any contact with my grandparents since I left. I had nothing to do with their murders. They may have been unhappy when I left, but they were the only family I had. I could never kill them."

Detective Marx leans back in her chair, her eyebrows folding in toward each other. "How, then, do you explain your prints all over the crime scene?"

Mic drop.

CHAPTER 27

GREG RIZZO

I'm following the game on Gamechanger as I speed down the long, winding road back to our hotel. It's the bottom of the second, and the game is now tied 2-2. Jake gave up one earned run and made a costly error when he overthrew his first baseman. It had to be a pretty wretched throw for the first baseman to miss — at only thirteen, he's already five-foot-nine and built like Gumby.

I don't feel good that Jake isn't doing well. I thought I would, considering it should have been Cam on the mound, but I don't at all.

All I can think about is the text.

The ten-minute drive takes less than five. I veer off the road several times and barely manage to slow down at the very last second when I pass a police car. I screech into the parking lot and shift the vehicle into park so abruptly I'm sure I've given myself whiplash.

I sprint through the parking lot into the entrance of Foxcroft. The police are mostly gone now. The lobby is buzzing with resort-goers headed in all different directions — to the restaurants, pools, and spa. I'm struck by how enjoyable a place like this might actually be if not for our current predicament.

I glance at the reception desk to find the manager glaring at me. *Glaring.* I'm not sure what *he's* so angry about. I'm the one who should be pissed here, shouldn't I? It's my son who went missing from his hotel. Perhaps he's just mad about all the unwanted attention our visit has brought. I'm sure this situation is far from ideal for Foxcroft and, by extension, for him, but it's not like I'm the one who is responsible for it.

I'm tempted to go to the front desk and give him a piece of my mind, but a screaming match won't accomplish anything. And as my phone buzzes again in my pocket, I'm also reminded there's somewhere else more important I need to be.

Still, I can feel his eyes trained on my back as I head through the lobby, and I'm overwhelmed with that same sense of déjà vu that our paths have crossed before. I wonder if it's paranoia getting the best of me. Let's see: my son has been missing for over twelve hours; my wife received threatening notes; and her grandparents were stabbed to death. I'd say I have pretty darn solid grounds for paranoia.

I don't bother waiting for the elevator. I burst through the stairwell door at full speed, heading toward our room.

When I get there, I bang my fists against the door so forcefully that I dent the wood. My knuckles turn red and start to bleed, but I keep hammering away. Panic shoots through my body like electric shocks.

The thought, running a marathon through my mind — *Please don't let me be too late.*

I slam my shoulder into the door, and it shifts on its hinges. I go at it again. And again. And again. Until I hear a crack, which knocks the wood askew in its frame. I squeeze my body through the opening and rush into the room.

It's empty. The bedroom is empty.

I check my phone for a fourth time just to be sure I haven't made a mistake. Because if I'm being honest with myself, I've made plenty of mistakes.

But no, it says to meet her in our room.

"Gabby?" I call out, cautiously. *Where the hell are you?* By the looks of it, she's not here.

I slump down onto the edge of the bed and drop my head into my hands, attempting to gather my harried thoughts. A jolt of pain shoots up my back — a sharp object stabbing into the base of my spine. I rise to my feet, tossing the duvet to the side, and spot the offending suitcase, which I hadn't noticed in my haste to collapse dramatically on the bed.

Might as well have a look, I figure, pausing for a moment in a panic that she's in the suitcase. I shake my head. This isn't *Seven.* I'm not Brad Pitt. Gwyneth Paltrow's head isn't in there.

I quickly rifle through its contents — socks, underwear, a black dress — thankful not to find Gabby's lifeless eyes staring back at me. Why is Gabby's luggage packed on the bed? Was she trying to leave?

Perspiration bubbles on my upper lip. There has to be a logical explanation for all this. And then I hear it — the shower running in the bathroom.

I lunge toward the bathroom door, but think better and turn back to grab the crystal vase off the dresser. I empty its contents — water and roses — dying the carpet a blood red. Whatever, let them charge me for the damage later. After what we've been through, I'd like to see them try.

I take a deep breath, count to three, and then kick open the bathroom door.

It takes my eyes a minute to adjust. The room is cloaked in a film of thick and heavy steam.

I can almost see my son through the mist.

When Cam was two, he had a terrible case of croup. I remember Gabby cradling him in her arms for three nights straight — back and forth from the steam-filled bathroom to the crisp winter air outside. My heart aches. I miss my son. I miss my wife.

I see her, naked, huddled in the bathroom corner, slumped against the wall. My feet are no longer working. I'm frozen in place.

"What are you doing here?" I ask, now confused beyond all belief.

Susie is rocking back and forth, her arms tightly wound around her knees.

"We should talk, Greg."

I turn off the shower and flick on the fan to clear the moisture from the room. Then I grab a towel and throw it at her.

"For goodness sake, cover up."

I should ask if she's okay, but I don't. I expected to find Gabby here, not Susie. Susie must have texted me from Gabby's phone. How did Susie get in here? Why isn't she at the game? Why does she have my wife's phone?

Where is my wife?

"Look," she says, pointing toward the mirror.

I turn and see it, vitriol dripping through the mist.

Die Bitch.

I wonder, for a moment, if the bartender did this. Did he sleep with Susie and then leave her here, a crumbled mess on the tile, a nasty note scrawled on the mirror for good measure? It wouldn't be the most disturbing revelation over the past twenty-four hours, that's for sure. But what could this possibly have to do with me? With my wife? With our son?

"What happened, Susie?"

"Steven Miller," she offers, matter-of-factly, as if that should explain this all.

"I thought the bartender's name was Chip? Why were you with Steven Miller? In my room?" My upper lip is trembling, my disgust for Susie palpable. Throw yourself at the bartender at your son's 13U baseball tournament and then go home with another man — the father of another player, no less? I feel a stab of sympathy for Matt. He's not perfect, but then, none of us are perfect. He doesn't deserve a philandering wife like Susie.

"I'm sorry to be the one to have to tell you this, Greg, but it's time you knew the truth. Gabby has been having an affair. For the past six months. Steven Miller is her lover."

It feels like I've taken a punch to the gut. I'm going to be sick. My wife has been carrying on an affair with someone we *know* — a man we sit with at the tournaments, grab food with during game breaks, travel with. *No, no, no.* This can't be true.

My wife, who wears her hair in a messy top bun nearly every day and rarely leaves the house other than to chauffeur our son, grocery shop, and attend her therapy sessions. Quiet, introverted Gabby.

Gabby, who hid a positive pregnancy test in our kitchen drawer.

Looks really can be deceiving.

"You've known this for the past six months and didn't tell me?"

"What was I supposed to do, Greg? She's my best friend. And Lord knows she's kept plenty of secrets for me."

I shake my head because I can't even begin to imagine what Gabby has on her. I'm hot and nauseous, the room spinning, but something isn't adding up. The text. The text came from Gabby's phone.

"Why do you have Gabby's phone? Where is she, Susie?"

"What are you talking about, Greg? I don't have her phone. Gabby has her phone. They released her from questioning an hour ago."

And she didn't call me?

Sent a cryptic text — *I'm ready to talk.*

"How did you even get in here?"

"The door was ajar, Greg, I thought she was in here. I mean, why would she ask me to meet her here and *not* be here?"

Unless she left in a hurry. Unless someone forced her to leave in a hurry.

I run a hand through my hair. This doesn't make any sense. Why would Gabby summon me and Susie to our room? Unless was she planning on dropping a bombshell? Was she planning on leaving me? Is Susie here because she was afraid of how I might react to this bombshell?

No, it's not possible. Gabby would never leave me. She would never abandon our son. Unless — was she planning on taking Cameron with her? Hiding him away so I couldn't stop her?

I feel Susie's eyes burning a hole in my skin as she watches me process my marriage's demise and my son's abduction. My eyes find hers. It's all starting to make sense, the missing pieces of a puzzle coming together to form a picture.

Except for Susie.

"Where is she, Susie? And why were you here, in our shower?"

"Look, I'm not proud of my actions last night. Gabby texted me to come here, and I came directly from his room."

"Whose room?"

Susie looks at the ground, as color rises to her cheeks. "Coach Bob."

"You're kidding me!"

"Listen, I made a mistake. The door was open, but Gabby wasn't here when I came. I felt like I needed to wash the night off if that makes sense. And then I heard something while I was in the shower and opened the curtain to this." She motions toward the mirror. "I think Gabby was here and she did this. She's completely gone off the rails, Greg. She's been acting so erratic lately. Think about it — the signs were all there."

They were, weren't they? Why is it so damn hard to see what's right in front of your face?

Still, something doesn't feel right. "Susie, why are you curled in the fetal position on our bathroom floor?"

"I collapsed when I saw the message on the mirror, Greg. I'm afraid of her. I really am. There's something you need to see."

Susie lifts herself from the tile, her towel falling to the ground, exposing her naked body. God, she's something to look at. But just as I realized long ago, that's all she is.

I follow Susie from the bathroom into the bedroom. My head is fuzzy and confused; all I can think about is how bad this looks. The door is partially hanging off its hinges, giving any passersby a front-row seat to Susie in all her nakedness, bending over the bed. I'm ready to throw a — "This isn't what it looks like." If Gabby has gone off the rails, catching me with her naked best friend is the last thing she needs to see.

I quickly go to the door and secure it back into place. I twist the lock, which lets out a relieving click. Then I turn to Susie.

I watch as she reaches into Gabby's luggage and pulls out a book. A journal. I recognize the brown leather cover. Because I've seen this journal before.

It's Gabby's.

She slips it into my hands.

"Go ahead," she says. "Read it."

TWELVE YEARS EARLIER
GABBY'S JOURNAL

Greg is home on the injured reserve list. He's just had his Tommy John surgery to repair the stubborn injury that's been nagging him since college. The doctors are confident he will be back on the mound in little to no time.

Except, I don't want him back on the mound in little to no time. I don't want him back on the mound at all. Is that so terrible? I want him here at home with our child and me. Is that too much to ask?

If I thought things were bad before, I can just imagine what it will be like if all goes off without a hitch. They are talking about calling him up to the big leagues. If that happens, I will see my husband even less. He will be jet-setting from city to city, doing God knows what in his off time while I'm at home raising our son.

I can't let that happen.

I won't let that happen.

I've often thought about what we'll do if (when) Greg's baseball career comes to an end. Because, of course, one day, it will. You never know when your body will quit on you when you play a sport, when you'll take a ball to the wrist that will be your last, or if some other unfortunate circumstance will befall you. Thankfully, besides being a rocket on the mound and a monster at the plate, Greg is a brilliant man. He majored in business management and fielded multiple offers from financial institutions and baseball organizations.

It was never really a choice for him, though. Wells Fargo could have offered him one hundred thousand a month's salary, and he still would have chosen to play baseball for free. I joke that baseball is Greg's one true love. But behind every joke, there's a kernel of truth. When his cleats are hung up, and his jersey retired, Greg will think of baseball as the one that got away. I'm not sure he'd choose me if I forced him to make a choice. That's why I would never come out and ask him to do that.

But I can do something about it. I have to do something about it.

Drugging my husband — it sounds worse than it is, or is it worse than it sounds? I'm doing it for us. For our future. For our son. He deserves to have his father around.

CHAPTER 28

GREG RIZZO

It feels like I'm stuck on a rollercoaster — strapped into the seat, crawling up the track. I'm desperate to get off before we plummet three hundred feet toward the ground below. But the operator is just smiling, laughing at me.

All the color has drained from my face. The room is spinning. I think I might be sick.

I try to get my bearings. This must be a joke. A sick, fucking joke. My eyes search the room for a hidden camera. *Where are you hiding, Ashton Kutcher?* Gabby would never do something as horrible as this. It couldn't be. She wouldn't drug me, shatter my dreams like a stone thrown at a house made of glass.

Would she?

I can't deny what I saw. It says so right there in Gabby's journal. So apparently, she would. Apparently, she did.

God, I was so stupid. I may as well have drugged myself. I certainly made it easy enough for her, didn't I? Took my pills diligently from the Sunday through Monday pill organizer she purchased without a second thought. Because I trusted her. What reason would I have not to? Why would my wife do something like this to me? *Why*?

I think about the mistakes I've made in the past. We all make mistakes. But I've tried to be a good husband to her. I've tried to help her. And all she's done is lie and betray me.

Susie silently stares at me as I take it all in. She bats her eyelashes in her Susie way, and I find my gaze lingering for longer than necessary, as it often does. Susie has the biggest, bluest eyes I've ever seen. A deep Caribbean blue that looks like they can't possibly be real. But they are. Probably the only part of her that's real.

There's a magnetic connection between us — opposite poles pulling toward one another. I was foolish to believe Gabby hadn't noticed, to think she wouldn't care.

Perhaps this is all my fault. Did I push my wife straight into the arms of another man? And have I completely underestimated her? Is Cameron paying the price for our games?

Because I wonder, if Gabby sensed it, does that mean Matt did as well? Could he be the mastermind behind whatever is playing out here? I flashback to the smug expression on his face as I confronted him at the game. Is he in on this with my wife? Or is it Gabby's lover? Who helped my wife kidnap our son?

The possibilities weigh so heavily on me that I can barely stand straight.

"Greg, I think it's time you're honest with yourself, that we're honest with each other. You don't deserve this. Gabby is not the right woman for you. She never was. She never will be." Susie walks around the bed to where I'm standing and rests a hand on my shoulder. She lays her head against my chest, and her perfume tickles my nostrils. I wonder if she can feel my heart beating a mile a minute.

Part of me is screaming, *don't do this.* Banging against my rib cage to get my attention, to stop me from making a mistake I will no doubt regret for the rest of my life.

The other part . . .

No, no. I can't.

I push Susie away.

"I love my wife, Susie. You're supposed to love her, too. She's your best friend."

Susie huffs, "Best friend, huh? Yeah, well, you might want to keep reading."

> *I have a confession — I hate my best friend. I absolutely despise Susie Baker with her perfect face and perfect hair and perfect body and perfect everything. Sometimes, I wish . . . I wish she would just disappear. People disappear all the time, don't they? I would feel bad for Matt, of course, because he'll be the one who'll be blamed. Because it's always the husband. But then, really, I'd be doing us all a favor, wouldn't I?*

"This doesn't prove anything, Susie. So she said she hates you. You probably had a fight, and she was venting. That's what people do when they're upset. I'm sure she didn't mean it. She probably said at times she hates me, too, sometimes."

"Oh, she did, Greg. And I'd hardly qualify her threatening to make me disappear as 'venting.'"

I hurl the book across the room.

"I don't need to see any more."

Because I don't, I really don't need to see any more.

"You do, Greg. There's a bunch of stuff she wrote about her grandparents and Cameron, too. I read the whole thing. She killed them. Said so herself. I think she's done something with Cam."

For the thousandth time since yesterday, all I can think is, *no, no, no.*

I can't let myself believe what Susie is telling me because that would make the mother of my child a monster. A monster who killed her grandparents in cold blood and orchestrated the disappearance of her own child. Of our child.

"I know this is upsetting, Greg. Honestly, I'm just as shaken as you are, but the important thing here is finding

Cam. And to do that, you need to accept Gabby for who she is . . . a disturbed and dangerous person."

"Why do you have her journal, Susie?" I wonder if Susie has done something with my wife. Because what's her endgame here? *Me*? This time, I refuse to look away. I lock my eyes on hers, searching for the truth.

"She's been acting erratic, and I just wanted to make sure she was okay."

I open my mouth to protest, but then, I realize I would have done the same thing had I known where Gabby hid it. I would have read her journal as well. The pregnancy test, Cameron's disappearance, and the revelation of Gabby's past and her murdered grandparents have left me completely paranoid. Susie may be a shitty wife, but she's always been a heck of a best friend to mine.

"Where was it?" I ask.

"In between the mattress and box spring on her side of the bed. I saw her stuff it in there a while back when I was trying on clothes. So you know . . ." She shrugs her shoulders and then struts across the room, bending down to pick up the journal from the floor. The last time I watched a woman bend this way was at my thirtieth birthday party. All that's missing here is a pole.

And she's your friend. Your wife's best friend.

"Please, just read it, Greg. I'm not the bad guy here."

I grab the book from her outstretched hand and slump down on the bed. I run my fingers along the bound leather, flipping through the pages. I don't even know where to start. I've learned a lot in the past few minutes. My wife drugged me to destroy my promising baseball career. And she was thinking of making her best friend disappear. I'm not sure how many more surprises I can mentally process in one sitting.

My stomach flips as I think about what else might be in there. Did Gabby write about Steven Miller? Am I about to read sordid details about her affair?

I can't.

I look up, and Susie nods that I should keep on. I can't, but I know I have to. If Gabby did have something to do with Cameron's disappearance, I owe it to my son to find out. Several pages are dogeared, all recent entries judging by their location in the book.

I take a deep breath.

> *Why did they have to come back into my life? Why couldn't they just leave well enough alone? My parents are dead; there's nothing my grandparents can say or do to bring them back to life. I know they've always blamed me, but that's why I left and never looked back. Closure. So we could all have closure. Somehow, they've found me. I'm not about to let them destroy everything I've worked so hard to build for myself, for my family. I can't believe I'm writing this, let alone thinking about it, but my grandparents have to die.*

CHAPTER 29

GABBY RIZZO

Apparently, I'm the reason my grandparents had to die. Someone is framing me for their murders, attempting to destroy my life. Who could possibly hate me enough to do something as twisted as this?

And for how long can they keep me here without charging me with a crime?

I open my mouth to speak, but no words follow. Rick is sitting silently beside me, typing something into his phone. I can only imagine he's phoning it in, texting Greg to call for reinforcements. His corporate tax background has taken him as far as it can. Rick could handle the pressure of representing me when he believed I didn't do it. When they had no evidence other than speculation and wild theories suggesting I had.

But now?

I can just imagine the text he's composing and the look of horror plastered on Greg's face as he reads it.

Hey buddy, your wife's prints were all over the crime scene. Yeah, thinking you may want to invest in a criminal attorney. She's completely screwed.

He'd be right in saying all that, too. I'm completely screwed.

Rick flips his phone around for the detectives to look at, and I feel a twinge of hope like maybe I have this all wrong. He's animated, poking his pointer finger repeatedly against the screen.

"Of course, Gabby's fingerprints were all over the house. They're her grandparents. It was her primary residence for two years. Latent fingerprints can last up to forty years. It says so right here." He jabs again so emphatically I'm worried he's about to crack his iPhone screen. "Surely, you all must know that already." He leans back in his chair, a look of satisfaction spread across his face. I'm impressed. Rick is definitely a better lawyer than I gave him credit for. People are just full of surprises, aren't they?

"This isn't an episode of *Law and Order*, Mr. Prendergast. We are well aware of the ability of prints to linger on surfaces for decades in some cases. However, we're unaware of how your client's fingerprints found their way all over the murder weapon, which presumably has been washed and sanitized an infinite number of times over the past decade. Care to explain that?"

I flick my eyes toward Rick, whose face has turned a sickly green. This time when he looks back at me, all I can do is shrug my shoulders because I really have no idea what they're talking about.

"What was the murder weapon?" I ask, genuinely confused, though I've got knives, daggers, and fireplace pokers flying through my brain. They've already shown us my grandparents were stabbed to death. How *did* my prints wind up on the murder weapon?

"Does this look familiar, Mrs. Rizzo?"

The detective pulls out another 8x10 glossy photograph from her folder. It would appear she has an unlimited supply. This image is of a blood-caked knife preserved in a plastic evidence bag. There's a ruler positioned next to it for reference;

it's about eight inches long. A chef's knife. Serrated edges. A knife you might use to slice through a thick slab of steak or, apparently, to murder an elderly couple.

I scrunch my eyes, pretending to examine it. Of course, it looks familiar. I'd have to be pretty dense not to recognize the missing knife from my kitchen, wouldn't I? For a moment, I think, at least I know what happened to it. But that doesn't change the fact that I've no idea how it got there. I can't very well come out and say all this, can I? I'm not too keen on leaving this place in chains. I need to walk out of here untethered. I need to find my son.

"It looks like a knife," I say, pushing the picture across the table as far away from me as possible. I'd like to take it in my hands and rip it into shreds, but that would make me look guilty. I'm not guilty of what they're accusing me of. I didn't kill my grandparents.

Detective Marx rolls her eyes. "How perceptive of you."

I bite the insides of my cheeks until the metallic tang of blood fills my mouth. I cross my legs to stop them from vibrating beneath the table. My knee smashes against the metal, and my eyes blur. My anxiety has made its presence known, as it likes to do. I struggle to contain it. I can't break down here.

"Have you seen this particular knife before, Mrs. Rizzo?"

I focus my eyes again on the picture, which Detective Marx has so kindly slid across the table again. "It's a Henckels," I say, my eyes meeting hers. "Yes, I've seen a Henckels knife before. Many times. We have a set at home, like every other family in our neighborhood."

"Yes, it's a very popular brand, not just in your neighborhood. Popular wedding registry gift. But I have to wonder if any other family is missing their eight-inch chef's knife? The one used to commit a brutal double homicide of *your* grandparents. The one with *your* prints all over it . . ."

She lets the question hang in the air between us. The question that's not really a question. How could she possibly know that I am missing a knife?

I slam my fists on the table, sending papers flying everywhere.

"You have to believe me. I didn't kill anyone. Yes, that may be my knife. I misplaced it months ago. Someone must have taken it from my house. Don't you see — someone is trying to frame me!"

"Said every guilty person ever . . ." Detective Marx mutters under her breath loud enough so we can all hear her.

"But I'm not guilty! Rick, you know me. You know my family. I didn't do it!" He gives me a helpless look. *Do I know you?*

Detective Marx clears her throat loudly.

"Good luck trying to convince a jury of that." She leans back in her chair, folding her arms across her chest. She looks pleased with herself, and I can't help but wonder why she hates me so much, why she wants to see me fry. Because that's what will happen if I'm convicted of my grandparents' double murders. They'll send me to the electric chair to fry.

"Ladies . . ." Rick holds up a hand. Then he digs his fingers into my thigh, jerking me back to attention.

"I'd like a moment alone with my client, please."

Detective Marx shoots to her feet, practically knocking her chair onto the floor. I'd bet my freedom she'd like to hit me over the head with it. Not that it seems I'll have my freedom to wager with much longer.

She stomps out of the interrogation room, slamming the metal door behind her. I can't shake the feeling that this is personal.

Detective Wren also rises to his feet, though he does so in a far more controlled manner. His body language says cool, calm, and collected, but there's something that's shifted in his eyes. I wonder if Detective Marx and Detective Wren knew my grandparents personally. It's such a small town I escaped from; I wouldn't be surprised if they did.

Detective Wren quietly tucks his chair back beneath the table. He takes a deep breath, his eyes locking momentarily with mine.

Then he brings his gaze to Rick. "You might want to discuss *this* with your client," he says, handing over a manila folder.

Rick's eyebrows fold in toward one another. "What's this?" he asks as he opens it.

"Search warrant executed on Mr. and Mrs. Rizzo's house."

"Search warrant? But they're here . . . How did you get into their house?"

He shrugs his broad shoulders. "Dog walker."

"Fuck," I mutter under my breath.

If Teddy had a middle finger to wag at me, I'm sure he'd be wagging it right now. This is what I get for leaving him at home.

"Well, I'll leave you with these. There are some pictures in there as well. A beautiful kitchen you have, Mrs. Rizzo. A nice wooden block of quality knives. We noticed the empty spot. Searched the whole premises for that knife, we did."

My stomach flips. Of course, they did. And, of course, it wasn't there. Because if it was there, I would have found it.

Detective Wren lets himself out of the room, leaving me alone with Rick. My lawyer's mouth is hanging open, a look of pure shock on his face.

"Did you do it?" He whispers so low I barely hear him. I realize the detectives are probably on the other side of the mirrored wall, listening. Not that a private conversation between attorney and client would be admissible in court, but still . . . They already have enough ammunition against me without us giving them more.

Did I do it?

I rack my brain, wondering if it's possible. I've been so out of it lately, so confused. Sometimes it feels like I'm a spectator watching myself from the outside. But I don't recall watching myself stab my grandparents to death. Murdering two people is not something you blink your eyes and forget. Is it?

"Rick, I swear to you. This is all some big mistake."

"Yeah, well, it's not me you need to convince, Gabby. And taking into consideration all of this . . ." Rick spreads his arms and motions around the table to the evidence upon evidence piling up against me. "I'm not convinced."

I swallow the lump of desperation lodged in my throat. Even my lawyer thinks I'm guilty, and if I can't convince Rick of my innocence, how could I ever convince a jury of my peers?

I push aside another picture of the murder weapon and start frantically flipping through the stack of papers. I'm not sure what it is I'm looking for; I just know there has to be something here that Rick can use to exonerate me. Because I didn't do it, which by the mere process of elimination means someone else did.

I scan through a DNA report. There's a bunch of mumbo jumbo I don't understand, but then I see it. "Rick," I say. "Look at this." I point to a paragraph within the recorded findings, and his eyes widen again. "Am I reading this wrong, or is that another set of prints on the knife?"

"No," he says slowly, scanning through the document. "Unidentified DNA not belonging to either victim or Brittany Stone found at the crime scene on the murder weapon."

"Are you thinking what I'm thinking? I told you someone is trying to frame me. Why didn't the police mention this? Why haven't they looked into it?"

"Maybe they have," he says, looking unsure of himself.

"Rick, it's there in black and white. Another person had their hands on that knife. Another person that's not me or my grandparents. Those prints must belong to whoever is setting me up. We need to figure out who that is, Rick. Someone is trying to destroy my life, don't you see? Oh my God, Rick, they probably have Cameron."

My chest constricts as I try unsuccessfully to draw a deep breath. My pulse thrums loudly in my ears.

Rapping on the metal door sends all my hairs on end. The knob turns, and I hear footsteps approaching. I don't bother turning around. I already know who is standing there.

I feel the heat of a body hovering over me before I hear Detective Marx's voice.

"Gabby Rizzo, legal name Brittany Stone, we are placing you under arrest for the murders of John and Edna Smith. You have the right to remain silent."

CHAPTER 30

GREG RIZZO

Something clicks.

Gabby once told me I'm denser than an unmanicured yard filled with thistle. Book smart, she called me. I'd love to see the expression on her face now that I've put all the puzzle pieces into place.

Susie has finally put her clothing back on and is sitting thigh-to-thigh with me on the bed. She's rubbing my back.

My body tingles as she draws circles with her fingernails against the thin fabric separating her from my bare skin. I lean toward her so that we're face to face.

"Susie . . ."

She fixes her giant blue eyes on mine expectantly.

"I need you to tell me the truth. Is Gabby pregnant?"

Susie quickly looks away, but not before I catch the disappointment in her eyes. She probably pictured this conversation going in an entirely different direction. She was probably expecting more than conversation. What kind of man does Susie take me for? There's an Amber alert out for Cameron, and Gabby has been questioned as a suspect in the double homicide of her grandparents. I'm not about to make a pass at my wife's best friend.

There's an uncomfortable silence as my stomach settles into my feet.

"Susie . . ." I wrap my fingers around her upper arm, digging into the flesh of her tanned, toned skin. I want to shake her, to thrust her body back and forth until she tells me the truth. But I stop myself there because I've taken things far enough already. "Answer me. I know she would have told you. Is Gabby pregnant?"

Susie looks back up at me. Her eyes are glazed over, and a single tear slides down her face. "I'm so sorry, Greg, I am. I really am. The last thing I'd ever want is to hurt you. It feels even worse than betraying my best friend."

I don't even know what to say.

"If you want to know the truth, Greg, you need to read this. It's the only way you'll see it for yourself." Susie picks up the journal, flipping through a few pages until she locates what she wants me to see. She holds it open, pointing to a passage.

> *I don't know how often you can tell a person how much you want to have another child. I tried for years to explain to Greg that I didn't feel complete. But he didn't want to hear it. He always has excuses — it's not the right time, work is so busy, another child will take our focus off of Cam, and is that fair to him?*
>
> *Cameron has grown from a preemie to a teenager in the blink of an eye, and my desire to bring another life into this world has grown along with him.*
>
> *So, I've decided to have another child, with or without my husband.*
>
> *Greg left me no choice but to have an affair. And now, I have a man who loves me and the life growing inside me. A brother or sister for Cam. I have everything I've ever wanted.*
>
> *And hopefully, a fresh start for us all.*

"What is this? Gabby never said anything like this to me." I'm shaking as if the earth is shifting beneath my feet. The book slips from my grasp and falls to the ground with a thud.

I thought it couldn't get worse when I found the pregnancy test. Boy, was I wrong. The pregnancy was intentional — Gabby knew exactly what she was doing. I've grossly underestimated my wife.

Gabby was right; I am denser than an unmanicured yard filled with thistle.

I'm desperate to understand how this could have happened right under my nose, though the thought of my wife with another man guts me.

"Did you ever see Gabby and Steven together?" His name burns like battery acid in my mouth — the father of my wife's unborn child. I'm not sure I even want to hear her answer. It feels like I'm driving past a fatal car crash — I don't want to look, but I can't look away. Locusts swarm around my stomach like it's the plague.

"Once," she admits, laying a hand on top of mine. "You were out of town. Gabby asked if Cam could sleep at our house, and I dropped by unexpectedly to pick up his stuffed baseball bat. You know the one?"

My heart clenches. I nod, biting back the tears because, of course, I know the one. I bought it for Cam right before he was born — a six-inch stuffed baseball bat dressed in a Richmond Flying Squirrels uniform with a beaming blue face sewn on the front. Gabby wouldn't let Cam sleep with it until he was two. She was worried about him having anything in his crib that could cause suffocation. She was always so concerned about everything.

Ironic how much more she has to worry about these days.

My thoughts turn back to my son. I will never forget the first night we let him bring it to bed. He hugged that stuffed bat so tightly I thought he would never let it go. And in a way, he hasn't. At thirteen, Cam still sleeps with it clutched securely against his chest. I wonder if anyone checked his empty hotel bed for the bat.

My chest squeezes again.

How did we get here?

"Do you think Steven has done something to Cam? And to Gabby?"

Susie's face is sheet white, her eyes like saucers on her face. She shakes her head from side to side, seemingly unable to speak.

"Oh my God, Susie, what if they're together? What if they both had something to do with this?"

I'm picturing Gabby and Steven with my son in the back seat of his car, driving far away, off to somewhere in the middle of nowhere where I will never find them. Starting over without me.

"We need to find them," I say, convinced my wife and son are still somewhere in this hotel.

I rise from the bed, moving toward the door. My hand reaches for the knob.

A sharp pinch in my neck stops me dead in my tracks.

What the . . .

The room blurs. I lean into the door, but it shifts as I attempt to wrap my fingers around the knob. The whole room is spinning. I flip around, panic sinking in, spreading its tentacles through my body.

My eyes whip around the room, making me dizzy. I grab at the air, but it slips through my fingertips. I try to scream, but my mouth can't form any words. I'm woozy, the ground slipping and sliding beneath my feet.

My heart is beating so forcefully against my chest I hear it in my ears. Warmth spreads through my body, turning my limbs to dead weight. My hand flies to my neck. There's blood. Not enough for a knife wound. I put two and two together. Someone injected me with something. It feels like I've been given enough tranquilizer to sedate a full-grown horse.

My legs grow heavier with each step until they give out entirely, and I crumble into a heap on the carpet. I attempt to stand up but fall back down. Up and down. Up and down. Until I no longer have the strength to stand.

My gaze finds the door one last time wondering if I will live to find my son as my eyelids collapse into darkness.

CHAPTER 31

GREG RIZZO

I jerk in place.

My skull is pounding as if I just took a fastball to the head. My mouth is desert dry. Where am I? What happened? I dig through my mind, but there are only snatches of memory, nothing concrete I can grasp onto.

I stand up, but I'm pulled back down like the force of gravity on a roller coaster ride. I'm hit with a wave of vertigo so intense I'm suddenly thankful I'm sitting. I lift my arm to wipe the sweat from my forehead, but it pulls against something tangible. I twist my head around, and panic sets in. I can't lift my hands because they are tied behind my back, wrapped around the neck of a chair. My gaze falls to the floor where my feet are bound to its legs.

And then it all comes rushing back.

Susie. Where is Susie?

I try to scream, but my voice sticks to the sides of my throat. My eyes flit toward the door, finding hers.

"Ah, you're awake," she says.

"What's happening?" I manage. "What did you do to me?"

"What did *I* do to *you?*"

I'm so confused.

"Please, Susie. Untie me. We can talk. Pick up where we left off."

Susie laughs, a wide grin spreading across her face. I smile back, and hers just as quickly disappears.

"Where is it you think we left off, Greg?"

"I was going to look for Gabby and Cam and then—"

"This," she finishes my thought, waving an empty syringe in the air.

"*You* drugged me? Why would you drug me, Susie? And is this really necessary?" I roll my head around, indicating the restraints binding me to the chair. "I'm not going to hurt you. I would never hurt you. Please, untie me. We can talk. We can figure this out."

"You would never hurt me," she repeats, appearing to mull it over as she closes the distance between us.

My heartbeat quickens to an unreasonably fast pace. *She's going to untie me. She's going to let me go. She's going to help me find Cam.*

Gabby's right — I'm a terrible liar.

Susie leans in, her face so close I think she's going to kiss me. Funny how I fantasized for years about a moment like this — well, not quite like *this* — but now that it's happening, I would move heaven and earth to make it stop. She runs a hand across my cheek. Her fingers are warm, but her eyes are ice cold. She slaps a strip of duct tape across my mouth.

"Shut up, Greg."

Susie removes her hand from my cheek, and then brings it back hard across my face.

"Susie . . ." I scream, my cries muddled by the duct tape, my body thrashing wildly against the restraints. She turns her back toward me, storming out of the room. The door slams, and I exhale the breath I was holding. How could she do something like this? *Why* would she do something like this? The only scenario I can come up with is that somehow, Susie Baker is in on this with my wife.

I pull against the restraints, my skin chafing against the rope. There's barely a centimeter of space, and the movement sends searing pain through my wrists, hands, and arms. Inside though, I've gone completely numb. My son is still missing. My wife may have had something to do with his disappearance. She may have murdered the grandparents I never knew she had. What are a few inch-deep wounds in the grand scheme of things? Gabby's betrayals have cut much deeper than any rope or knife ever could.

Still, I give up after a few minutes because I'm getting nowhere fast. The rope won't give. All I'm doing is fighting a losing battle against Boy Scout knots. Cameron spent a few years in the Boy Scouts. His vest still hangs in his closet, every inch proudly decorated with an assortment of merit badges.

I shift my weight from side to side, in a futile attempt to dislodge myself from the chair. I have to do something. Gabby's words sting sharper than Susie's slap — "You do you, Greg, just like you always do." Is that what this is about?

The chair legs stick to the carpet, refusing to move. I give a violent shake, and the chair topples over with me stuck in it, hurling me to the ground. My face hits the carpet, and my teeth dig into the side of my mouth. I can taste the blood pooling.

And then I gulp as I hear it — the sound of someone at the door.

CHAPTER 32

GABBY RIZZO

"Wait!" I scream, jumping up from the metal chair and nearly knocking Detective Marx off her feet. She reacts quickly, pushing into my back, and I let out a loud gasp as she pins me face-first onto the interrogation table.

"You can't arrest me," I plead, my cheek stinging from the impact. "The reports. Have you seen the DNA reports? There's another set of fingerprints. Rick, please, tell her. Tell her about the prints!"

I catch Rick's expression out of the corner of my eye. The eye that's not pinned to the table. He looks like a deer caught in headlights. Legal contracts, litigation, collections, mergers, and acquisitions are his jam. Not DNA analysis. Not gruesome double homicides. This is not in his pay grade, that's for sure. But he is still here. He could have left, but he didn't. Wouldn't it be nice if I could say the same for my husband?

"My client is right. There's an unidentified set of fingerprints on the knife in question. Shouldn't you figure out who they belong to before arresting my client? I doubt you'd get a conviction that could hold with another set of prints on the murder weapon."

Detective Marx rolls her eyes, her patience visibly wearing thin.

"We've already run the other set of prints through Pennsylvania's fingerprint database, but there were no matches. I have a call into the FBI to have them run through its national database. That said, your client's prints were also on the murder weapon that originated in her house. And considering the once intimate, since strained nature of her relationship with the deceased, I'd say Ms. Stone — I apologize, Mrs. Rizzo — had a heck of a motive and opportunity to commit this crime. But don't worry, Mr. Prendergast — I assure you, we will leave no stone unturned."

Her lip quivers as if she's about to crack a smile, but she quickly composes herself. No stone unturned. How original, I think, like I haven't heard that one before. It was Stone Therapeutics' motto for crying out loud.

"I have an idea, a request if you will . . ."

"You have exactly sixty seconds starting now." She taps a finger against her Apple Watch. "Sit down," she orders, and I collapse back into the chair. I can't even begin to imagine what Rick is about to say. I mean, what can he say? She's right, and we all know it. This doesn't look good for me at all.

"What if — just hear me out — Mrs. Rizzo compiles a list of every person she knows and believes could possibly have had something to do with this? You fingerprint them and run them against the ones from the murder weapon. If none of them pan out, I have no issue with you placing my client under arrest and taking her into custody, pending the identification of the unidentified DNA."

"Rick!" I shoot him a look of death and kick him underneath the table.

"Trust me," he mouths.

I fidget in my seat, watching the detectives mull over my lawyer's unheard-of request. I mean, who says something like that? So hey, listen, would you mind holding off on arresting my client until you do this or that? Thanks, much appreciated. I wouldn't be surprised if they laughed in his face.

Especially Detective Marx, who looks like she would gladly strap me to an electric chair and flip the switch herself if given the opportunity.

I'm relieved when it's Detective Wren who responds. I've had enough of his partner for a lifetime, thank you very much.

"This is an odd request, to say the least, and I can't believe I'm even entertaining this, but . . ."

I hold my breath and wait. The seconds stretch like miles of empty highway.

Please, say something. I bite the inside of my mouth to stop myself from screaming out. My teeth push through the scar tissue lining my inner cheek, and the familiar sting comes before the blood coats my tongue.

Detective Wren rests both hands on the table, staring at me. "I'll admit, the unexplained prints unsettle me. You've got ten minutes to compile a list. We will hold off on transferring you to the Johnstown precinct for booking until after we've tested the DNA of the people on your list against the DNA in the report. I imagine this may take quite a few days. First, we'll have to get warrants and samples. In the meantime, you will be held here."

"But . . ."

This time it's Rick who kicks me.

"I don't like this, Wren."

"It's the right thing to do, Marx."

I look at Detective Marx. She's probably a decade or so older than me, but if it weren't for the hardness in her eyes, she could probably pass for younger. I can't begin to imagine what those eyes have seen. My own eyes flick to a photo of my grandparents, and my stomach turns because I don't have to imagine.

"Fine," she acquiesces, crossing her arms across her chest. "This woman is dangerous. Don't say I didn't warn you, Nick. She's your problem now. You can explain to our bosses why we are allowing a double murder suspect to call the shots here."

And the award for most dramatic actress in a police force docuseries goes to Rhonda Marx.

Detective Marx smooths the crisp white shirt beneath her navy blazer and shoots me a look of death before turning back to Detective Wren. "Good luck, partner. You're making the worst decision of your career. Don't say I didn't warn you."

And then she looks at me, stone-faced. "Mark my words. You will pay for what you've done."

"But I haven't—"

"Don't," Rick warns, placing a hand in the air to stop me from saying anything that could be used against me in a court of law.

Detective Marx storms out of the interrogation room, presumably to return to Johnstown without her partner. Detective Wren and Rick waste no time discussing the logistics of getting all the DNA together and submitting it to the lab for expedited analysis.

After a few minutes, Detective Wren rises from his seat. "I'll leave you to that list."

Rick nods. "Thank you, Detective."

The door barely closes before my mouth is in Rick's ear. "What the hell, Rick? You don't care if I go to jail? What kind of game are you playing with them? I need to get out of here! Cam . . ." I don't have it in me to finish the thought out loud. I've been here for hours, and still no word on my son.

"I was buying us time. The next request is a police escort to the hotel to search for Cameron. Hopefully, by the time they figure out who that other set of prints belongs to, we will have found Cam, and you will have been cleared of all charges. The ball isn't really in our court, Gabby. I'm working with what I have to work with here. I suggest you make it a long list. Once they extradite you to Pennsylvania, it's going to become a heck of a lot harder to get you out."

He pushes his notepad toward me and offers up a pen. It's an obscenely expensive pen — a limited-edition Montblanc with gold etchings wrapping around the cap like a snake. Wow, Greg must pay Rick a fortune. Another thing I didn't know about my husband. The thought is a punch to my battered gut but oddly makes me more confident in my lawyer.

I take the pen in my hand, running my fingers along the ridges while I think about who might have killed my grandparents and framed me for murder.

CHAPTER 33

GABBY RIZZO

Rick said I should make my list as long as possible to buy us as much time as possible before they stick me in the back of their armored car and haul me off to Pennsylvania. Nothing good will come of returning to the place I fled from, especially not in a police cruiser.

So I force myself to think about who might want to frame me for murder, a more difficult task than you'd think. Because for every person I can think of, I can come up with an excuse as to why they wouldn't or couldn't frame me for murder. That doesn't seem like a terrible problem to have, except that the reality is someone did this.

And I'm essentially tasked with figuring out who that someone is. Because clearly, no one else is doing it for me.

I begin to compile a list of everyone currently in my life, along with everyone I've ever met. Anyone I may have disgruntled. I start with those closest to me, though I know they surely couldn't have had anything to do with this — Greg, Susie, Matt, and Jake.

Jake is an impossibility by all stretches of the imagination. How would a thirteen-year-old have the means to travel from

Richmond, Virginia, to Johnstown, Pennsylvania, on his own, his absence unnoticed? And what would his motivation be to slaughter an elderly couple he's never met? And on top of that, to engineer his best friend's disappearance? It's a long shot at best. Still, I hope the mere mention of his name will get the detectives back to talking to him. Because while I know he didn't do this, there's no denying he is holding something back.

I tap the obscenely expensive pen against my chin, thinking. I scribble Coach Bob's name on the list, though it seems he's already been cleared of involvement in Cameron's disappearance. At least in the eyes of the law. I still have my doubts about him. But what would he stand to accomplish by slaughtering my grandparents? I can't think of a single thing, a single reason why he would have that level of hatred toward my family and me.

I quickly write out the names of every parent with a kid on Cam's team and every parent of every player he's played with since he was seven. Families I've known or heard of on opposing teams. Cameron's schoolmates. Greg's parents. My husband's business associates and my former coworkers from a decade ago. Our neighbors. My book club that's more like a gossip club.

Next comes Steven, his wife. Dr. Green. Friends of my grandparents and my parents. The other driver in the collision that killed my parents. She would certainly have the motivation to hurt me.

Could it be her? Could she have killed my grandparents and taken my son?

She's the obvious suspect, but I have my questions. How could she have possibly found me after all these years? And why wait this long to exact revenge? It doesn't make sense. The accident was sixteen years ago. Sixteen years is a heck of a time to lie in wait to get back at someone, but still, what happened to her — I draw a star next to her name.

Carla Miller is next up there on the list. Surely she'd want to destroy me if she learned about my affair with her husband.

But how could she know about my grandparents? Besides, she isn't here at the tournament. Or *is* she? I scribble an asterisk next to her name as well.

Then I add the staff at the hotel I've crossed paths with for good measure though we've only met — the manager, housekeepers, and bartender. I'm grasping at straws, but I have nothing else to grasp at.

I keep writing frantically. When I think I'm finished, I come up with another name. The list goes on and on and on.

Finally, I gently lay Rick's pen down on the table, satisfied that I've provided as inclusive a list as possible. I'm mentally and emotionally exhausted.

"Is that everyone you can think of?" Rick asks, examining the page-worth of names.

"Offhand. I think so. I mean, you're on it," I say, shrugging my shoulders.

Rick raises an eyebrow but doesn't say anything.

"You said, everyone."

"Touché."

The metal door opens as if on cue, and Detective Wren joins us at the table.

"Have you finished your list?"

"We have." Rick hands over the paper, which may or may not contain the name of the person who killed my grandparents, framed me for their murders, and kidnapped my son.

I don't know for sure that it's all connected. But then, how could it not be connected? Finding out who those prints belong to is essential on so many levels, not least of which is finding the person who has my son.

Detective Wren takes the list, his eyebrows furrowing together as he looks it over. "Mr. Prendergast, are you aware your name is on your client's list of possible suspects?"

Rick's cheeks turn a touch pink. "Yes, Detective. I told Mrs. Rizzo to make a list of everyone she knows. It could be anyone, though I can assure you, it's not me. I know you have to follow protocol, though, so have at it."

Rick holds out his hands so Detective Wren can fingerprint him. I nearly laugh out loud. Why would he bring a fingerprint kit into the interrogation room when he knows the suspect's prints were already identified on the murder weapon?

Except nothing about my predicament is funny.

Detective Wren wipes Rick's left hand down with alcohol. Once it's dry, he rolls each of Rick's fingers on an ink pad until they are sufficiently coated from tip to joint. Then he guides each finger across a fingerprint card. Finally, Detective Wren secures the card in a plastic evidence bag. I wonder if he'll even bother running it. Obviously, the perpetrator of this is not my lawyer.

"One down, ninety-nine to go," he says.

Rick nods in understanding. This is not going to be an easy task whatsoever. Detective Wren is really going out on a limb to help me. I'm not sure why he even wants to, considering how adamant his partner was against doing so. Maybe he has his own grown daughter, and I remind him of her. Perhaps he's just a really good-natured guy. Or maybe, he knows in his gut I'm innocent, and he cares too much about the law to watch an innocent woman go to prison for the rest of her life. Especially when her son is missing.

I don't care what his motivations are; I'll take the help in any way, shape, or form I can.

Now there's just the question of where I will spend the night.

CHAPTER 34

GREG RIZZO

This is not how I planned to spend the night. Hog-tied to a chair, I've blistering rope burns on my wrists and ankles and carpet fibers stuck in my throat.

I'm still trying to process my situation. Why would Susie do something as horrific as this? Was it for Gabby? Susie has shown she'd do anything for her best friend. But *this?* And I know I haven't been the perfect husband, but would Gabby really go to such extremes to hurt me? My head is spinning because none of this makes sense.

I listen for sounds outside the door, but it's quiet now. Whoever was there must have left. Perhaps after hearing a slight commotion, they ultimately decided to mind their business and go on with their evening. But where has Susie gone? Is she coming back? Or is she going to leave me here until someone discovers me? Will I be stuck here until tomorrow morning when housekeeping comes knocking? A ball of panic forms in my stomach — what if she hung up the do not disturb sign? If that's the case, I can't even imagine how long I'll be trapped inside this room.

I have to stop thinking like this.

But what else can I think about? My failed baseball career? Horrible life choices? What horrors may have befallen my son?

I'm about to have a good old-fashioned scream when I hear a knock on the door. Considering what she's done, I doubt Susie would knock. Which means, it must be someone else.

"Help me, please," I instinctively shout, flooded with relief that at least one part of this nightmarish trip is about to end. I'll be better able to deal with the other parts when my hands are not tied behind my back.

There's some shuffling outside the door and then the sound that brings tears of relief to my eyes.

Beep.

I hold my breath as the door swings open and in walks the hotel manager, Tomas.

"Oh my," he says, freezing in place and bringing a hand to his chest. "What do we have here? Are you alright?"

Okay, so Tomas is strange and kind of an asshole. I also blame him a little for what's happened in his hotel resort, but I've never been so pleased to see someone in my entire life. I am obscenely happy to see him. I want to hug him. I want to cry. I would lick his toes if he asked me to.

But first, I want him to untie these fucking ropes.

A niggle of doubt creeps in — *what brought him here to find me* — but I shrug it off as Tomas drops to his knees and pulls the duct tape from my mouth. Then he begins fiddling with the ropes.

"They're pretty tight," I tell him, but he ignores me and continues moving them this way and that, attempting to untie them. Finally, he throws his hands up in defeat. "Well, this isn't working."

Tomas rises to his feet, and I think he's going to leave to find something to get this rope untangled. I'm about to cry out, *please don't leave me here.* But he doesn't leave. Instead, he reaches into his black pants and pulls out a pocket knife.

Panic tears through me as he flicks open the blade. It's normal for a hotel manager to carry around a pocket knife, you know, in the event of an emergency, right? But what kind of emergency in a four-star resort would warrant a pocket knife? And wouldn't maintenance handle such emergencies?

And then the knife makes me think about what Gabby said about the rat — the three-inch gash lining its underbelly. Surely it couldn't be. Why would Tomas murder a rat in his own hotel?

I watch in horror as he squats back down and brings the knife to the rope. Another bang on the door stops him mid-cut.

"Just a second," he says as he once again rises to his feet.

My breath hitches and my heart stops beating as he yanks open the door.

Susie is standing on the other side.

"She did this," I scream as Tomas's eyes flit back and forth between Susie and me. "Listen to me, please!"

It quickly becomes clear Tomas is not listening to me as he moves aside so Susie can enter the room. He closes the door behind her and slips the chain lock into place. And then, I look on in shock as Tomas gently places a hand on the small of Susie's back, ushering her further into the room. There is something familiar in the gesture that I don't like. They clearly know one another intimately.

What does that mean for me?

Tomas has a crazy look in his eyes and a stupid grin stretching from ear to ear. Something isn't adding up. I'm missing something here. As the thoughts run amok in my head, I try to process what's happening.

I'm interrupted by Tomas cutting through the air with his knife, maniacally talking to himself. I watch in horror as he grabs a chair and carries it over to the chained door, where he jams it underneath the knob.

Then he turns back to look at us.

"Now, who's ready to have a little fun here?"

CHAPTER 35

GABBY RIZZO

"It's time to go, Mrs. Rizzo." A uniformed officer is beside me, helping me to my feet so he can slip his dangling handcuffs around my wrists and escort me to my cell. It would appear I have the answer to my question — I'm spending the night in jail. I can already feel the awkward pull of my arms behind my back, the cold steel against my skin.

Rick abruptly stands and holds out a hand. "Hold on a second," he tells the cop. He turns back to face Detective Wren. "Listen, I have an idea. Please, hear me out."

Who knew Rick had such a set of balls? Well, other than his wife and Susie, that is.

Detective Wren throws his hands up in the air, like *seriously, now what?* As if he doesn't already have enough to do. By agreeing to Rick's insane request, the detective has created more work for himself than he probably knows what to do with. And nonetheless, without a partner to help. I bet at this moment, as he waits for the next thing to come out of Rick's mouth, he's regretting saying yes to his unorthodox request in the first place.

"Look, I know my client is technically under arrest, but given the extenuating circumstances, I need bail to be granted, erm, like now."

Detective Wren shakes his head in disbelief. "Let me get this straight. You're telling me you want me to let a suspect in a double homicide *go*? Because you need bail granted *now*? Do I have that right, Mr. Prendergast?"

It sounds insane to me as he repeats back the request, and I'm the suspect under arrest for a double homicide. But Detective Wren doesn't further protest, so clearly, Rick has, at minimum, grabbed his attention.

"Listen, I know technically Mrs. Rizzo needs to go before a judge before she can get bail, but there's no time. She needs to be at that hotel while the police search for her son. And who knows, perhaps she can be of assistance in helping you identify the people on her list. So this might actually wind up helping you exponentially."

It's a twisted way of putting it, but he kind of makes a valid point. I could help find the person who did this because, really, I'm more motivated than anyone to find the person who did this.

Detective Wren's eyes shoot back and forth like pinballs among me, Rick, and the officer waiting for instruction. Does he take me into custody or not? Am I spending the night here or at the four-star luxury Foxcroft where my entire life was flipped upside down?

"I don't know, Mr. Prendergast. How can you guarantee your client isn't going to pull something and try to escape custody? You're asking me to put my career on the line. And for the record, just because I have my doubts as to whether Mrs. Rizzo committed this absolutely heinous crime doesn't mean I don't also have my doubts as to whether she didn't."

He narrows his eyes at me and grows silent. He hasn't said no, which means he's thinking about it. I can't believe he's actually thinking about it! Now I know why Greg pays Rick so well — he's a freaking genius.

I take a deep breath before laying it all on the table. "Please, Detective. I need to find my son. He's the only thing in this world that matters to me right now. I promise you, I'm not going anywhere. I need to be there when he . . ." I choke back a sob ". . . comes back. When he comes back . . ." My voice trails off with an anguished cry.

Rick passes me a box of Kleenex, and I greedily grab a wad of tissues. I'm going to need them.

Tears trail down my cheeks as I stare into the dark eyes of the man who holds my freedom in his hands. For now, at least. If we don't find a DNA match for that extra set of prints, there will be nothing more he can do. I can all but kiss that freedom goodbye.

We may never find Cam.

But we're in this moment now together, where hope still exists. Where I may be vindicated. Where Cam may still be alive and well, and coming back to us. Where Greg and I haven't yet said our goodbyes and agreed to the dissolution of our marriage.

"What I'm about to say is crazy. Certifiably insane." He looks at the officer standing on alert next to me, examining his badge. "What time are you on until, Johnson?"

"Just started my shift an hour ago, sir. I'm on for the next twelve hours."

"And how do you feel about working overtime?"

Officer Johnson is young, with a baby face and a thin gold band around *that* finger. I'd bet he's just recently married, maybe even a brand-new father. I can't imagine they pay extraordinarily well in a small precinct like this, where crimes of this nature are unheard of. At least, not until the Rizzos came ripping through their quiet, once peaceful town. Of course, he wants the overtime.

"I'm happy to help, sir. In any way that I can."

"Well, there we have it. Johnson, I'm going to speak with your superiors, and then I'd like you to escort Mrs. Rizzo back to Foxcroft. You'll be her shadow for the next twenty-four hours."

His attention shifts back to me. "Mrs. Rizzo, I'm giving you twenty-four hours to find anyone you think might be a match to those prints, but after that, I will have to place you in custody. No funny business, understand?"

There's no way in hell we'll be able to track down everyone on my list in twenty-four hours. But twenty-four hours out there are still twenty-four hours not spent here behind bars. Twenty-four hours for me to find my son.

"Thank you so much, Detective Wren. No funny business. I understand."

He nods in Officer Johnson's direction, seemingly satisfied that we've sorted it all out. If you could call my son missing and unidentified fingerprints on a murder weapon used to slaughter my estranged grandparents sorted out.

"Give me a minute to get your release processed."

"Should I cuff her, Detective?"

"My gut tells me that won't be necessary."

CHAPTER 36

GABBY RIZZO

It won't be necessary. I meant what I said about not going anywhere. Not without my son.

My heart is beating a mile a minute as Officer Johnson navigates the winding roads leading back to our hotel. The drive takes nearly an hour, and I'm once again struck by how stuck in the middle of nowhere this place really is.

Despite my current predicament, I find Officer Johnson's presence soothing. It's as if nothing bad can happen to us now, even if the damage has already been done. As if, somehow, we can strip back the layers upon layers of damage to reveal the new growth beneath.

The afternoon is slowly transitioning to night, the sky bursting with the ribbons of pinks, purples, and oranges of a setting sun. It's a blaring contrast to the turmoil we've experienced over the last forty-eight hours.

My stomach gives a loud rumble, and it registers that I haven't had a bite to eat in two whole days. Not since I finished the cookie before we left the house. But who could eat at a time like this?

God, I miss Cam. I don't give a shit about the dance anymore — I fully intend to hug and kiss him and squeeze him indefinitely when I have him back in my arms. I don't care who sees my outward displays of affection or how embarrassed or angry Cam is with me for bestowing it upon him. Though I have a hunch, he'll be just as happy to see me as I am him. Either way, I'm never letting my baby boy go again.

Greg, on the other hand . . .

This time, I feel a sharp twinge of sadness when I think about my husband because it feels like it's the end of the line for us. Despite everything that's happened, it's still hard to imagine it being the end of us. But I remind myself very few things in this world last forever.

As we pull into the hotel parking lot, I try to put Greg from my mind. Officer Johnson shifts the police cruiser into park and walks around to my side of the car. I notice he's sweating a bit, and I suspect it's not just from the oppressive heat of a late Georgia afternoon. He's barely a year on the force — a tidbit I learned during our car ride. I'm sure he's worried I might take off running as soon as he opens the door to let me out of the car. And what will he do then? Chase me down and tackle me to the ground? Force his knee into my back as I mourn the literal loss of my son?

Officer Johnson doesn't want to do that. He doesn't want to hurt me. He's got a two-month-old baby boy of his own at home, his picture proudly displayed on the dashboard of his police car. I bet he's imagining what he'd be capable of doing if someone did something to him.

Wondering what I am capable of.

But he needn't worry. I've run for long enough. I'm done running away.

Once I'm out of the car, and it's clear I'm not going to sprint into the tangle of woods surrounding the parking lot, Officer Johnson motions for me to walk toward the hotel. Despite my evident cooperation, he still sticks as close to my side as possible without jumping into my arms.

We both quicken our pace. The fierce heat only adds to the sense of urgency electrifying the air around us. The clock is ticking down.

As I mentally scroll through all the possible scenarios and people who might want to hurt me, I keep coming back to Steven. I saw it in his face when he kicked me out of his hotel room — I hurt him. And now, I strongly believe he is doing anything he can in his power to hurt me back. It doesn't explain the double murder of my grandparents, but it does explain the disappearance of my son.

The Futures lost their first game and were eliminated from the tournament. I'm sure most of the players and parents have packed up and headed home. But not Steven. No, he's still at Foxcroft. I feel it deep in my gut. There's no way he simply left the hotel and traveled back to Richmond without putting up more of a fight. Yes, his emotions were raw, and he was angry as hell at me. But Steven also loves me. He said so himself. I guess it's true what they say — sometimes we hurt the ones we love.

"What's the room number again, Mrs. Rizzo?"

"It's 2012. The room next door to mine. We'll start with Steven Miller. He's on my list."

The lobby is pumping with people returning from the beach or fields, heading to the pool and spa. I peek into the bar as we walk toward the stairs, half expecting to find Susie perched on the barstool where we left her. Chip is back behind the bar, but it's otherwise empty.

As we approach the stairwell, I prepare myself for the ugly scene that's about to play out. I broke up with Steven, tore up his heart, and now I'm about to show up back at his doorstep with a policeman in tow.

I'm not sure if it's the adrenaline coursing through my body, but I feel more clear-headed than I have in ages. It's as if a veil has been lifted.

Officer Johnson opens the door for us, and I obediently step into the stairwell. It's dimly lit and narrow, but we scale the steps side-by-side. As I clear the final step and reach for the exit door, he places a hand on my elbow. "I want you to know that even if you did what you're accused of doing, I'm not going to rest until we find your son."

I smile weakly.

While I know some people will do anything to win — in business, baseball, and love — I believe there is still goodness in this world. Detective Wren and Officer Johnson are proof of that. Hopefully, their goodness is enough to bring Cameron home and to clear my name. Hopefully, justice will be served, and whoever did this to my family will pay.

Life won't look the same after this trip, but I sense Greg and I both knew deep down, well before Cam disappeared, that this was the case.

We walk down the hallway in silence to room 2012. I've got too much on my mind to make casual conversation. Instead, I'm trying to figure out what we will find when we get inside. Steven? My son? The front desk was abandoned, housekeeping long gone for the day, so we don't have a key. I wonder if Steven will open the door for us or if my police escort will be forced to break it down.

We will find out soon enough.

Halfway down the hallway, I pull Officer Johnson to the side.

"I know you know what you're doing, but I think you should let me knock. Maybe stay off to the side."

"Remind me — who do you think is inside of there?"

My cheeks flame. "My ex-lover. Maybe my son?"

I break eye contact.

"My job isn't to judge you, Mrs. Rizzo. It's to make sure you're in my custody and safe. It's to enforce the law."

"Thank you." I feel myself relax ever so slightly.

"Besides," he adds. "I'd rather not have to break down a door tonight." The corners of his lips twitch into a brief smile.

We reach room 2012, and I take a deep breath. I clench and unclench my fists a few times to stop my fingers from shaking. And then I raise my hand to the door, and I knock.

CHAPTER 37

GREG RIZZO

We all jump at the knock.

It sounds like it's coming from the room next door, which means someone is in the hallway, within earshot.

Tomas swivels his head toward the door, his eyes crazed. He holds a finger to his mouth and whispers, "Not a word," brandishing the pocketknife for emphasis.

As if I'm not going to scream bloody murder.

I get out, "We're in—" before his thick black boot connects with my cheek. Searing pain rips through my face. I run my tongue over my teeth and find one of them is loose, dangling in place. I look up at him with utter contempt. He broke my freaking tooth. I spray red on the carpet since I can't physically move my finger to flip him off.

But I don't scream again. I seal my lips into a tight line. Tomas is eyeing me like a rabid animal, circling, waiting for the opportunity to pounce again and rip me to threads. Under normal circumstances, I could shatter every bone in his body with my eyes closed. But these are far from normal circumstances. With my hands and feet bound behind my body, I can't do a thing.

Besides, where will screaming get me other than dead? The way he's waving that knife around, there's no doubt in mind that he won't hesitate to use it to kill me if I push him too far.

Satisfied he's quieted me — *for now* — Tomas moves swiftly toward Susie, and the lump in my throat expands.

The next knock that comes is at *our* door.

I feel a flicker of hope. Maybe he'll let me go? Untie me and then open the door and act like everything is normal?

Or will he let the door go unanswered? Kill me?

Who's to say what a psychopath is to do?

A second knock has Tomas pacing around the room like he's in the final mile of a marathon. He runs into Susie, and she stumbles back. "Are you okay, love? Have I hurt you?" he asks.

My heart momentarily stops beating. I couldn't have heard that right. I must have a concussion from the kick I took to the head; it's making me hallucinate. Lack of water and blood flow is causing me to see things that aren't there.

But something *is* there.

It's in how he reaches out a hand to her face and gently strokes her cheek. It's in his expression that no longer screams, I've been sucking on a sour lemon. And it's in how Susie is gazing back at him, her big blue eyes swimming with adoration. There's a familiarity between them that turns my blood cold.

I watch as he leans down, kissing Susie's forehead. She's smiling ear-to-ear until her gaze meets mine and her lips fall. And then I catch it — a glint of recognition — something I wish I could unsee in her eyes.

FOURTEEN YEARS EARLIER
GABBY'S JOURNAL

I waited up all night.

Greg went out with some of his teammates to celebrate their big win. He invited me to go with him, but none of the other girlfriends were going, and I had an early Saturday morning real estate class.

In retrospect, I should have gone. It's not like I got any sleep by staying home.

The bars here close at two, and while we attend the occasional after-party, it's rare for Greg to go without me or me without him. We are each other's everything.

Were.

We were each other's everything.

Until he didn't come home last night.

When 2.30 a.m. rolled around, I started to worry. We are only a ten-minute walk from the bars, maybe fifteen, stumbling drunk. I tried calling Greg, but his phone went straight to voicemail. He wasn't answering my texts, either. That wasn't like Greg at all. At least not the Greg I thought I knew.

By three, I entered panic mode, pacing around our six-hundred-square-foot basement apartment. By four, I had left messages for all of Greg's friends and was ready to start calling hospitals, the police, and even his parents.

Because something was wrong, which became more apparent with each tick of the second hand on my watch. Deep down, though, a part of me knew Greg wasn't dead in a gutter. A woman's intuition, I guess. I cried myself to sleep on the bed we'd shared since our sophomore year. If he wasn't home by morning, I would make the necessary calls and begin my search.

Part of me wished I hadn't been right, that Greg was concussed somewhere on the pavement sleeping it off. Because he did come home. Greg was wasted when he finally stumbled through the door. The sun was filtering through our haphazardly thrown-up window shades — two old, dark pillowcases nailed up on the wall — casting an ominous haze over our shoe-box apartment. I knew right away where he'd been. My knight had a crack in his armor — lipstick on his shirt, scratch marks down his back.

Son of a bitch.

Greg was crying and desperately apologetic. I'm sure they usually are. His words were slurred, and the stench of booze mixed with perfume permeated every cell of my body. He said he didn't remember what happened, but isn't that just a thing people say when they don't want to admit what they've done? Can you actually forget being with another person?

I wasn't going to give him another chance; there was no way I'd take him back, but I guess we all make mistakes.

I'm not perfect, either.

But I'm not sure I'll ever be able to forgive him for his betrayal. He might not remember, but I will never forget.

CHAPTER 38

GREG RIZZO

I remember.

CHAPTER 39

GABBY RIZZO

'Did you hear that?' I mouth quietly to Officer Johnson. His back is pressed against the wall between rooms 2010 and 2012, a hand resting on the solid black gun in his holster.

He nods; he hears it, too.

So I'm not imagining the voices carrying through the door. From the room next door. From *my* room.

Arguing.

We walk the few steps to room 2010, and I knock on the door. I wait a minute, but no one answers.

"Look," I whisper to Officer Johnson, pointing to where the door is slightly askew in the frame, as if knocked off its hinges and then hastily pushed back into place.

He nods in understanding and then motions with his eyes and chin for me to continue, so I knock again. I rap my fingers against the wood, harder this time in case the arguing drowned out my knock on the first go. Though my gut tells me it was the other way around, that my knock was the catalyst of the argument.

A knot forms in the pit of my stomach. It's impossible that it was less than two days ago I awoke to Matt and Greg arguing about Cam in the hallway. I wish I could go back in time and warn myself how gut-wrenching the next thirty-six hours would be. Prepare for my entire world to come crashing down all around me.

And it will only get worse if you don't find out who did this. If you don't find Cam before they take you into custody and transport you to Johnstown, Pennsylvania.

I press my ear against the door, straining to make out the conversation. The voices are lower now, as if not wanting to be heard in the hallway.

"Who's in there? Greg, is that you? Open the door, please. It's Gabby."

There's a loud shuffle behind the door as if someone is moving furniture. The desperation is building inside of me.

Who is our room? Why won't they answer?

"Open the damn door!" I'm screaming now. Officer Johnson is in the corner of my eye, waving his hand, warning me to calm down. How can I possibly calm down? There are people in my room. Greg? Cameron? *Steven?* Why won't they open the goddamn door?

"Open this door NOW!" I kick the wood with my sneaker, sending a jolt of pain through my toes up my leg. It doesn't stop me — I bang harder.

If they don't open this door, I will hammer my body against it until it fully falls off the hinges. I feel it in my bones — someone I love is in that room. I've never been more sure of anything in my life.

A hand on my shoulder pulls me from my frenzy. Officer Johnson. His face is a mix of concern and irritation. I step aside, not wanting to piss him off. I need him on my team.

Now it's he who bangs forcefully on the door.

"Police, open up."

More shuffling.

Officer Johnson's walkie-talkie pierces the air. I immediately recognize the voice on the other end — Detective Grady. My heart skips in my chest. They've found Cam. They must have found Cam.

I hold my breath, waiting.

I'm not expecting what comes next.

"Where are you located, Johnson? We need to speak with Mrs. Rizzo immediately. The Richmond P.D. reached out to our precinct. They've got two officers in the hospital after searching her home."

"After searching my home?"

"She's right next to me, Detective Grady. We're on the second floor, outside of room 2010. Did you get that — 2-0-1-0? Go on, please. She's listening."

"The officers were both admitted to the hospital. They were exhibiting signs of unexplainable fatigue, lightheadedness, and vomiting. Another officer on the scene reported witnessing them both take a cookie off a tray on the kitchen island. Quite an embarrassment to be caught with your hand in the cookie jar, but in any event . . ."

Static.

"The cookies?" I can't believe what I'm hearing. "What about the cookies?"

"Detective Grady, do you read me?"

"Yeah, I'm here. We sent the cookies to the lab for testing, and they came back positive for potentially lethal levels of Ambien."

"Sleeping pills? Why would there be sleeping pills in the cookies?"

"That's what I wanted to ask you. Why would there be Ambien in your cookies? Just who were you trying to drug, Mrs. Rizzo?"

The hallway spins, and I place a hand on the wall for support. I can't answer Detective Grady's question. I can't speak, for that matter. My head is spinning wildly.

The cookies. The giant batches of chocolate-chip cookies Susie regularly bakes for me with extra dark chocolate chips because she knows how much I love them. The cookies I eat on a daily basis because they're a staple on my kitchen island. The cookies Greg and Cameron never touch because their palates are salty and sour, not sweet. The cookies Susie never takes a bite of because she's always watching her figure.

There must be some mistake. Susie wouldn't.

All these years . . .

I'm going to be sick.

"Susie Baker," I manage. "You need to find Susie Baker."

CHAPTER 40

GREG RIZZO

"I remember," I say, seething. "You . . ."

This is where I'd point my finger at the culprit, except I'm still laid on the carpet, my hands tied behind my back. I can only stare at this perfectly diabolical woman in disbelief.

The smile is back, spread across Susie's face. I've never seen her look so pleased with herself. "What's that Gabby says about you?" she asks as she hovers over me, brushing her foot against the side of my face, where I can feel a bruise starting to form. "Right, denser than an unmanicured lawn filled with thistle."

Heat rises to my cheeks. What hasn't Gabby told this woman?

"That night . . ."

"I thought you'd never remember, Greg. All these years, living next door, flirting with the possibility."

"With the possibility of what, Susie?"

"With the possibility of sleeping with me, Greg. Don't be coy. I see the way you look at me. Gabby sees it, too. We both know you've thought about it. I bet you're kicking yourself now that you remember."

"But that's the thing — I don't remember anything after the bar. We were doing shots, and then I woke up in your apartment. I was completely disoriented when I left. I wanted to come back to talk to you. To find out what happened. To apologize for whatever I might have said or done. But I couldn't remember where you lived. I couldn't even remember your name. What happened that night, Susie?"

"I was watching you at the game that day, Greg. Remember the game? You probably don't think about it all because why would you? You only think about yourself and your perfect little family. When I saw you at the bar that night, celebrating, *celebrating*, while my boyfriend lay broken in a hospital bed, I knew what I had to do. We had big plans for our future, you know. And you destroyed any chance we had at happiness. And now, you will pay for what you've done."

Susie reels back and forward, her shoe connecting with my nose. Stars dance before my eyes as the room shifts from light to dark. A gush of warmth pours from my nostrils down my face, coating my lips.

"You're out of your mind," I tell her, spitting blood as I speak.

"You seem to have a thing for women who are out of their minds, don't you?" She makes a valid point. I want to defend my wife, but how can I?

All I can do is ask, "But Gabby? She's your best friend. How could you do this to her?"

"Payback is a bitch, Greg. Sometimes, innocent people are hurt along the way. Though I doubt the police will consider your wife innocent. I made sure of that."

"We, darling. We made sure of that."

Tomas. I'd almost forgotten he was in the room. He slips his arm protectively around Susie's shoulder. I stare at them in complete disbelief. I wonder again if they injected me with a hallucinogenic, and this is all some bad trip.

"Have you met Tommy, Greg?"

"The manager, Tomas?"

"Tommy Piccola." The manager extends a hand before pulling it back and laughing. "Oh right, you can't."

I stare at his name tag, Tomas. And now I know why he looked so familiar — because he is so familiar. Senior year, the player from App State that I hit with my fastball. Would he have gone pro had that not happened? Probably not, but who knows? Stranger things have happened. What might have happened doesn't really matter. What matters is they seem to think so. And now, after all these years, he's come back to destroy me.

They. They've come back to destroy me. To destroy my family.

I turn my attention back to Susie.

"Why are you so angry at me, Susie? You're the one who broke up with him."

"Yes, I did, Greg. You ruined our plans, and I panicked. But Tommy and I kept in touch all these years. When this opportunity presented itself, we both decided it was time for a comeuppance."

"What about Matt and Jake? Your family, Susie? How could you do something like this to them?"

Susie rolls her eyes. "Have you met my husband, Greg? Ours is a marriage of convenience. Matt doesn't love me the way Tommy does. No one loves me the way Tommy does. We had a perfect future ahead of us until you came along. You ruined our lives, and now we're going to ruin yours. Fair is fair. Wouldn't you agree?"

"At least think about Jake, Susie. Your son. Think about what this will do to him."

Susie tosses her head back and laughs. "Do you honestly think I could have pushed a baby out of this body and still looked this good? Wake up and smell the coffee, Greg. Jake isn't my son. Matt and I were having an affair when his wife met an untimely death right after she gave birth to our bouncing baby boy. A terrible accident, really. I jumped in to help with his newborn baby; the rest is history. He owed me."

"So he knows about all this?"

"My husband won't drive more than five miles over the speed limit. You think he's capable of this?" She shakes her head. "Matt just knows he needs to do whatever I ask him to keep me happy. Maybe you should have done the same for Gabby. You might have had a different outcome here."

I push past nausea rising inside of me like a tidal wave. Susie Baker is out of her mind. Out of her fucking mind.

"Please, Susie. At least tell me what happened between us. I honestly can't remember anything after the bar."

"Of course, you can't, silly. I slipped a little something into your drink. You were drunk as a skunk. Too drunk to do anything, but drunk enough to believe you had. Drunk enough for Gabby to believe you had."

"So I didn't cheat on her?"

"Not unless there's a secret woman you're not telling us about." She pauses, looking me over. "Nah, I would know. I've been tracking your every move for years. Gabby's too. That necklace with the built-in tracker I got her sure has come in handy. How do you think I found out about Steven?"

Tears spring to my eyes. All these years, believing I'd done something terrible I hadn't done. Thinking I was the one who destroyed my wife. This was all some horrible mistake engineered by a psychotic woman and her equally psychotic ex-boyfriend.

I've never wanted to see Gabby so badly in my entire life. Tell her I never cheated on her, even if she has me. I'm sure it took a lot to get her to that point. I'm sure Susie was pulling the strings all along, lurking in the background, building this wedge between us.

I know my wife still loves me. And despite everything, I love Gabby, too. Now, if I could just get out of here, find my wife and son.

"Cam? What have you done with Cam?"

"I was going to ask you the very same question, Greg. We haven't done anything with Cam *yet.* We haven't been able to find him. Where is he hiding? Tell me, or I'll have to kill you right now."

Tommy passes Susie the knife. She flips it open and straddles my body, angling it over my neck.

CHAPTER 41

GABBY RIZZO

Officer Johnson calls for backup.

Then he bangs on the door again.

"It's the police." I said, *"open up."*

I don't need to state the obvious — whoever is in my room is not going to open the door. I consider all the scenarios in which someone wouldn't open the door to the police. Do they have Cam in there? What will happen if the police break down the door? Will they harm my son? Or worse?

Shouting from down the hallway interrupts my frantic thoughts. As it travels around the corner, growing louder, I expect to see the police storming the place. But, instead, it's Matt and Jake running full speed, screaming my name.

"Gabby . . ." Matt is breathless by the time he reaches my side, his words coming in harried gasps. "Thank goodness I found you. Jake has something to tell you. Tell her, son. Tell her what you told me."

Jake is standing at my side, staring at his feet. I close the space between us and pull him in for a hug. None of this is his fault. He's just a kid. A thirteen-year-old shouldn't have to process something of this magnitude. Yet that's what he's had to do.

I pull back and look him over. Jake's big brown eyes are glassy. He looks exhausted and scared. I take a deep breath. "It's okay, buddy. I'm not upset with you. You aren't in trouble. But, please, tell me what you know."

"I'm so sorry I didn't tell you the truth before. I was just trying to protect Cam."

"Protect him from who?"

Jake breaks eye contact, looking at his dad before looking back at me. "From my mom."

"From your mom? I don't understand, Jake. Why would you feel you need to protect Cameron from your mom?" As I say this, I think about the Ambien-laced cookies, and it's crystal clear why he would need to protect Cameron from Susie. What's not clear is why she would want to hurt my son and me in the first place. And Greg? I wonder where my husband is and if he's safe — if he's given up on us.

"Let me talk to Aunt Gabby, Jake. I'll tell her everything you told me."

"I'm so sorry," Jake says again. I bring my hand to his face and wipe a tear from his cheek. "It's okay. Everything will be okay." I hope I'm right.

"It's a long story . . ."

"I'm listening."

"A few weeks ago, Jake overheard Susie talking to someone on the phone about getting some sort of revenge on your family. He didn't know what to do. He was afraid to confront her and afraid to come to me. But he told Cam. He also told Cam when he found your journal in our house, hidden in Susie's nightstand."

I nod, understanding but not. Because why would Susie want to get revenge on us? And what could she possibly be doing with my journal?

"There's more. Jake overheard Susie talking about doing something to Cam. She said it would happen here on this trip."

My heart lodges in my throat. Even when you think they're not listening . . .

"Has she . . . has she done something to him?"

"No," Jake says. "He's hiding."

"*Hiding*?" Surely I must have heard him wrong.

"I helped him hide out. I told him to stay away from the hotel until we figured out what was happening."

"You mean, he's alive?"

"Yes, but—"

"But what?"

"But he was supposed to show up this morning for the game, and he never came. I started to worry, and I finally told my dad."

"Where is he, Jake? Can you take me to him?"

Jake nods, his fluffy dark hair spilling over his forehead. His mannerisms remind me so much of Cam's that my heart squeezes with affection.

We all turn toward the shuffle of feet barreling down the hallway. Backup has arrived, and not a moment too soon. Officer Johnson quickly gets the police up to speed. Then he turns to me.

"They'll handle this. Let's go find your son."

* * *

The parking lot is an ocean of darkness. We follow Jake and Matt out of the hotel into the vast expanse of black. Officer Johnson flicks on his flashlight, illuminating the parking lot and the woods that stretch beyond. It's in those woods, Jake tells us, where Cam has been hiding.

Jake hasn't seen or heard from him since he went "missing," and I can't help but fear the worst. He should have shown up for his game. Thirty-six hours in ninety-degree heat with no food or water, with the elements bearing down on him. I'm not sure in what condition we will find him. A part of me wants to rip his head off for doing this to us, but the other part is too flooded with relief that he wasn't kidnapped or murdered to be angry. There's no question that the latter will win.

"I have a question, Jake," I throw out as I struggle to keep up with him. "Why wouldn't Cam come stay with us if he was afraid your mom might do something to him?"

"We were worried it would tip her off, and she'd find another way to hurt you all."

"Okay. But how did you boys sneak out of the hotel without being seen?"

"My dad was distracted looking for my mom. We took the back staircase, and then I snuck back in before he came back. I didn't know he was going to check on us. My plan was to sneak back out and try to figure out what my mom was up to."

I shake my head, processing what these boys have been through.

"I forgive you," I say, meaning it. "You were trying to protect your best friend. We're gonna have a long talk after this, though, about making better decisions, okay?"

"Okay."

"One more question, Jake."

"Sure."

"The notes?"

"It was me. Well, me and Cam. I was trying to tip you off. I thought you would think they were from my mom, that you would start to figure things out on your own without me telling you."

I shake my head. Susie was the last person I would ever suspect of sending me threatening notes. But how would Jake know that? He has seen glimpses of his mother through a different lens than I have. For him, it was glaringly obvious. I was too blinded by the image of the perfect best friend I had cultivated in my head.

"Wait," Officer Johnson interrupts. "Do you hear that?"

The subtle moan of a wounded animal blows like a breeze through the trees. We follow cautiously toward the noise, uncertain of what we will discover. There are plenty of animals in these parts — gators, snakes, and bobcats. My heart stops beating momentarily in my chest because Cameron is somewhere out here as well.

And then I see him, propped against a tree, curled in the fetal position, whimpering.

Cam.

CHAPTER 42

GREG RIZZO

Tomas has his ear pressed up against the door; Susie, the sharp end of the knife pressed against the skin of my throat. She pushes down against my body with her own, increasing the pressure until I cough.

"Susie, please, you don't need to do this. Can't we just talk?"

"And why would I want to do that, Greg?"

"I promise you; I won't say anything. No one ever has to know about your involvement in this. It was Tomas, not you. Gabby will probably spend the rest of her life in prison. You can leave Matt; we can finally be together. I think we both know deep down that it was always you."

I have her attention. Susie pulls back slightly, and my breath returns in painful spurts. I have to keep talking, convince her she doesn't want to hurt me.

"Think about what a charmed life we would live, Susie. I can give you the world."

"What about the baby?"

"It's not mine."

"Of course, it's not yours. We haven't slept together, not yet, at least."

"Wait . . . what do you mean?"

"I assume you found the pregnancy test in your drawer where I left it, right? I figured, either way, one of you would find it and assume the other was cheating. Gabby isn't pregnant; I am."

I'm gripped with the sensation of plummeting in a free fall. This whole time I thought Gabby was pregnant. I would kick myself if I could. All I had to do was talk to my wife, but instead, I let my anger and pride get the best of me. And now, I fear it may be too late.

"We'll raise your baby together," I say. "Untie me, Susie." *So I can wrap my hands around your neck.*

Susie pulls the knife from my throat. She's considering what I said. She's thinking about my big house and all the things that fill it, how I will spoil her like I do Gabby, and how much better her life will be with me.

It seems we've both forgotten about Tomas. He is upon us in a flash, pushing Susie off me so forcefully that she stumbles backward and smacks her head on the floor. He grabs the knife from her hand and hovers over me.

"She always was a dimwit," he says, looking her over with disgust. "But hot as a sauna, if you know what I mean." He winks conspiratorially as if we are both in on some knee-slapping joke involving Susie.

Then he circles me like a shark, ignoring the cacophony of activity outside our door.

"She always had a thing for you, you know. Ever since she met you that night at the bar while I was in the hospital. I'm not sure why I thought she might choose me over you. But unlike you, Greg, I'm okay with second place. Runner-up. If, for any reason, the winner cannot fulfill his duties, the runner-up shall take over. Hard to fulfill your duties if you're dead, Greg."

"The door, Tomas. The police. You're not going to get away with this."

"I don't care about what happens to me, Greg. I care about what happens to you."

With that, Tomas lunges toward me, knife outstretched. I curl myself into a tight ball, instinctively attempting to protect my major organs. The blade connects with my thigh, and blood-searing pain rips through my leg as my scream rips through the air.

He pulls the knife from my flesh, sending a fresh wave of pain through my body. I watch, horrified, as he throws his arm back, readying himself to strike again. I close my eyes and say a prayer.

The blow doesn't come.

The sound of a tree trunk splitting in a forest stops him as the door to the hotel room caves in. Twenty uniformed officers descend upon the room.

It's complete chaos and confusion. I watch as one of the officers tackles Tomas to the ground. Quickly enough to stop him from stabbing me again, but not quickly enough to stop him from driving the knife into his own chest. For a moment, the room goes still. He lets out a final scream from the ground as he pulls the knife from his chest and a pool of blood spreads on the carpet.

I pull my eyes from Tomas's body to find Susie inching toward the broken-down door.

"Don't let that woman out of your sight. She was in on it." I warn the officer undoing the knots around my wrists. At the same time, another officer radios for emergency medical services and attends to the bleeding on my leg.

I catch Susie out of the corner of my eye, all white teeth and cherry lipstick. She bats her eyelashes at the officer speaking with her. I worry that she may talk her way out of this. Because that's what manipulative people like Susie do — they spin situations to look like the victim.

The officer smiles back at Susie as he slips his cuffs around her slender wrists and places her under arrest.

Not this time, Susie Baker.

Susie will spend a long time in prison for this. I'm sure she will be the queen bee and the life and soul of the party in jail, at least until all the Botox and fillers wear off and her roots begin to show. Who could have guessed the evil she hid behind that beautiful face? I hope I never have to look at that face again.

"Ambulance is on the way," an officer tells me as he wraps a thick strip of gauze around my wound. I draw a deep breath as I wait to be transported to a hospital.

His walkie-talkie roars to life. "You're not going to believe this. We found him — the missing boy."

"They found the missing boy — my son?" I try to sit up to grab the walkie-talkie from his hand.

"Easy there," he warns, lowering me back to the ground. "You've lost quite a bit of blood." His voice has a faraway quality to it as if my head is submerged in water. I sink into the carpet as the room starts to go black.

He brings the walkie-talkie to his lips. "Can you confirm the name and current condition?"

"Cameron Rizzo. He's with his mother right now in the woods by Foxcroft. He's severely dehydrated, with some facial and body burns and lacerations, but it looks like he's going to be just fine."

This time, I actually hear the angels sing.

This nightmare is finally coming to an end.

CHAPTER 43

GABBY RIZZO

The nightmare is over. Well, part of the nightmare.

I practically hurl myself onto Cam's body. He's worse for the wear, but he's alive. All that matters is that he's alive.

"Mom," he whispers, voice wavering, as he folds into my arms. I pull him as close to my body as humanly possible. We remain huddled like this for a while, my tears of relief dripping onto his hair, Cam's tears soaking my shirt.

"I'm so sorry," he cries into my chest.

I peel him off me, holding his face in my hands. "You listen to me, Cam. You have nothing to be sorry for. You were scared. This isn't your fault."

Cam's eyes grow wide. "I love you, Mom."

My heart explodes in my chest.

"If you thought I was a helicopter mom before, just wait . . ." I warn him, unsure if I'll survive another swell of affection.

Our Hallmark moment is interrupted by ambulance sirens approaching the hotel. Red and blue lights dance across the trees and, for a moment, I truly believe everything will turn out okay. Because no matter what happens, I have my son; in the end, that's all that matters.

Almost all that matters.

Officer Johnson speaks into his walkie-talkie. "We're about 100 meters into the woods off the main entrance."

"Roger. There's another ambulance arriving in the next few minutes. We've got two vics being taken out right now. One is DOA."

All the color drains from my face, and my heart thumps in my chest.

"Two vics?" I ask, choking on my words. "As in victims? DOA? Dead on arrival?"

"Can you release the names of the victims?"

"We're still sorting it all out. It appears the deceased is the hotel manager. The injured victim is Greg Rizzo. Stab wound to the leg. He's lost a lot of blood but appears to be stable."

The second round of tears streams down my face for the second person I love most in this world.

* * *

The paramedics load Cameron into the back of the ambulance. I am about to hop in to ride with him to the hospital when Matt grabs my arm.

"Oh, Gabby," he says. "I'm so sorry. I had no idea."

"None of us did, Matt."

"Is Cameron going to be okay?"

"The paramedics seem to think so. I've got to get in, to head to the hospital."

"I just want you to know, Gabby, I will make sure Susie pays for what she's done to your family."

"*Susie*?"

"You haven't heard? She was arrested for murder. They ran her prints against those found on the knife used to kill your grandparents, and would you believe it was a match?"

As if on cue, Detective Wren's police car screeches to a halt by the ambulance. He jumps from the vehicle and runs to my side. "Mrs. Rizzo," he says, breathless. "I wanted to let you know we've dropped all the charges against you. You're a free woman now." He smiles as he peers into the ambulance. "A free woman reunited with her son."

I smile back.

Thirty-six hours ago, you couldn't have paid me to believe Susie was capable of something like this. *Now?* As I step into the ambulance and sit next to Cameron, my head spins. Matt and Jake slip into their Suburban to follow us to the hospital.

I think about my best friend the entire ambulance ride. How could she have done this to me? How could I not have known?

Why?

By the time we arrive at the hospital, my stomach is in a state. Emergency room physicians immediately attend to Cam. They hook him up to an IV to rehydrate him and run a battery of tests, which Cameron passes with flying colors. Because, of course, he does. He's Cam.

We sit in wordless silence, absorbed in our thoughts, as the IV drips and the machines monitor Cam's vitals. I wonder what he's thinking about.

"Mom?"

My eyes meet his. "Yes, honey?"

"What happened with the game?"

I chuckle out loud. That's Cam for you, lying in a hospital bed after going through hell worried about a baseball game. "They lost, sweetie."

"That's a shame," he says. "I really hoped they would pull it out."

I've never been more proud of my son than I am at this moment. Because it's true what they say — it doesn't matter if you win or lose, it's how you play the game.

"Why didn't you go, Cam — like you told Jake you would?"

"I got lost." I know what he means, in more ways than one.

Once the doctor has assured me that Cam is safe and well, I gently kiss his forehead and slip out the door of his room.

As I make my way to the elevator, my flip-flops echo on the linoleum floors. I press the upward arrow and wait. Dozens of scenarios about how this could have ended, about how this will end, fight for space.

The elevator doors open, and I step inside, my heart pounding forcibly against my rib cage. I sense it will take a while for the paranoia I've carried with me to go away. But I have to believe that one day it will.

Despite what's happened, I feel better than I have in years. I press the button to the fifth floor and hold my breath.

* * *

Greg is barely recognizable. Cuts and bruises line his face, and his wrists are wrapped in soft white gauze. One leg is stretched out on the bed in a thick brace. I watch the slow rise and fall of his chest from the doorway. And then I tiptoe into the room so as not to wake him. I can wait a little longer. Lord knows we've both waited a long time for this.

Greg's eyes flutter as if sensing my presence in the room. I wonder how he will receive me after everything that's happened. As his lids open and his eyes find mine, my heart stops beating for a moment. The corners of his lips rise, and relief washes over me.

"Gabby," he says before he starts coughing violently. I turn on my heels to get a nurse, but he grabs my arm to stop me. He points to the table where a pitcher of water sits, and I pour him a glass. I bring it to his lips. Eventually, the coughing subsides.

"Thank God you're okay." He runs his fingers along the top of my hand. Goosebumps line my arms.

"I'd say it's the other way around. You look like you've been through the wringer."

"In more ways than one."

"I think it's time we talk," I say, pulling up a seat next to Greg's bed.

CHAPTER 44

SUSIE BAKER

Oh Gabby, you really should be more careful who you trust.

I'm not sure how she didn't figure it out. Poor naive Gabby. *Come on — no one is that* nice, *girl. Really* — weekly batches of chocolate-chip cookies? Who am I — Martha fucking Stewart? At least it made her a little fat.

Good thing no one else touched those cookies except for those unfortunate policemen.

I've been crushing up Ambien in the batter for years, steadily increasing the dose — the perfect cocktail to induce daytime drowsiness, headaches, confusion, and all the other lovely traits my best friend exhibits. *And you wonder why you're so tired, Gabby?*

There were enough sleeping pills in the last batch to tranquilize a grown horse. I was hoping Gabby would bring them to Startown with her, but you can't control everything, can you?

And to think — Gabby says Greg is denser than an unmanicured lawn filled with thistle. Pot, meet kettle.

On second thought, he may not be *as* dense as his wife, but I've no idea how Greg didn't recognize my voice on the other end of the line when he thought he was talking to Gabby's grandmother. Difficult to talk to someone who's been murdered. Oh well, nobody's perfect.

Certainly not my "best friend" Gabby Rizzo.

Sixteen years. It was a heck of a time to wait for revenge. I'm not sure how or why I waited that long, but I quite enjoyed it.

I was only slightly older than Gabby when the accident happened. I was driving home from my boyfriend's house on a dark, windy road when her car appeared out of nowhere. People didn't venture out this late in those parts. Except for that night.

I watched in horror as she swerved out of the way, and the second car appeared. There was no time to react, nowhere for me to go. The impact was deafening. *Literally* — I lost thirty percent of hearing in my left ear as my head slammed against the airbag. A few moments later, my car burst into angry flames. As I struggled to free myself of the vehicle, I watched the headlights of her car fade away. I saw her face, eyes steeled on the road ahead.

She didn't even try to help. Did she call an ambulance as she sped away or just leave us all there to die? Only Gabby knows the answer to that. I bet right about now, she's wishing I had died. I certainly came close. Burns covered nearly half of my body. I spent the next six months in a rehab facility and underwent more surgeries than I can count.

Being laid up in the hospital gave me plenty of time to think, to do some detective work of my own. It wasn't hard to figure out who she was. The papers talked about the victims' minor child involved in the crash. All it took was a little research and *voila* — I had a name.

I tried to move on, though. I did. I went to college. I fell in love. Tommy and I were going to get married. We were going to have an amazing life together. What were the chances I would see Brittany Stone at a baseball game and then her boyfriend would be the one to destroy my life for the second time? Apparently as high as the chances of a car driving down that lonely road in the middle of the night. They say lightning never strikes twice. I'd beg to differ.

Twice, she killed any chance of happiness I had. And so I vowed — however long it took — I would kill hers.

EPILOGUE

SIX MONTHS LATER
GABBY'S JOURNAL

It's been one heck of a morning.

I was standing in the grand foyer of my house, my naked toes freshly manicured, a wide grin plastered across my face. The sun was streaming through the glass panels flanking my double doors, casting a warm glow on the open space. We recently painted the front doors a striking cobalt blue to match Greg's Porsche.

It's all about compromise. Greg's even taken to washing the dishes every once in a while.

It's baby steps for both of us.

Besides, I've no reason to hide now that the truth about my past is out.

The marble tiles felt cool against my feet, a gray and white pool devoid of coffee stains. It cost us a small fortune to get those stains out. Worth every penny.

Susie's trial was swift. A group of her randomly selected peers unanimously found her guilty of two counts of first-degree murder in the fatal stabbings of John and Edna Smith. The judge handed her two consecutive life sentences in prison without the possibility of parole.

She gave birth in prison.

Well, that's what would have happened if she were pregnant in the first place. It turns out you really can purchase anything on Amazon, including a positive pregnancy test to pass off as your own or someone else's whose life you wish to destroy. We never figured out why she told Greg she was pregnant in the first place, but who's to say what a psychopath will do to get what they want?

Or what a psychopath will do simply because they're a psychopath? Remember the rat in our room — it turns out Tomas planted it there to screw with us. Susie allegedly had nothing to do with it. I'd love to ask Tomas what he was really hoping to accomplish with that, but I can't ask him, since he's dead.

They really did deserve one another.

It feels like we've only begun to scrape the surface of what Susie has done to break up our once happy union, to destroy our family.

As for Greg and me, it's been a slow but steady climb regaining our trust and getting to know one another again, this time with a clean slate. I've returned to real estate part-time and feel like a different person, in large part because I started taking better care of myself and stopped eating Susie's dark chocolate-chip cookies. Turns out her secret ingredient was Ambien. Also turns out I wasn't the only one she drugged. Susie admitted to tampering with Greg's medications, as well, swiftly ending his promising baseball career. Ergo the positive tests for performance-enhancing substances.

I still see Dr. Green, but only once every few months for maintenance. It turns out I just have a run-of-the-mill case of anxiety coupled with years of being unnecessarily medicated. Taking my childhood into consideration and what I've been through since, I'd say that's a reasonable diagnosis. I am much more invested in our sessions now, and it seems to be paying off. Well, that and not being plied with an inordinate amount of sleeping pills.

Oh, and how could I forget? I started volunteering! I spend a few hours a week at the local hospital, helping out in the NICU by holding babies. I have that itch again, and this time Greg is on board — he has an appointment to reverse his vasectomy! Yes, he admitted to that. We've told each other everything.

Well, almost everything.

Cam is happy as can be. He's still playing baseball, obviously. And he's still ranked as one of the top pitchers, hitters, and shortstops for his age bracket. But he's the Cam he used to be — he smiles more, and he's back to being less sour-than-sweet. That's a win-win for all of us as far as I'm concerned.

Now that Susie's gone, Matt and Jake spend a great deal of time at our house, and we are all happy to have them. Matt is like a brother to us, an uncle to Cam.

We are one big, happy, no longer dysfunctional family.

Steven, on the other hand — I heard from him once after word got out about what had happened at Foxcroft. He told me that he never wants to see or hear from me, my crazy family, crazy friends or crazy neighbors ever again. Colton was cut from the Futures the following season. Well, that made it easy.

Coach Bob is still coaching, only for a different team. It turns out he wasn't satisfied with coaching thirteen-year-old boys, as I'd suspected. He may not have done anything to Cam, but I still believe he was the one who alerted the press when he went missing. Cam's disappearance and the wild events that followed garnered more media attention than anyone could have ever imagined. Dateline even ran a two-part story on it. And although the Futures lost their first game and were eliminated from the tournament, the offers came rolling in. Coach Bob wasted no time as he greedily snatched up a position as head coach at a D1 school.

I've kept in touch with Officer Johnson. He just welcomed his second baby, a girl, into the world. He regularly sends me pictures, and she's as cute as a button, just like his son.

Detective Wren called once to check in on how we were all doing and make arrangements to return my journal. Susie had taken the liberty of writing in it, as verified by a handwriting analysis. Not that it'll add time to her sentence, but it's further vindication for me. I didn't do any of the things she made out that I had done. Closure.

I think about Detective Wren often, how he put himself on the line for me. I also think about Detective Marx. Because it turns out, it was personal. She was fresh on the force when my parents tragically perished in the car crash, and she was one of the first to arrive on the scene. I'm sure the image of my charred parents is seared in her brain.

The thing about detective work is it's a crapshoot. Some investigators are meticulous; others are lazy, and then some believe enough in their intuition to give you a chance. In the end, it's the toss of a coin which kind of detective you get.

What can I say? Lady Luck lives in my corner.

They never checked the brakes.

THE END

ACKNOWLEDGMENTS

Pinch me. I must be dreaming.

I'm so grateful for you, reader. Of all the amazing books you could choose from, I am humbled that you chose mine.

Thank you.

Thank you to all my beta readers, friends and family who are not afraid to give (very) strong opinions and point out any errors they can find. Thank you to my editor, Traci Finlay, for your keen eye for detail and for making this book so much better than it was before you touched it. Thank you to my husband for getting up with our kids and bringing me coffee so I can stay in bed and write on the weekends. Thank you to my parents for your unwavering support. And to my five children — you inspire me every single day. It really does take a village.

I hope you enjoyed this story!

You can follow me on Instagram @dlfisherthrillers for information on upcoming releases and to reach out. I would love to hear from you! Wishing you peace, love, and an abundant supply of thrilling books.

XX

D.L. Fisher

THE JOFFE BOOKS STORY

We began in 2014 when Jasper agreed to publish his mum's much-rejected romance novel and it became a bestseller.

Since then we've grown into the largest independent publisher in the UK. We're extremely proud to publish some of the very best writers in the world, including Joy Ellis, Faith Martin, Caro Ramsay, Helen Forrester, Simon Brett and Robert Goddard. Everyone at Joffe Books loves reading and we never forget that it all begins with the magic of an author telling a story.

We are proud to publish talented first-time authors, as well as established writers whose books we love introducing to a new generation of readers.

We won Trade Publisher of the Year at the Independent Publishing Awards in 2023 and Best Publisher Award in 2024 at the People's Book Prize. We have been shortlisted for Independent Publisher of the Year at the British Book Awards for the last five years, and were shortlisted for the Diversity and Inclusivity Award at the 2022 Independent Publishing Awards. In 2023 we were shortlisted for Publisher of the Year at the RNA Industry Awards, and in 2024 we were shortlisted at the CWA Daggers for the Best Crime and Mystery Publisher.

We built this company with your help, and we love to hear from you, so please email us about absolutely anything bookish at feedback@joffebooks.com.

If you want to receive free books every Friday and hear about all our new releases, join our mailing list here: www.joffebooks.com/freebooks.

And when you tell your friends about us, just remember: it's pronounced Joffe as in coffee or toffee!

Made in the USA
Columbia, SC
12 May 2025

57810465R00155